LIGHTLINE

Dayana Stockdale

BANNER ROOTS

Cover Art by Gabriel Stockdale
Cover & Book Design by Julie Valin,
  The Word Boutique, *www.TheWordBoutique.net*
Author Photo by Todd Anderson

For information, contact:
Banner Roots
www.BannerRoots.com

Printed in the United States of America.

To Mrs. Markovich, for planting the seed.
And to Gabriel, the one who watered me.

1

Joanne

THE RESCUE BOAT must be one of those dinky yellow rowboats on the side of the ship.

I'm waiting for the razored teeth of every shark in the ocean to rip me open.

I'll die if I continue screaming. Maybe that's the best route. Every time my freaked out body tries to punish itself with air, instinct takes over and I have to bring my head back down.

My heart jumps. What is that? It's bright and orange, almost as red as my hair, but shiny and flashing...

All the agility of my legs is wrapped into one front-to-back pulsating bulk that's keeping me afloat.

This is breathing. Why is this breathing?

I breathe more and more water, trying to understand.

Air is what brings the agony. Every time I lift my head out of the water, I feel like I'm going to die. Choking, gasping, wheezing.

I try to call for them. "Mom! Dad! Tessa!" But a high-pitched shriek consumes my voice. Air chokes me. A wave crashes into my mouth and brings relief.

2

Syedahl

I HEAR SOMETHING AND TURN to my right. Then again and turn to the left. Strong, smooth arms envelop me, holding my bare waist just below my cobalt blue top.

Coming from a squat house behind me, a single funnel of light shows the jagged edge of the city foundation. I sit with my flukes folded up.

This clearing has gotten smaller and smaller. If just two more houses are built, this little section of Southern End will no longer be our meeting place.

Only when I wrap my arms around him, folding over the fin that trails down his spine, does he let me go and swim in front of me. I can barely see his smile in the dim light.

"Hello, Alinx," I say. I bring my flukes in front of me but keep them parallel with the city foundation, not wanting to let them hang into the unimaginable depths below.

He hovers vertically. "Syedahl, aren't you supposed to be meditating?"

"In fact I am. Aren't you supposed to be killing someone?"

He shakes his head, his short brown hair flinging from his smirk like darts. "There's no one to kill."

"It doesn't seem that way to me."

After he got home from last night's council meeting, Father was mumbling frantically, devoid of the calm demeanor that everyone else sees. He wouldn't answer any of my questions.

"Is there anything you can tell me?" I ask Alinx now. "Why the king is keeping my father even busier lately?"

"Sorry. You'll know more than I do soon." His golden eyes flash anger and I look towards home. His expression changes. "If you have to go…"

"No. Not yet."

Alinx has dropped down so that only his torso is above the level of the foundation.

"I never get to see you anymore," I say.

He avoids offering a solution and inverts himself, showing me his wide flukes with their pale golden-brown scales. Alinx's coloring is like sunlight through seaweed, a sight I've seen but once.

"Where are you going?"

I can't see him at all, and my heart starts to race, remembering the anglerfish that chased us back up the foundation moons after we had first met. Alinx had the tip of his fluke clipped by its fearsome teeth. The tip never grew back.

"Why don't you follow me?" he calls, his voice as distant as I had feared.

"What are you doing?" I say to the darkness.

"Come down here."

"No. Please come up here."

"I think I see a skull," he taunts. The foundation is made of wars past.

"Alinx! Of course you can't see anything! I'm sure your head hurts…doesn't it?"

I hover near the edge and peer over. Behind me, an ala comes out of her house with her lightfish in a net. She swims off, taking away my only source of light.

"It's creepy down here. And slimy," he calls, from too far down.

"Alinx, stop. The *boundary*."

"Fine." His voice reaches me, but there's no sound of movement.

"My father will know," I plead. He can sense when anyone enters or leaves the city, and he knows that this spot at Southern End is my hideaway.

I swish my flukes to back away from the edge. Alinx's energy hits me like a current, forceful and steady. The sound, the smell of him...

Metal scratches on metal, the bands of his wrist swords coming together.

"Please don't make this any harder. My father knows I'm here. If you leave the boundary, he'll know that you're here too."

The exhale from his gills stirs my hair as he moves forward, guiding me back over the city foundation.

"I can't believe we started meeting in the morning," I say.

"I can't believe we're not together all the time."

All my efforts to please him are worthless—never enough. I come here. We talk about everything that has passed since we last saw each other. Sometimes our lips touch. Neither of us makes such an effort today.

The siren sings her wake-up call, and grumbling old alees begin to emerge from the houses around us. Most of them can't afford to buy lightfish, so they exist in near darkness all the time.

Alees are the males of our kind, alas are the females. Our species in general is called alu.

"Inward reflection is the gorgeous gift of darkness," the siren sings, drawing out the last note for what seems like an eternity.

Alinx holds me, making me feel insignificant and tiny. I pull away, kissing him on the cheek. "See you in three days," I whisper.

He swims off to the remote training area. As I navigate my way to the castle, I pass patches of bioluminescence, but mostly it's the sound of flukes and voices, as well as my own memory that guide me through the darkness. "Memory is greater than light," the siren sings each morning. The grayish cast of day would be nearly imperceptible were it not for her voice.

The Temple glows an eerie blue. The white walls shine with it. Scanning the tall statues and tablets, I finally see the Teindahn's head poking out from behind a plain stone.

"Syedahl, come here!"

He gestures for me to lie down beside him.

I sit facing the Teindahn, our tails laid out side by side on the pale stone floor. His is blue like mine, though saturated with age. In the sunless waters of Ezkine, the tails of the wise are colored, and those of the newborns are almost see-through. My scales are still quite pale, tinged blue around the edges.

He raises his black, half-circle eyebrows a little higher on his round and hairless head. He must be 110 at least. All of the wrinkles on his face accentuate his smile. "What's bothering you? You seem preoccupied."

My heart beats faster. I'm always preoccupied. Usually I'm better at hiding it, but today the tension between us was strong. Alinx and I weren't a tender escape for each other.

The Teindahn may be kind and understanding, but I can't confide in him. Though he's a mediator between my kind and royalty, I understand whose side he is truly on. So I don't dare ask, "Is it true that I won't love Alinx after I'm initiated?"

Alinx is my childhood best friend. Because he's not an heir to magic like I am, we can never be together.

The Teindahn clears his throat, tiny bubbles rising up towards the apex of the ceiling. A lightfish pulses red, standing out among the glowing blue jellies that are netted and strung up next to it.

I've agonized over my answer for too long, and now must offer something important or he won't believe me. I think of the person I'm not allowed to meet. "My mother…"

The Teindahn rustles, his tail creaking with movement, a crooked finger zooming to his lips to shush me.

I prop myself up with my hands. "Please. Tell me anything that you know about her. Did she ever come here?"

He shakes his head. Father is the only Hea in our city. Soon I will get lava power and join him in serving the king. For this reason I am the envy of everyone, especially royalty. They would steal my blood if it could possibly give them Hea power, because only a Hea heir can withstand the burn of lava.

"You know that isn't how Hea matings proceed." The Teindahn puffs up his frail unclad chest, suddenly seeing the opportunity for a lesson. "What did I teach you?"

I exhale deeply, hating to cover up my personal question with impersonal information. I haven't thought of my mother in a long time, but now that I've spoken of her, I desperately want answers.

My tone is flat as I respond. I feel no pride for having been born of the magical Hea race. "The Tribe of All Seas mediates between the rulers of two cities to pair Hea couples, so that all heirs are directly descended from the first 400 Heas. The Tribe records all couplings to minimize incest. The alee travels to the city of the female Hea."

I pause, fearing this inevitable moment. At least I can be

comforted knowing that Alinx isn't allowed in the castle, and won't have to meet my mate.

I continue, "He meets with the ruler and council of the city, feasts and celebrates, and mates with the female Hea. She keeps their first child for her own city's heir. Two years later, the male Hea returns, mates with her again, stays throughout the gestation, and takes their second baby back to his city as his own heir."

I have an older sibling who lives with my mother. Did my mother sob when I was ripped from her breast?

The Teindahn is staring at me intently, holding my soft hand in his small, bony one. "You ask about her because you are concerned for yourself."

I bow my head, immediately embarrassed. "Yes."

He squeezes my hand tighter and lowers his voice. "It will be alright, Syedahl. That's a few years off still."

A stone of guilt and unease settles in my stomach.

"It takes so long to arrange," he says. "All the negotiations. Trading more than just heirs…it's all very political. It took your father four moons to swim to your mother's city, so there is travel time as well." The Teindahn covers his mouth as if to take back that escaped secret. But when I catch his eye, I see that his gasp of surprise was feigned, that he fully intended to reveal it. I raise an eyebrow to question him further, and he shrugs regretfully.

That is all he knows. It took Father four moons to get to my mother's city. The longest swim I ever took, and the longest one I'll ever be allowed to take, is but a journey of four days.

"It *will* happen though," I say, not comforted by the Teindahn's list of procrastinations.

He nods without compassion. "Yes, it will."

3

Joanne

Rows of teeth are coming to shred me.

I stay as still as I can and focus on the sound. Somehow I can *hear* what it is, hear its size even.

How is that possible?

My stomach does flips with the waves. It's food. My flukes are twitching, getting ready to chase it, but I don't want to swim lower. I want to go home to Mom and Dad and Tessa.

Oh, Dad. Please find me. Why didn't you see me fall in? I was there with you leaning against the railing. Where were you when I needed you? Why didn't you save me?

Save me now. Don't let me die.

These fins take over, driving me towards the sandy bottom. My hands shoot outwards towards a creature I've never seen before, not even on TV. It's the length of my forearm, with round eyes and smooth gray skin. I grasp it.

This is not *me* doing this.

I squeeze it tightly, consumed by the smell of blood. I bite into it, past the thick fatty skin. It's still squirming. I bite in further and crunch something. It stops shaking finally and I work my teeth and nails through the soft stuff.

I savor the eyes.

When I'm done, I want to throw up. But I don't.

I'm down here, caught between the sand and the surface. If only Dad hadn't insisted we go on this cruise from Reykjavik to London. Would this transformation have happened if I had been back home in LA? Dad says SoCal winters are nothing, but I *need* my hot baths in January. Would I have sprouted fins in the tub?

I stare at the surface, wanting to go back up there but knowing there's no point. What am I supposed to do?

One time I lit a candle and tried to meditate with my best friend, Lily. We just ended up laughing at the dancing flame. Well, now I have to give it my best shot. I try to clear my mind, to think of a plan. What comes is every mermaid movie I've ever seen. Don't they always get thrown in a tank? That's what humans would do to me. They would catch me, trap me, and experiment on me.

Not even Dad can save me now.

I like it better down here than at the surface. No waves. The eerie stillness. So I stay here, floating as motionless as I can.

Running my tongue along the inside of my mouth, I try to make peace with these new teeth. The front top and bottom are pointed, like extra canines. The rest feel like molars.

A stupid memory flashes back to me. Our recently sworn-in vegetarian friend Shawnda bragging about health benefits. Lily pointed to her front teeth and said, "Fruit." Then to her canines… "Meat." Her back teeth… "Vegetables."

I tap my tongue against my pointed teeth and think *Fish*. Lick my molars and assume *Seaweed*.

Why don't I know what the hell happened to me? I thought mermaids only existed in cartoons and my backyard pool when I was like five. Last thing I remember is leaning over the railing with Mom, Dad, and Tessa, waiting for the circus show to start and wishing Mom would let me drink some wine.

I don't remember falling off the ship—or transforming. I don't know why no one saw me fall in, why the cruise ship or a rescue boat wasn't around when I woke up with blood-orange flukes and gills that collapse painfully above water.

Not even my naked torso looks the same. I have a circular scar on my left side.

Not even my face is the same. Scales spread around the outside of my eyes.

I can't go to land. My only hope is to find other mermaids and get some answers. So I start swimming down the slope of sand.

4

Syedahl

I GUT A COD in our kitchen. Father has gone to fetch King Ezkun, so I'm to enter the Half Sphere alone. I've spent the morning in meditation with the Teindahn. Two days have passed since I last saw Alinx, and another day will pass before I see him again.

I take the tunnel that connects our house, set deep in Ezkine's foundation, to the Realm of Court.

Bioluminescent light shines in between the bodies that block the audience entrance to the Half Sphere. A funnel of light emerges from the performers' entrance on top of the black dome.

I move around the secretaries and councilors, their wives and children. They react to me in one of two ways, either hushing the conversations that were surely about me or else uttering a curt hello.

Dipping through the low entrance, I squint my eyes against the brightness. One hundred lightfish wiggle in the space between the floor and the tightly woven net just above it.

One half of the immense theatre is filled with rows of positioning sleeves, pairs of curved metal tubes. Ignoring the stares and whispers, I go to the pair I always take, in the middle of the second row. I make sure not to hit the ala in front of me with my flukes as I place my arms in the sleeves, relax into them, and hang comfortably.

The Half Sphere is my favorite place in Ezkine. In general I loathe the castle because Alinx can't come here. The king's guards garner more respect than our warriors, who mostly serve the city through brute-strength tasks, assisting with fishing, building, and emergencies. Some of the nobility don't see the need for warriors, but the common citizalus—and King Ezkun as well I'm sure—prefer to be prepared.

In the Half Sphere, the exclusivity feels like a blessing. I don't have to worry about seeing Alinx or how to react. He tells me that I'm absolutely terrible at hiding the emotions on my face.

The Half Sphere is my only escape. Here I imagine what life is like in the warmer Seas and how increased visibility might change everything.

Today the performers are from Hisa, the city of actors in the Raisgan Sea, the sea of artists. Yesterday Father let me watch as he sent purple orbs zipping around the room to ensure that when the actors speak Raisgan, the audience hears Ch'tlan, our native tongue.

Almost all of the 150 pairs of positioning sleeves are filled now. I look around and notice with a pang that there is only one empty pair available to the audience, and it is next to me. I'm envied but avoided. Respected but never befriended.

Everyone rises simultaneously. I hover above my sleeves again, careful not to hit the ala with my flukes. The swishing behind me stirs my long black hair.

King Ezkun swims above Father across the room, their undersides glistening from the light below. They take their sleeves on the other side of the room, facing the audience. Someday soon another pair will be constructed there for me, and I'll never again see a play in its intended form.

I look up, expecting an actor to come down. No one does. Then I look to the right, at the dark room tacked onto the Half Sphere, once again expecting an actor to emerge.

The plump King Ezkun looks exasperated, his fingers and face twitching.

Someone enters the room. Alinx. My heart pounds. I want to scream at him to leave. What is he doing? What is he thinking, coming here? They'll kill him.

I lift my arms out of the sleeves, but someone else is faster. Commander Wortahl rises and joins Alinx in the center of the room. Wortahl is going to escort him to the dungeons! What can I do?

I am powerless.

My worry is interrupted. "Kind nobility of Ezkine, allow me to present to you our newest officer, Alinx," says Wortahl.

I ease my arms back into the sleeves and clutch my stomach. My whole body goes limp. My mouth can't pull in enough water to match the speed that it leaves my gills.

Alinx meets my gaze.

Once I'm initiated, we'll have to attend many of the same council meetings. We'll have to pretend to be nothing more than ex-friends.

Why did he have to make this harder? Couldn't he have declined?

The entire audience is shocked, but for a very different reason. No one expected Alinx to rise in the ranks. In our city's 250 years of existence, every officer has been born within our waters. Alinx wasn't even born in the Ch'tlan Sea. He and his mother are from the Hieste Sea, giving him that slightly darker skin and lighter hair that I love.

That I love.

Water rushes out of my gills. A councilor's wife slides her eyes in my direction.

Alinx and Commander Wortahl turn to the king and bow, both bending in half, nearly inverted. King Ezkun makes a low guttural sound and the audience cheers.

I notice again the empty space beside me and feel the blood rushing in my veins. Wartohl returns to his sleeves and Alinx crosses the expanse. I shift to look at Father, seeking advice, but he's busy peering into the performers' room, muttering under his breath and shaking his head. What could he have to say to an actor?

Alinx approaches the pair of sleeves to my left. I catch Father's eye. He gives me a stern look that says very clearly: *Stay put and be calm.*

Alinx drops in beside me and rests in the sleeves, his back straight and his face barely concealing a grin.

I hang my head in defeat. How can we go on this way? Our lives have collided. He's now permitted into my sacred space.

Alinx's defined arms are so close to me that I want to lean in and brush against him, but the sleeves hold me in place. I want to touch his forearm with my fingertips. I could clasp his hand right now. I could touch the side of his face.

I steal a glance at him, vaguely hearing the actors' voices booming in the center of the Sphere. Alinx's golden eyes ignite my heart, making it beat faster than I ever thought possible.

I snap my head back to the performers. An ala and two alees. A common Hisan play about a sister, her brother, and her suitor. I've seen it twice before. It's one of the few plays that King Ezkun permits.

Alinx leans in and I feel the water from his gills against my own. "Aren't you going to congratulate me?"

I plead with my eyes. Not here. Not now. Don't be so reckless. But he will not right himself, or look away.

"Congratulations." I'm certain that I've said it too loudly, that everyone has heard.

But the performers are speaking much louder, and no one is looking in our direction.

Satisfied, Alinx watches the play.

I'm completely consumed with dread and excitement. My whole body feels tainted with poison: skin gritty, innards sharp, blood thick.

How will I pretend in all of the meetings that we will have to attend together? Will I be able to listen to Alinx, speak to him nonchalantly, in front of Father, the king, the Band of Thrones?

A scream from the ala actress shakes me from my panic and into hers.

The suitor's skin turns green, and his tail morphs into what I've been taught to call legs, joined together by a slimy membrane. His hands are webbed, as are the ends of his legs. He has big round black eyes, tiny holes for a nose, and a wide slash of a mouth that grins to bare pointed teeth. The suitor has morphed into a slinu, that other half-man, half-fish species that lives in the unfathomable depths.

Most of the alas in the audience scream. The alees stiffen, wanting to protect them. Alinx clenches his fists.

The slinu slices the brother's neck with his claws and grabs the sister. I want to cover my eyes as he holds her and rubs the fins behind his ears against her soft cheek, but I am too curious. I've never seen a slinu before, not even an illusionary one. This is beyond all the tales I've ever heard. Beyond fright and disgust.

So *real*.

Certainly some Hea has infused this magician's wand.

No regular alu could ever perform such a seamless illusion. I look towards the dark room but see only a shaking arm—thick and heavily scarred and much paler than I'd expect a native of Raisgan to be.

But I don't have much time to ponder. Another character, a strong young alee, dives down from the top, slays the slinu, and kisses the ala. The audience cheers as the actor within the slinu illusion flees. The handsome alee pulls away from his victory kiss, renewed terror on his face.

A green orb appears out of nowhere over Father's and King Ezkun's heads. The mass moves to the center of the room and grows larger and larger, writhing like a school of fish. Fifty hungry slinus, their eyes glowing red, come to the center of the room. They dart this way and that, breaking formation. The ala screams. Even the alee begs for his life. The slinus are wild, snarling. They lick and bite and claw with the nails on their webbed hands.

I smell blood. A slinu looks straight at me and smells my fear.

Alinx whispers, "It isn't real."

But the slinu is coming at me, ready to attack. What have I to live for, anyway?

All the slinus are moving towards the audience now. A clawed hand reaches for me and I scream, louder than anyone else in the room. Alinx jolts out of his sleeves and covers me. I pant into his chest.

The audience lets out a collective sigh.

Alinx releases me. The smell of blood is gone. The sound of their hunger is gone. No more green skin.

And everyone—everyone—is staring straight at me. I'm too scared to look at my father.

The actors who played the slinu and the brother return. They all swim around and around the top of the Half Sphere, creating a vortex.

Humming their approval, everyone rises above the sleeves, hair flowing in the same direction. Strands of short gray hair cross King Ezkun's wide grin. Father rises and the two of them pass under the entrance and into the Realm of Court. As soon as Father's pallid green flukes can no longer be seen, the whole Half Sphere comes alive with movement.

The usual friendly chatter can't conceal the hushed murmurings. As I rise, I feel the room watching me. Alinx waits, as if we could reasonably leave the theatre together. I glare at him intently until he swims off.

Faces turn in my direction. I ignore a councilor's friendly attempts to get my attention. I pass him and curve around a young child, the daughter of one the Overseers of Structure. She moves slightly to let me pass. Once out of the Half Sphere, I take a deep pull of water and am greeted by the dim expanse of the Realm of Court.

No one is near me. This is my chance.

I angle upwards and swim fast. The boundary of my father's protection charm pushes against me and I pulse my flukes to break through.

Normally I would never leave unless I'd already asked his permission to get some exercise, but right now I don't care. I'm too deeply embarrassed and horrified that I nestled into Alinx's arms. Nothing could have been worse. And at such an influential time too—when I haven't been officially chosen as the next initiate in the Ch'tlan Sea!

I take deep gulps to calm myself, enjoying the utterly empty darkness. Ezkinian citizalus keep a great distance from the boundary. They fear sharks, humans, and other alus, but they should know that when you live on a deep seamount far from the shelf, you are mostly forgotten.

I hate the poor visibility of the city. I can usually see only three arm's lengths out around me. From this height, Ezkine is a haze of white-green light and particles that fall forever.

When I wander around Ezkine, I'm constantly reminded that there is so much I can't see. Up here, just above the city but still in the dark, there's nothing to miss.

I haven't been out of the boundary in moons. I wonder what would happen if I just kept going up, if I took Alinx with me and said goodbye to the possibility of power.

To see bright sunlight for the second time in my life. To pretend that I'm not a Hea heiress so that I can eat forbidden foods—steamed or mixed with seaweed and sauces. To be surrounded by another language. To maybe even see that human contraption called a ship. To discover the sea and city of my mother. To meet her.

Dreaming is my favorite form of self-torture.

Once I'm initiated and hot lava is mine, I'll never be allowed to leave. My power won't really belong to me, but to my king.

I'm denied sunlight and love and freedom. Everyone wishes they could have the power I will receive. I'd give it freely, if it were mine to give.

5

Joanne

I SWIM SO FAST the sand looks like static. The water dims to gray, and I can't tell if it's nighttime or if I've followed the shelf down really deep.

Suddenly the shelf disappears, leaving me staring down into a darkness I've never known.

Oh no. No. *No!* I dart back around, forcing these orange flukes to obey.

When I'm over the shelf again, I take a deep breath and try to convince myself that the shelf equals safety.

All I've eaten for three days is that one weird gray thing. All I've seen for two days is dirt and little red worms that don't look the least bit appetizing. My stomach is a fist that won't unclench.

I'm going to do whatever it takes to get out of here. And that means finding other mermaids. Ridiculous, I know. But humans would try to experiment on me. I need to ask other mermaids if my condition is temporary. Will I turn back soon? And if I do, will I drown?

I try to hold onto home. Things have been completely messed up since Dad got diagnosed with colon cancer, so everything I remember—the look in his eyes, my mom's exhaustion, Tessa's helplessness—runs through my mind again and again.

I wonder if Lily is still at my house. She's supposed to be house sitting. I've been a mermaid for at least three days. Does Lily know I'm missing? Did my family go back home? I hope they're still looking for me, even though they can't help me. I'm not giving up hope, so I don't want them to either.

Especially not Dad.

I get no relief from avoiding the drop-off. Instead I feel worse.

Soon the water is black all around me, so it doesn't matter any more. It's all dark now. But big creatures—sharks and whales—live down there, so of course the shelf must be safer.

Still I'm compelled. I don't have a choice. I keep swimming past the drop-off and into the deep! A flash of silver light pours over me and slick skin brushes past. I shiver and the memory goes away, just like that.

I try to figure out what the memory means. I know it has something to do with the giant snake monster that I dreamt of last night. Somehow I know this monster was a she.

Was she really only a dream? Why does the drop-off remind me of her?

Why is a word I shouldn't let into my brain. All that matters is getting home. Daddy is dying. Not saying goodbye scares me more than anything. I have to be there for the six months to a year that he has left.

I try not to let myself blame him, but I don't succeed. Here's your cruise, Dad! Is this what you wanted?

We were all leaning against the railing together, so why didn't they see me fall in and get me out? Did we all go to the circus show? Did I fall in after?

I don't remember.

I notice again the oval scar on my side. It is raised and splotchy. Touching it makes me mad. Infuriated. I swim faster and harder than ever before, farther past the shelf. No turning back.

I didn't have this scar as a human. I'm left wondering not only what the hell happened to me, but also how long ago it happened, since this wound is completely healed.

I want to kill myself. But that wouldn't get me back to land. It would just end my life.

Really.

Seriously.

This is *me*.

What I don't understand is *why* I'm swimming out here past the drop-off, *why* this body tells me to do exactly what my mind doesn't want. Is this instinct?

Just ahead the water brightens, freaking me out with a greenish glow. My first thought is that it's a submarine, but that just doesn't feel right. I guess the light is too hazy and dissipated—not directed like a man-made light would be.

Then I think of anglerfish, those creatures with the big teeth and the light bobbles on their heads. Maybe this light is a horde of them. Could I have swum that deep?

Some insane obsession washes over me. I chug along, kicking my flukes down into the faint light. After being alone in the dark, the glow feels like an escape.

6

Syedahl

I'M LEANING AGAINST THE CUTTING BLOCK, dead fish in hand, knife discarded and stomach growling, but Father won't relent. "Stupid ala!" he's shouting at me, his lips pulled back. His anger is so great that his sentences aren't fully formed. "Ruined everything!"

He turns away to regain his composure and when he faces me again, his long black braid whips across his pale chest and falls over his opposite shoulder.

"Father, please."

"This isn't punishment. This is nothing! Did you not see her? Did you not even *notice*? Are you that daft? Ah! Ah!" He emits a disgusting sound, as if trying to clear me from his throat. Then he smiles, a terrible, cool smile, and I know the real insult is coming. "It's the Tribe's fault. They set me up with your ridiculous, frivolous, irresponsible mother."

I sink lower down the stone, my shoulder blades pressing against it. I don't even know my mother's name. All I know is that I must have her face. His coloring, but her features. Soft, where he is sharp.

Father's voice rises as he continues, "I told them she wasn't adequate to make the heir I needed to turn this city from forgotten to elite."

I interrupt him with a soft whisper. "Notice who?"

He sees the hope in my eyes. "Oh, useless Syedahl! Your mother wasn't there. Is that what you thought?"

I harden, clenching my teeth, narrowing my eyes, and straightening my posture to protect myself from this alee who has never once said he loves me. "Then who *was* there?"

"Had you been doing what you were supposed to, speaking with everyone present, mingling, acquainting yourself with the motives and desires of every alu who in some way or another affects this city…had you been looking anywhere other than *down* or at *Alinx*…" Father pauses, trying to calm himself enough to speak. When he succeeds his voice is calculating, chilling. "Had you been paying attention you would have noticed that foreign ala. Pale, but not as pale as we are. Chunky. Much better fed. *Clearly. Not. From. This. City.*" He looks deep into my eyes. "Did you notice her?"

"No."

He frowns before continuing. "She was a messenger for two parties."

My heart quickens, and I fear it will explode from the day's excitement.

"A messenger for Queen Tilas," he continues. "As well as for the Ch'tlan Court. Queen Tilas has promised you Sarta and the Court has approved."

A weak smile forms on my quavering lips.

"Before, you may have only needed to perform some simple rite of passage, but now…*oh now, Syedahl!* Surely that messenger will report your embrace with Alinx, and the Court will have to require something more revealing of your dedication." Father circles the kitchen once. "Your devotion. Something that requires patience. Time." His eyes deepen with rage again and I expect him to resume his shouting, but instead he says, "Henna and Dawein won't be easy to please."

Father's face is unnervingly close to me now. I've never met Henna, but I've heard her name in conversation about the city of Tila. I can't recall the city of the Hea Dawein.

"What do think my rite of passage will be?" I ask.

"I'm not sure yet, but I sense the answer will present itself soon."

When I face the cutting block again, Father says to my back, "You will not meet with Alinx anymore."

"You knew."

"I suspected it. Today I was certain."

"What am I going to do?" It is a whisper to myself.

Father answers, "A quick, obvious breakup will only make this worse."

Finally, I turn to face him.

"Don't tell Alinx that you've been chosen," Father continues, his voice surprisingly soft. "Treat him as you treat the other warriors. He is an acquaintance now. I've let this go on too long." Even though his words seem kind, I know he did not interfere sooner because he was too busy, not out of love or pity.

"It really is time?" I ask.

"It really is. You need to be here now, in the castle. You're not even to go to Southern End alone."

"What? Why not?"

"For the sake of appearances," he mutters. "You've caused enough commotion today. Until Sarta's corpse is within our waters, we cannot be too careful. Anything could change if unfavorable rumors about you upset the Ch'tlan Court. It's over, Syedahl. You and Alinx—" Father closes his eyes and falls backwards as if driven down by an invisible force.

When he rights himself, he speaks urgently. "Someone has

just crossed the boundary, coming in!" He inclines his head towards the south, listening to something no one else can hear. "Go to Southern End. Now!"

"But the guards will interrogate—"

"Go now. Go there *now!*" He shouts until I rush out of the room. I take my usual route, sick from his terrible words. I don't mean to be so dissenting. Is it even possible for me to stay away from Alinx?

The Teindahn says it will be easier when I'm initiated, that I won't be able to concern myself with such common things. They say that Heas can't love. All I know for certain is that they aren't allowed to. Is love only for common citizalus? Is it not magical?

I come to our clearing, assuming this is where Father wanted me. I'm confused, but his reasons for sending me here are far from my mind. I settle in near the edge of the foundation and peer down into the great expanse.

Who can I talk to? Maybe Henna. I recall who she is now, the youngest Hea in Ch'tlan and our most recent initiate, even though she has had power for ten years. I remember how worried everyone was when Father left for her initiation. He worked hard for several days to keep the city's protections up, and life went on as usual. Maybe I'll have a moment alone with her. Maybe being a Hea is different for an ala than it is for an alee.

When Sarta dies, Henna will be left alone to do her ruler's bidding. That will happen to me someday, too. What will be worse, working under Father or being the only Hea, utterly alone? But by then I will have a child, as Henna probably does. That will be better…to not be alone. Even so I desperately don't want to create such a child.

I can't think about it, it makes me so sick.

When I sense someone coming from above, I remember

the slinus and shudder, instinctively scooting back farther from the edge of the foundation, folding my flukes under me and stirring up dust.

I look up and speak his name. "Alinx. Alinx," I whisper, letting the words morph into a thin wail.

Out of the haze, a tan-skinned, red-haired ala about my age appears, still angled downwards from her descent. Her coloring is absolutely shocking. Her eyes are so wide that I feel instantly afraid. Did she see real slinus?

"Are you alright?" I ask.

She stares at me with her huge bright eyes and stays suspended, her face above mine.

"Come into the city," I say, moving to the side, embarrassed for her that she has lost her manners.

She stays above me and emits a high-pitched sound. A monosyllable.

"Excuse me?" I ask. My pain over Alinx burrows deeper within me and I'm filled with the fear in this ala's aquamarine eyes.

7

Joanne

PLEASE LISTEN TO ME. Just listen. I try to speak. Help! Help!

But all I get is "Eeeeeee," and this mermaid looking at me with pity, like it's obvious something really bad has happened to me. Like I'm a trauma victim.

I'm not supposed to be a mermaid! But my words don't come out. I point upwards, trying to tell her that I come from up there. She mimics me.

Do you get it?

She just looks confused and sad. Her lavender eyes are the shape of sideways teardrops, and she has pouty baby doll lips. Her skin is as white as ice. Her long hair is as dark as the deep sea.

Help me!

I sink down to the dusty floor. What is this place? All I can see are two little brown domes. Why did I think it would be easy? She's a mermaid, but she can't help me. We can't even understand each other!

I don't have the words. It isn't just my voice that won't obey, it's my brain.

The mermaid says a string of syllables, grabs my face with

both hands, and inspects me. I think she's going to rip my head off, so I push up off the floor with my flukes. When she looks at my torso, I feel embarrassed because she's wearing fabric around her boobs and I'm naked.

She touches my scar and I shriek. Do you know what happened to me?

When we lock eyes, I can tell that she doesn't. She touches her chest and says, "Sydaaaal."

She says it over and over again, and then touches my chest. I pull away. Her whole face is a question. I try to say "Joanne" but what comes out is "Joaviz."

She giggles and smiles. "Joaviz."

No. *No!* I shake my head, but she keeps repeating it, touching herself and then me. "Syedahl. Joaviz."

Call me whatever you want, just get me the hell out of here!

Her eyes light up. There are lavender and baby blue scales in a curving pattern on her temples, like crazy eye shadow. I touch my own eye scales and wonder what color they are.

My love for all things beauty makes me think *cool,* but I shake the compliment away. Nothing about this situation is cool. Nothing.

Syedahl grabs my hand and pulls me towards the domes. For some reason I came to this place. She can't seem to help me, but at least maybe she'll feed me. And then I have to find somebody who knows what happened to me.

I think of the snake monster from my dream and shudder. I can't picture what she looked like exactly or how I know it was a she. I remember the feeling of her. The memory of her is scarier than being alone in the ocean, scarier than swimming past the drop-off.

Scarier than swimming straight down to a mysterious light.

I pull my hand away from Syedahl and follow her because I have nowhere else to go. All these ugly brown domes appear out of nowhere and I try to dodge them, try to keep track of Syedahl's light blue flukes, but it's too dark. I lose sight of her and scream.

Syedahl's white face appears, grimacing at me. She opens her mouth, revealing her pointy front teeth. She's going to bite me! But instead she speaks.

I run my tongue over my own pointy teeth and shudder.

She turns away and I follow, hearing my way around the next few domes. But it's too hard. I can barely focus and almost run into one. Why not just swim over the tops? So I swim over the next one. Syedahl grabs my flukes and yanks me back down. I want to hit her, but then I see how mad she is at *me*. When she sneers, I cover my head with my arms. She peels my hands away and I shut my eyes, not wanting to see what she's going to do next.

She tugs my eyelids open. Her face is too close to mine. I scream and she darts away, invisible now.

I don't want to be alone! I can't see her or even hear her.

She appears in front of me again and covers my wailing mouth. I unclench my jaw to bite her, but she whips her hand away. We stare at each other for a long while. When she turns around, she does it slowly. I follow and try to obey.

The domes morph into rectangles, buildings lined up to create halls. We go through a hazy narrow canal, passing many white faces with black hair that steal looks at us. They're totally freaky, popping into view. I consider asking for help, but I don't want to talk to *them*.

The sound of movement gets louder. I take Syedahl's hand. So much talking and shouting and creepy grinding noises and whining babies.

Babies!

How cute. How *disgusting!* Their tails are totally see-through. I dart backwards.

We get closer to all the noise, surrounded by more and more merfolk. Why do I look so different, with my tan skin and bright hair? Why isn't my tail that pale or my hair that dark? Why can't I *speak?*

I get the feeling right away—I don't know how—that none of these merfolk has ever been human. And that terrifies me. Their faces are so…dead. Like they don't care about anything. Slack mouths. Motionless eyes.

A fat glowing blue fish snaps its jaws and lights up the space around it. I want to scream, but I don't want any more stares than I'm already getting. I squeeze Syedahl's hand tighter, and she points up at the thing. A closer look shows it's tied to a pole with a net. A lamp!

I try to suck in deep gulps to calm myself down, but I hear fast movement coming from behind and it only makes me pant. I whip around and come face to face with two mer-men.

They've all finally noticed me. They're cannibals!

I run my tongue along my own sharp teeth. I'll bite back!

Strong hands grip my arms as I thrash and scream. Sye-dahl is shouting at the two young mermen. They point clubs lined with shark teeth at my face. I squirm and wriggle, but their grip only gets tighter on my arms. This busy place goes silent. In the darkness and around the fish lamps, they're all listening in.

Let go! Let *go* of me! I don't stop fighting until I feel a prick at my neck. Syedahl pushes a guard away and stares into my face, shaking her head. She looks concerned for me, but I don't care. She's one of them.

Let me GO!

I'm not crying, just trying to breathe, but I can't get

enough water. A memory flashes back to me. Sitting in my dad's green chair, smelling the mint and cologne and hint of tobacco on the arm covers. Waiting for that final opinion. I cried the whole time he was away in San Francisco because I already knew. I cried because he wasn't home and I didn't have to be strong for him anymore.

I feel myself relaxing, giving in. Just eat me already. Syedahl takes my chin in one hand.

Something about her expression calms me down.

Just as I start to breathe regularly again—well not *regularly*—a third merman comes up. He's not as pale as the others, but he's not as tan or colorful as I am. He talks to Syedahl, and then the guards release me.

I pump my tail to get straight up and out of here, but Syedahl is too fast. She's got me by the fluke.

8

Syedahl

"WHO IS THIS?" ALINX ASKS. I feel a sharp twinge of jealousy every time he looks at her exotic naked body, even when I can tell that he's only paying attention to her horrified face.

Instead of explaining that Father sensed her at the boundary, I say, "I have to go back."

"Wait." He takes hold of my hand and I yank it away. I don't know what to say to him. Father urged me not to tell him that I'm to be the next initiate, but we've always been honest with each other.

"I already know," Alinx says.

Joaviz tugs on my hand and I squeeze hers, begging her to leave me be. She lets go and peers at Alinx from over my shoulder.

"You do?" I ask.

"Congratulations." He looks past me, disgusted. I'm closer to that inevitable moment when a Hea from another Sea will travel here and I'll conceive an heir for Ezkine. Then someday, he'll take our second child from me.

Why must Alinx be so cruel, when he knows there's absolutely nothing I can do? Now he's staring at me, waiting.

Can I break away from him, or is it impossible for us to stay apart?

Will we be drawn back together again, like the last time we tried to break up? That separation only lasted one moon.

Joaviz stays obediently by my side and then cowers behind me when activity resumes in Polar Square. Her eyes dance with every cackle of the traders and every desperate plea.

"What do you think happened to her?" I ask, certain she has been attacked or suffered something awful. "Slinus?"

Alinx shakes his head, his dark brown hair stirring around him. "She's just a lost foreigner...and you know that wasn't real."

I shiver with remembering. "Then why did they perform it? Why was it allowed?"

Not caring to analyze the play, Alinx looks at me with something painfully close to disappointment. It's a reaction I know all too well, but never before from him. Father was wrong about avoiding an abrupt ending. A quick break is the only way for us.

"It's over," I say.

Alinx exhales audibly and watches the dust swirl beneath us. "I know." When he looks up, the shine in his eyes is subdued. "I won't bother you anymore. You can have Southern End. I'll never go there."

"No, Alinx. You can go there. I won't." I'm whispering despite the fact that Polar Square is alive with trade.

"You love it there," he says.

Southern End is his territory, close to his home and certainly not intended for the powerful likes of me. Before I met him, I never even left the castle, so Southern End should be his, as it was before. But I can't stand to see him so sad, so in an effort to console him, I nod.

Maybe by the time I get my power, Alinx and I will have

healed a little and being in meetings together will come easier. "I'll still see you all the time," I say.

"Not really. You'll be different. Maybe they're right. You won't be able to love anyone. It already seems to be happening." Alinx's jaw is set tight, resolved. I've never heard him speak so sullenly.

I want to collapse and never rise again, but I force myself to hover feebly. This sense of loss is my destiny, soon to be fulfilled.

"Maybe you're right." I don't want to believe it.

I take Joaviz's hand and guide her away, but Alinx says something that stops my heart. "I'm going to Kalein tomorrow."

"For how long?" I ask.

"I don't know yet. Maybe it will make this easier."

"Is that why you're going?"

He doesn't take his eyes off me. "I have to deliver a message."

"A message? You're an officer, not a—"

"It's highly confidential. Your father's personal mission, in fact."

So that *is* why he's leaving—to make this easier on us. Father has given him this message for my sake. "I..." How can I say what I need to? There's too much...and he knows it all already. "I'm sorry."

"I know."

"Be safe."

"Of course."

I nod curtly, grab Joaviz, and leave.

9

Joaviz

SYEDAHL STUFFS A BIOLUMINESCENT FISH into a net on top of a tall pole.

In the dim eerie light I can see four other, shorter poles with braided seaweed hanging off of them. That's it. No windows. We're inside the tower, or the seamount, or whatever the rest of the city is on top of.

A merman comes in. It must be his voice that I heard when we swam straight down the tunnel and into this room. He looks me up and down and rushes towards me with outstretched hands. I dart to the side to get past him, but he catches me around the shoulders and slams me against the back wall.

I feel my nakedness and panic. I thrash and bang my fists against his chest. He holds my hands behind my back and squeezes me tight against him.

Syedahl is shouting at him, but I can't guess the tone of her protest because I'm screaming so much louder. When he lets go of me, I stop.

Syedahl asks him a question, and he snarls back an answer.

She glides towards me, but he shouts again, stopping her short. I move side to side and he blocks me every time. His eyes are pale green, hollow and empty but shining. I want to gouge them out! I want to strangle him.

But I can't *move*. I'm still as a statue. My body won't listen to my brain. What is happening to me?

Syedahl hovers, staring at me, trying to apologize.

I hate you, Syedahl! I wish she could understand. You and that cute merguy saved me from the ones with clubs. You acted like you were going to feed me, and now this?

The merman grabs my head. My mouth and eyelids close. He presses his thumbs against the scales on my temples and makes all my thoughts and memories go black.

Blankness.

Darkness.

Nothing.

But then…

One image comes to mind. I'm walking on the ship at nighttime, stepping slowly towards the railing, possessed.

It's windy and the emptiness of the ocean draws me in.

The merman pulls away and I slide down the wall, the green glow of the room returning. My muscles work again. My head aches.

I stare down the triumph in his tired eyes. He's panting. It took all his energy to send me to that dark place. What I don't get is why he did it. It almost felt like a memory, but I think he created it to torture me.

He smiles and turns to Syedahl, who comes to my side. I push her away and try to leave again, but she grabs me. As I struggle to get free, she holds my face and apologizes with her eyes.

I hate you, you know.

This is her father. That's what she's trying to say. I can tell by how she looks at me. Pleading. Obedient. Well, I don't care. I would never let *my* dad attack anybody.

He speaks and leaves. I exhale.

Syedahl grabs my hand and I yank it away. She tries again. This time I let her, not knowing what else to do. I follow her into another room. One glowing fish strung up in the corner illuminates a few others, bumpy and orange-brown, trapped in a net tied to the wall.

Syedahl grabs one and stabs it with a knife, tranquilizing me with the smell of the oils. It makes me sick how excited I get to watch it die. She slices it, guts it, puts the guts in a stone jar, turns the fish inside out, and cuts the meat into cubes. When she hands me half the cubes, I don't accept them right away, just to show her that I'm still really mad.

After I've taken a few delicious bites, she holds up a hand to tell me to wait and then leaves the room.

I should try to get away. But my head is still throbbing and dizzy.

And I *have* to stay here, because that merman knows something I don't. I stare at the chopping blocks and little stone jars and dull fish eyes until Syedahl comes back holding a piece of yellow fabric with four strings. She ties it on me.

Ugh! Yellow.

I look like a frickin' sunset—red hair, orange tail, yellow top. Great. Some wannabe fashion designer I am.

When I've had my fill, I let her guide me back to the first room. She shoves me into the center of the four short poles and I wish I hadn't been so trusting again. Her dad rushes in and whispers something that makes me go completely still.

I'm stuck here, floating all rigid, watching them tie me up with seaweed and there's nothing I can do. I try to breathe but can't even do that.

All of a sudden I'm free of his magic and squirming, breathing deeply, but now I'm trapped in this seaweed. He's gone from the room.

I scream. Syedahl covers my mouth. I bite her hand and draw blood.

She whips her hand away from me, narrows her eyes, and leaves, taking the green fish with her.

I sob for a long time—the aching without the tears. My brain burns behind my eyes. After a while there's nothing left. I go totally still. That's when I fall asleep.

10

Syedahl

THE SIREN SINGS her wake-up call, but I'm already
awake.

All day yesterday I thought about Alinx as I lay in my
wrappings in the utter darkness, mourning the loss of our
relationship and ignoring Joaviz's screams. I had intended to
spend today in the same tortured, self-indulgent manner, but
the Teindahn's visit has brought me out of my stagnation. My
rite of passage will be the longest and most tedious the Teindahn has ever heard of, but it must be done to prove to the
Ch'tlan Court that I am dedicated and patient.

I must teach Joaviz to speak. Father could do it with a
wave of his staff, but I must do it alone and without power. I
wonder how long it will take. Father says she doesn't have a
mother tongue. He couldn't read her mind or a single memory because she can't speak. Father's weakness is interpersonal
magic, but he claimed that shortcoming had nothing to do
with it. Joaviz has no native language, but she is not mute or
deaf. How is this possible?

She must be wild, then. Certainly she has no manners. I
give her food and wrappings to sleep in, and she responds to
my hospitality with a bite!

I only worry a little about my task. Mostly I long for Alinx. We usually go three or four days without seeing each other, but now I know that everything save politics is finally over between us. No one to complain to. No one to ask for advice. No one to hold. No one to kiss. No one to dream with.

The last time we tried to separate was more like some silly experiment, a joke, but this time it is real and necessary.

Does Alinx believe what he told me, that I may not be able to love?

The Teindahn believes it, but why? He's such a merry and light-hearted soul; how could he believe in something so cruel?

And yet Father is the only Hea that I know. Love is what he is least capable of.

Joaviz resumes her wailing. She has learned how to say my name. "Syedaaaaahl."

Father comes into my room, calm and well rested. I realize he must have cast a spell to block the sound from entering the Hea room.

"You've had enough time to mourn him. You must begin your task," he says and then leaves.

He's right. I can no longer lie here, my muscles weakening. I do feel awful for not even trying to console Joaviz, but how can I possibly comfort her?

More importantly, why can't she speak?

Father said he doesn't know, but I don't believe him. I saw an unusual look in his eyes when he attempted to read her mind. I'm sure he knows something about her. Why else would he keep her here? We have never, in all my life, had a guest before.

The way she screams makes it quite clear that she considers herself less a guest and more a captive. Poor thing has been left alone in sleep wrappings for over a day.

I begged him to teach her to speak himself, but he refused. Our creator told him that she is my rite of passage, but this shocked me only because Father never speaks of the Great Volcán.

The only thing to do is obey. I decide to take the Teindahn's advice and give Joaviz a tour of Ezkine. He said it would benefit her to get familiar with her surroundings, and would also help me see Ezkine with new eyes. With Joaviz's eyes, meaning frightened. I already see Ezkine with frightened eyes. Dedication. Duty. Eternity.

Ezkine haunts me.

I unwrap myself and bring a lightfish into Joaviz's room. I can tell she's relieved, even though she attempts to mask it with anger. It takes me a long time to untie the knots because her thrashing has left them tighter and more intricate. I feel terrible for having imprisoned her. Initially it was only to hold her in her sleep, but I kept her tied up all day yesterday. I didn't want to deal with her, nor did I want to risk her escape. I didn't even untie her the one time I gave her food. Instead I chose to feed her myself.

When I have finally set her free, she points at the wrappings and at me, shaking her head vigorously.

"I apologize," I say.

She is still frowning, but she follows me into the kitchen. I butcher a fish for us. When we are full, I lead her around the Realm of Court. I point up to the softly glistening castle, but Joaviz isn't paying attention. Her eyes shift between me and slightly past where I'm pointing—the pure darkness of the unseen surface above.

She pushes water out of her gills with a great rushing sound and flicks her flukes to swim up. I grab her tail and pull her back down. She scratches my face with her nails.

I stare at her in complete shock. She looks at me without

remorse and points up. She wants to leave. I shake my head to tell her I won't let her go and she buries her face in her hands. "I'm sorry," I say.

Her eyes are like daggers.

Stupidly, I begin the tour. In front of the carved white castle entrance, I tell her its stone stories: Ezkun the First broke off from the shallow city of Kalein 250 years ago, killed most of the slinus who lived here on this massive slinu tower, and then forced the rest to build our alu city. For many years he kept them on as servants, but eventually he grew tired of having to monitor them and so had them all publicly slain.

The Realm of Court is encircled by the homes of the Band of Thrones. These conical towers provide the support for the king's castle high above. The effect is darkness giving way sparingly to smooth white walls that reflect whatever shade of bioluminsence squirms near them. I seek out the carvings by memory and tell their stories. King after king. Counseled by Throne after Throne. All to the same aim: keep Ezkininans alone and autonomous in the undesirable Deep.

I grow tired of the shining white pinnacles and domes of the castle. This is useless. How many moons will this take? What keeps me talking is my real desire to communicate with her, to know her secrets and find out what she remembers. I still suspect that she has seen slinus.

Father refuses to discuss the play with me. I don't know why such a violent performance was allowed. Slinus have not attacked for 1000 years! It can be no coincidence that two days after a play about slinus, I meet the second foreigner of my life, and the most frightened ala I've ever seen.

I guide her through the castle entrance and down into Deep Rise Tunnel, then into a rich neighborhood inhabited mostly by shop owners and fishing managers. The houses here are large and decorated with a few imported shells, a topic of controversy among those who care about our embargo on outside trade. King Ezkun the First took over this cylindrical seamount to create an autonomous city, one that was uninvolved in the matters of the Ch'tlan Sea. The current king would like Ezkine to remain this way forever.

I wonder what this neighborhood—and this city—would be like if we could see more than a body's length away.

Joaviz looks as numb as I feel, until she notices a group of alu children zooming over a bowl and dropping stones into it with precision. She smiles, then frowns again when she sees me watching her.

That frown freezes in place when a loud wail—the siren's shark warning—pierces our ears. The children dart into the nearest house. Joaviz rushes to follow them but I grab her hand, swim to the next house over and motion Joaviz inside. This way we won't be so crowded.

Darting around the room is a stout old alee with a yellow tail and hefty, heavily scarred arms. His wide-set eyes are round and black.

"We ask for your protection," I say in the customary fashion.

"And I'm glad you're here," he says with a grin.

I've never before heard anything other than the standard response, which is "It is my duty and pleasure to protect you." Noticing again his yellow tail, stereotypically signifying a rebellious personality, I don't give his brashness another thought.

He shakes his hand as if something has bitten him, and a tiny silver wand morphs into a Hea staff, full of dancing, bright-colored orbs. Before I have time to react, he points the staff at Joaviz, who screams and turns to swim outside. Muttering, he forces her to spin back around and be still. I am as motionless as she is.

He wraps her throat in yellow light.

I recognize that I am completely defenseless against him. Instead of rushing towards them, I hover vertically and cover my open mouth with my hand.

Joaviz's movements are horridly contorted as she tries to wriggle out of the telekinetic restraint. The result is a shaking seizure that makes me whimper with sympathetic pain.

Her stunted screams turn into words. "Stop! Stop it!"

Joaviz's scrunched up face relaxes and then stretches into a huge, ecstatic grin as the yellow light fades. "I can talk!" she says in perfect Ch'tlan.

The old Hea and I lock eyes. We both ignore Joaviz as she rattles on about how strange it feels to speak our language.

"Who are you?" I ask him quietly, not wanting to anger him, lest he decide I deserve a spell of my own.

His voice is gravelly and bemused. "Ah yes. Now you finally get to know! I'm Hasat. Still mad at Cualt for not telling you about me."

The way he says it so nonchalantly enrages me. I lose my sense of calm.

11

Joaviz

MY STOMACH IS RIPPLING. Now I can tell them what I am, and they can tell me how to get back! I wave my arms around, but they don't even notice me. They're busy staring each other down.

"I'm human!" I shout.

Hasat's black eyes shine, then go dull real fast. "Shush, pup. Keep it down!"

Syedahl laughs! I don't like the sound. It's the first time I've heard her laugh. It's cruel and mean and I...

"But I am. I'm human." I stare at Hasat, his sympathetic smile, and I know that he believes me.

I stop feeling sorry for myself. It's time to get answers. It's time to go home! "How do I change back? Can you do the spell? Will you take me to the shore and do it there? Let's leave right now."

"Joaviz, stop." Syedahl has both her hands up. She reminds me of my mother, of anybody's mother when she doesn't believe in the scaly monster or the invisible friend.

Syedahl doesn't believe me.

"We're here to help you, but you have to tell the truth. It was a slinu, wasn't it? You were traveling and your family was attacked, but you survived and found Ezkine. And you were in shock."

I twist away from her and grab Hasat's big hands. "I don't know what she's talking about! You can help me. You believe me, right?"

Hasat's huge chest deflates and his shoulders slump. He's the kind of male you'd expect to have wiry white hair on his chest. In his nose and ears, too. But his skin is smooth except for those big nasty scars. "Yeah, I believe you. Can't turn you back, though."

I smile.

He's joking.

He seems like that kind of alee.

But he hasn't taken his eyes off me.

"You're lying. You can do magic. You...you..." I ram my finger into his chest. "...Can help me."

He covers his face with his hands and breathes deeply. "This is hard." When he finally exhales, he looks at me. "You're the first one I've met. This is harder than I thought. I'm sorry. I can't help you."

What is he talking about? Ohmygodno. This is supposed to be...

He's supposed to...

Mermaids were supposed to know!

"This is absurd," Syedahl says.

I want to slap her. I want to shout at both of them.

But I just let myself fall to the ground and curl up. Drape my flukes over my arms.

"So this is why I'm here," Hasat grumbles at the floor. "Thank you. Thank you. It's clear now." He explains to Syedahl, "This is why the Great Volcán sent me."

I want to crawl out of these scales and into my skin. Legs. Normal lungs. My life.

But I'll keep the eye scales.

Hasat's white hair dances around his head and he mumbles more quietly now.

"Please say you can help me," I plead. "Who did this to me?"

I'm stuck on this idea that it was a she, but I don't know why. I used to remember something about the moment of transformation, but now it's gone. There isn't even a blur. It's a sharp cut. On the boat at sunset with my family. In the water at sunset, a mermaid. Alone.

There was something I used to know, something that Syedahl's dad was looking for or that he gave me or forced on me. Something I knew that he didn't. Or that he wanted me to know.

Syedahl is staring at us, absolutely shocked.

"I don't know who did it to you," Hasat says, hanging onto metal circles on the ceiling. "I can't help you."

I heave hot tears that aren't tears at all. Just aching pressure and heat.

"Sorry, pup," Hasat says.

"You're lying!" I shout.

"Hey! Keep your voice down." His own voice is loud and gruff. His black eyes dart in all directions. "No. I'm not lying."

Syedahl rubs my shoulder. I swat her hand away.

"Are you really a human?" she whispers.

I turn around, lying with my back on the floor. "Are you really mean?"

Syedahl retreats. Hasat's eyes narrow at her reaction. I need him to help me, so I can't let him think that this tension is *my* fault. She's the mean one, not me.

"Her dad attacked me," I say.

Hasat's face goes serious and stern. "Cualt knows about her?"

Syedahl nods and pouts.

Hasat grunts. "Now it all makes sense."

Nothing makes sense to me. Except one thing: I'm not buying it. It's not impossible to transform me back.

I won't be stuck in the water. I'm going to find out whose fault this is and then ask them to fix me. Politely or rudely. Whatever the situation demands.

12

Syedahl

"HOW MANY LIKE HER ARE THERE?" I ask. Many have tried, but no Hea has ever accomplished High Transformation. If Joaviz really is a human, then to my knowledge she's the first one to ever become an alu.

Hasat furrows his brow at me, incredulous at my question. Then he nods with something like respect. "Oh, I don't know. She may be the only one."

They're both waiting for me to speak, Hasat already understanding, Joaviz needing verbal proof. I oblige. "I believe you."

The words come out smooth and natural, full of honesty. She was so afraid! She had no mother tongue, and didn't know how to properly cut up fish or wrap herself to sleep. Father took an unusual interest in her, and said that he couldn't read her thoughts. This is hard to believe, even considering Father's lack of skill in interpersonal magic. Reading memories takes dedication or natural inclination, but thoughts ought to be easily accessed by a Hea of Father's age and training.

Joaviz is clinging to my tail as if for life, begging for my help.

"I'm sorry," I say. "It's impossible." I'm clinging to my past knowledge, not ready for my world to crumble.

"Obviously, it's not." She motions at her tail.

"Hasat, are you *sure* you don't know?"

He stops drifting around the room. Though he now hovers before me calmly, he seems poised to attack. His movements are jerky and unpredictable. "Syedahl, listen to me. Listen!"

I try to entertain him but it's not easy, for my mind wants to reject everything he says and does not say.

"You have to protect her," Hasat says.

That statement is utterly ridiculous, as if I had control over my father. The only word to break through my thoughts is a very flat "What?"

Joaviz has let go of me and is now sniveling in a corner of the room, which is completely empty save the circular holdings on the ceiling. This is not his home. It is no one's.

Hasat is wringing his hands, his whole body alive like a current swirling around the room. When he stops to look at me, his gaze is so intense I wish he would start swimming around again to release his anger.

"Your father is going to experiment on her, just you wait!"

"Experiment?"

"He's greedy for power. He wants to learn High Transformation."

"Did *he* transform her?" I ask. If the answer is yes, then Father would be the most powerful being in all the Seas, and if that were the case, I doubt that even he, loyal as he is, would take orders from the king.

Joaviz's head is still hung, presumably in mourning for the world she'll never see again.

Hasat narrows his eyes. "No. He can't do High Transformation. But he wants to. Oh he wants to. It's what he wants most." How can Hasat know the dream my father holds most dear, when I can't even name a single thing he enjoys?

"Who, then?" I ask, once again failing to convey everything that's going on inside of my head.

The scars on Hasat's arm are pale and iridescent in the light from the fish overhead. "I don't know," he says.

"How do you know he wants to learn High Transformation?"

"Because he asked me to help him figure it out. Even though it's pointless. No one has ever figured it out...*ever.*"

Still lying against the wall, Joaviz pleads, "Don't help Cualt." Her cries are soft and half-hearted, as though she knows the words are a waste but can't keep from saying them. "Help me! Please, just help me."

"It was you," I say to Hasat, remembering the slinu play, the heavily scarred arm that protruded from the performers' room and created the illusions that terrified me so.

He throws up his massive hands. "I didn't want to. I didn't have a choice."

"You did this?" Joaviz demands.

"No, pup. No...She's talking about a *play*...Cualt caught me! I came in undetected but then he sensed what I was doing and...I had to do what he wanted or he would have sent me back to Queen Tilas."

So many terrible things are spinning around in my brain, confusing me, but this comment sends a clear thought into the center of it all. Hasat *left* his city. He fled. He *escaped.*

"Queen Tilas?" I ask.

"She was my ruler."

"But Sarta—"

"Is my brother," he says. "My twin brother. By accident. The other city got the first heir, so when my mom got pregnant with twins, my dad got two heirs. Tila got two heirs. Both of us got initiated—him before me—but when Queen Tilas chose his daughter over mine..."

The insanity starts to fit together. "Henna," I say. "She's your niece. She's to be one of my initiators. So that's why you left? Because Henna was chosen, and not your daughter?"

"No, not really. I wanted it that way. The Great Volcán wanted a different life for us." Hasat grabs me by the shoulders and says very rapidly, "There isn't much time. You've been here too long. Initiators will know you saw me, so don't decide yet. When the time comes, you have to leave. As soon as you get your power, leave Ezkine. It's what the Great Volcán wants." Hasat points a thick finger at me. "You must learn to listen to him."

I pull myself from Hasat's grasp, and allow images of fleeing Ezkine with Alinx to fill my mind. The two of us together, living outside of city boundaries. This in itself is a punishable offense.

The thoughts are too painful. I've made my decision and accepted my fate. My life belongs to King Ezkun.

"Let's go," I say to Joaviz as I rush out of the house, overriding a desire to stay and listen to Hasat ramble. I hear a trickle of movement behind me and turn to see him shouting at me to come back inside.

In the light of the fish strung up outside the house, I watch as Hasat's eyes enlarge and spread farther apart on his face. At the same time his skin turns gray and the ridge along his back peaks into a sharp dorsal fin.

The shark moves towards me, jaws set in a tight line. As the siren renews her song of warning, I hear shrieks of terror coming from the houses around us, but see no faces in the openings. The neighbors can hear the pursuit. Hasat gets closer. I turn and look over my shoulder at a blunt snout and wild eyes, and I can't be sure how much is animal and how much alee.

I dart into a hall and then turn left into another alley.

When I come to a dead end, I do what only King Ezkun and Father are permitted to do: I swim over a row of houses. Hasat comes at me from the left, so I turn right. The memory of his true face leaves me. He is all predator now.

He rushes forward and charges me from the left again.

The children's stone bowl lies forgotten in the alley. A familiar ring of shells adorns an opening. Joaviz's terrified face draws me in. I push her out of the way and tumble into the room.

The large snout slams against the opening and starts a crack on the inside wall. Just as quickly as before, the transformation is over, and a heaving Hasat plunges into the room, taking in large gulps of water in an effort to control himself.

Joaviz skitters away from him.

"I'm sorry," Hasat says to us both, light gleaming off of his yellow scales. "I had to catch you and didn't want to be seen. Some citizalus will remember descriptions of me. Couldn't let them see me. I'm sorry."

After a lot of heavy breathing and scrambling to stay as far from Hasat as possible, Joaviz's eyes light up with hope. "You *can* transform me!"

He smacks his hands on his stocky tail, as if to check that it is really there. "It's different. High Transformation is between two human or half-human species. Alu. Slinu. Human. Dessa."

My senses are still hyper-aware, so that every slush and slither, every trickle and tiny current caused by the slightest movement renews my fear. "Dessa?" I ask. Tales of half-human and half-octopus creatures that glide through the Deep are mere folklore—silly stories told to frighten children.

Hasat looks at me strangely, opens his mouth to explain, but then shrugs and turns back to Joaviz. "Can't do that kind of transformation. Can do this kind because animal magic

57

was my principle skill and I've worked hard to master trans-formation too. *Regular* transformation. Animals. Inanimate objects."

Joaviz looks at him fiercely, as if she still thinks he's lying, and exhales with frustration. She clenches her fists into tight balls and hits the ground three times.

Hasat is still heaving deeply. "Sorry, Syedahl. Didn't mean to scare you. I...*listen to me*. You have to get her out of here. It's what the Great Volcán wants. But only after you've got your power. Your dad will teach you how to tune him out. You might not be able to tell the Great Volcán's voice from your own. It's different for everybody, but eventually you have to learn how to hear—not ignore—him. So listen to me. I've worked hard at it. Soon as you get your power, leave."

I can't imagine living in constant fear of pursuit. "How did you manage all these years?" I ask.

"Spend most of my time as a shark. Only turn into an alee when I have to go into a city whose Hea is so good at animal magic that he can block out predators. Barely ever live as an alee. I do what the Great Volcán asks me. Do what I can to survive. You have to protect her. No matter what. Don't let him do anything else to her! He'll cut her brain into a million pieces trying to figure out how to do it."

Joaviz whimpers and pleads.

"Not supposed to mess with humans," he says. "The Great Volcán doesn't want us to transform them. That's why we can't do it!"

I have no feelings or thoughts anymore.

"The Great Volcán sent me here to ask you to leave," he says, trying to bore his mission into my empty mind.

I refuse to think about leaving. "Who transformed her?" I ask.

Hasat's black eyes grow wild again and I fear a second

transformation. "I don't know."

Something about the way he says this reveals to me that he is lying, but I don't press the issue. He has his reasons I'm sure, and whatever they are, I've gleaned enough about him to assume that nothing I could say would get him to change his mind.

Perhaps he thinks I wouldn't believe him. He's probably right.

"What about this?" Joaviz asks, pointing to the nasty-looking scar on her side. "Do you know—?"

Hasat interrupts her with a resolute, resounding, "No."

13

Joaviz

SYEDAHL COMES INTO THE ROOM and puts a flat palm over her own mouth to remind me to shut up. I don't really get how we're going to keep this from her dad, even if he is bad at reading minds.

I have to hope that she'll take me away from here. I could try to leave by myself, but then I'd be back to square one—all alone with my dying memories.

The smell of Mom's cinnamon rolls. The sound of Dad playing the piano. Sharp, distinct flashes—just pieces of my life. I can't visualize movement, though. I can't remember what it's like to walk. I see the footsteps ruining Mom's vacuuming, but I can't imagine the motion that created them.

How did Tessa do gymnastics? How did I dance?

In a mosh pit for sure, or maybe grinding against some guy but…

I can't remember. All I see are faces floating in the dark haze.

Syedahl swims over the hole in the floor where her dad does magic.

I hesitate. Those deathly white hands, grabbing me…

But I realize Syedahl's going into the kitchen, and I'm so

freaking hungry that I zoom across the empty space, shaking.

Syedahl cuts up fish for us and my fear follows me. Cualt is in the room!

I try my best to look confused as he tells her that her initiation is tonight. They fight over something, about how her rite of passage isn't done. Syedahl is having a fit over it, pulling at her hair, but Cualt tells her it doesn't matter, and then they argue about somebody named Henna.

"You'll spend the day alone in meditation, in your room," Cualt says, but he's looking straight at me.

He leaves.

Syedahl and I eat in silence. I want to ask her what *I'm* supposed to do, but I have to be quiet.

She goes into her room and I go into "mine." They're identical and yet mine's a dungeon.

I wrap myself up the way Syedahl showed me last night and just go limp, not worrying about or even feeling my body.

I have to worry about my mind. Something is wrong with me. I can't remember what walking looks like and it really freaks me out. Feet picking up and slamming down? But no. Too forced. All wrong.

I'm still pissed at Syedahl. I don't like her and I don't really know her, but I want her to come with me. She's all I've got.

A white face appears in the opening. Syedahl?

Oh no.

Cualt rushes into the room. Those white hands are coming for me! He's holding his staff, pointing it at me.

I scream. No words. Just a scream. I shake myself out of the loose wraps as yellow orbs come to the top of Cualt's staff. What happens if the spell is done twice?

"Stop!" I shout.

He backs me into a corner of the room and holds his staff

against me like a bar. He smiles, his pale gums showing in the corners of his mouth. Syedahl's so stupid! He already knew Hasat did this to me! He could tell. Or maybe I just told him. Either way, she's not here to help me.

"Why did she send you here?" he asks.

She.

His face is ridiculously close to mine. There's nowhere to go.

I scream for Syedahl even though I don't want her. I want my own family. I want Sunday mornings and Saturday barbeques. I want to sneak out and get in trouble. I want to be a rebellious 17-year-old girl who gets bad grades. "Syedaaaaaahl!" As soon as I say it, I realize she's as afraid of him as I am.

"Hush! You think she'd risk defying me on the night of her initiation?" His sneering tone tells me that he's not that confident in her, that he's not so sure himself.

"Let me go. I'll leave. I'll leave right now. Just let me go!"

Cualt shakes his head slowly. "I can't let you leave." He looks at my forehead. "There are secrets inside of there that I must get out." The hungry look in his eyes makes me shiver.

"Please let me go."

"Be quiet!" Cualt says. "I'll ask you once more. Why did she send you here?"

"Who?" I ask. "Who are you talking about? I swear I don't know anything. I just want to go home!"

Somewhere deep inside of me I'm so afraid. Afraid of fear. Of endless darkness. Of someone other than Cualt.

Who is *she*?

Cualt's laugh is haunting. "You can pretend if you like. Doesn't matter. I'll get what I need from you. Isn't she the most terrible? Wouldn't you rather work for me?"

I don't know how to answer. I stumble over a bunch of

words that don't make any sense.

He grabs my head, my eyelids slam shut, and he shoves his thumbs into my temples. Everything is dark again. My gut is sickly hot. I'm in that deep place and I'll never get out of it. I'll be in fear forever.

I'm not alone.

Someone is with me. Someone terrible. The darkness of the night pushes in on my head, crushing me. I'll be trapped forever. I deserve all of this.

I'm lifted back into the room.

Cualt is shaking and panting, glaring at me. When he finally lets go of my head, I slide to the floor, hurting everywhere.

He's doing this to me. Why. What. How.

I watch what he takes and what he leaves. The lightfish is gone. Stripes of red light stretch across the opening.

I swim to the bars. Solid and real. I'm trapped—all alone in the endless night with no one to pull me back up.

14

Syedahl

WHEN FATHER APPROACHES MY ROOM, I tighten my grasp on the ceiling holdings. A long time has passed since Joaviz stopped screaming. If I'm this selfish without power, how will I be with it?

I hesitate a moment longer—my mind lingering between what it's seen and what it knows—before letting go. No matter what I decide to do, I will need power to do it.

Before I leave my room, Father says, "Henna has agreed to tell the Ch'tlan Court that you taught Joaviz to speak on your own."

"She'll lie to them?"

Father gives me a weary look and rubs between the middle of his eyebrows. "Yes."

Suddenly, I'm overwhelmed with the desire to tell Father how I'm feeling and to ask for his guidance. I stall. The two of us face each other, me inside my room and he in the entrance, slightly closer to my fate.

"I know that you know what she is, Syedahl." The sternness in his voice surprises me. His patience has vanished.

"Why did you want me to teach her?" I ask.

Father leans against the opening to my room, propping his elbows on the curved rim. The gesture is so informal that once again I want to tell him of my anguish and see how he responds, but I stay silent.

"She needs someone to hold onto," he says. "Someone to trust. I wanted you to calm her while I tried to reach the memory of her transformation."

"How did you know what she was? Does Henna know? Will Henna tell the Court? How many humans are there? Who—"

Father lowers his head and looks up at me from beneath his heavy brows. "I'm not sure what Henna knows, but she will tell the Court that Joaviz was wild—just as I told her to. There will be plenty of time to talk about all of this. Now though, we must go to your initiation." As Father turns away to swim up to the Realm of Court, I approach the opening, but then he spins back around and I pause. "What did you think of Hasat? I hope to have him as our...guest a little longer before I return him to Queen Tilas."

I breathe in sharply and my heart seems to stop. Father has just asked me openly about the most terrifyingly exciting moment of my life. "I...I thought him despicable to be honest, Father. To have left his city! Abandoned his citizalus and queen. I don't see why we should keep him, now that I'll be able to help you."

I keep eye contact with Father until he turns away with a slight smile.

"Wait," I say. "Are you upset that I didn't complete a rite of passage? That Hasat did it for me?"

Father answers without turning around. "No. You'll prove yourself in time. It's all politics anyway." He peers over his shoulder, showing me the sharp lines of his profile. "I did not complete one, either." He waves his hand.

I'm momentarily shocked by this news, but then I recover, for I can't recall a single story about his rite of passage. I only remember my constant fretting over what mine might be. It has certainly exceeded my imagination.

I follow Father up the Hea Tunnel and out into the Realm of Court, with its freshly polished stones. They shine brighter than ever before.

"Syedahl, come along."

Father's voice is far off. I tear my eyes away from the stones and fix them on him, two lightfish ahead. I cross the light and darkness between us to find him laughing at my procrastination. I've never seen him act so pleasant.

After tonight, he won't be alone anymore. Ezkine will once again have two Heas for the first time since my grandmother died.

Agonizing over what my principle skill might be, I follow Father across the Realm of Court. Sooner than I would have liked, we're past the Halls of Conference. I remember how Alinx and I used to zoom through the Halls when his father brought him to court—back when his father was welcome.

A golden glow emanates from the opening of the temple, spilling down onto the columns below it. I study them intensely. I never before took interest in the columns, but now I want to read every carved story, touch every defeated slinu, and search for the face of the Great Volcán.

"Syedahl."

"Yes, Father."

I swim up, keeping my eyes on the tall, arched opening.

Father is already inside, waiting for me. My nervousness turns to dread. I don't want to promise my life to King Ezkun. Or deny my love for Alinx. Or accept that someday I'll be forced to mate with another alee.

I wish Alinx were here with me. He's so courageous. I

imagine him behind me and turn around to see the illusion. I listen as his deep, smooth voice tells me to look past the fear.

"But how?" I whisper aloud.

"Figure out what else is there. What are you feeling besides fear? That's what I do." This is what he would tell me, if he were really here.

Doubt, guilt, and vulnerability are the only other things I can name.

"Syedahl."

Father is in the entryway, full of patience and understanding and forgiveness. These feelings smooth his features. Perhaps my apprehension is a normal response. Besides, he must have guessed that Hasat told me something scandalous.

I can't hover here any longer.

I imagine Alinx giving me a firm shove, but the movement only pushes me a little bit forward.

It is I—not Alinx or Joaviz or Hasat—who goes inside. The only way to describe my decision is that I actually don't have a choice. All the years of my life have brought me here and the last few days can't undo them.

The Temple isn't lit by the usual lightfish, but is instead glowing with a glass bowl full of hot swirling magma on a table in the center of the room.

Father gathers black orbs in his staff and directs them at the opening, where they spread, ooze, and crawl. They fill every gap, closing us off from intruders and distracting noises.

I exhale and move farther into the room, my eyes darting to the ala statues settled into the walls. The Teindahn isn't here. He's only a Hea scholar, not a Hea, and so he's not allowed to be a part of this moment of my life. I can't relax in the comfort of his kindness.

There are two Heas here that I've never met. I don't even

pay attention to them. Only one thing in this magnificent temple draws me in, and that is the promise of my power.

"Welcome," Henna says, smiling widely.

Dawein laughs. "Seems she's eager to bring the number back to 400." There are always 400 Heas in the Eleven Seas, but now with Sarta dead and me as yet uninitiated, the number is 399.

I notice Father relax slightly, relieved that they didn't deem my hesitation suspicious.

I can barely pull my eyes away from the swirling mass, so it must be obvious that I want this.

Red exchanges with gold in ever-changing whirls. I've never seen anything like it before. I've never even seen lava, let alone lava that hasn't cooled in thousands of years—and never will.

I'll finally be part of a group. No longer stuck in the limbo of not belonging.

"Are you ready?" Henna asks. I tear my eyes away from the gorgeous glow and survey the three of them, across from me and nearly blocking my view of the Great Volcán. His majestic image takes up the entire back wall and sets the shape of the temple.

I nod in response.

Henna is dainty, with dark brown eyes that are heavily hooded. She laughs, a light sweet sound. "Unfortunately there are things to take care of first."

"Unfortunately," I say, again enraptured by the lava that was inside of Sarta. I was not allowed in the temple while they extracted it, so I don't know how the lava gets removed from the body.

Nor do I know how it gets in.

The three of them are whispering, torturing me with suspense.

"Of course," Father says, more audibly, though I don't know who or what he is responding to.

"Syedahl," Henna says. The lava is reflected in her eyes. "I have to read your memories, to ensure that you completed your rite and check that there is nothing to suggest that you would betray Ezkine."

Was Father wrong about her lying or does their agreement simply not include Dawein? I vaguely recall Hasat mentioning memories. It isn't my fault that Hasat urged me to leave!

Though my thoughts churn, my body is still. "Of course," I say.

Henna moves around the table towards me. She appears to be in her late twenties. I wonder if she's ever been in love. No, Alinx! Don't bother me now. You'll never be allowed in here.

Henna takes hold of my head. I've never been read before, not even by Father.

Her hands are small and soft. My eyelids fall as if stones had been tied to my eyelashes. My teeth slam shut and I bite my tongue.

For a long while everything is dark. A searing pain flashes across my entire skull as I'm thrown back into the conversation with Hasat. Again I pass through being incredulous, then believing, then angry with myself for such a treacherous belief. Empathy for Joaviz overwhelms me, giving me what I imagine storm sickness to feel like: a longing for calm and a sense of loss. Once again, I imagine myself leaving Ezkine.

It's then that Henna pulls away from me, and I take a much needed breath, an awful sucking sound that would embarrass me were I not so hopelessly disoriented.

My eyes seek out the lava and there it is. To say that it calls to me is an understatement. We want each other. We belong together.

I've been waiting for this my entire life.

Please, Henna. Don't deny me.

"Did she complete it? The wild ala...?" Dawein asks, waving his hand in lieu of completing the question.

"Yes," Henna breathes. "The ala forms basic sentences now."

"Anything else?" Dawein asks, disinterested.

"No," Henna says with a smile. Father is staring at her but she doesn't return his gaze. Henna touches my shoulder. "Of course there was nothing." The gesture is motherly, sisterly I suppose. My desire for feminine affection saddens me. Mother. Sister. I can't imagine what that would be like.

Could Henna advise me about Alinx? Is she already the mother of a Hea heir?

I sigh and silently thank her. Receiving the lava quickly after Sarta's death means that my initial training comes more quickly as well. Father didn't even give me enough time to complete my rite. I care less about why Henna doesn't mind lying and more about whether or not a rite truly matters.

The lava swirls, red and golden. The royals all know that my blood keeps me from dying, but I know that it doesn't protect me from pain.

"What now?" I ask.

They all laugh.

I'm certain I've never heard my father laugh half as much as he has today.

"Now you make your vow," Dawein says.

They're all lined up again on the other side of the table, Henna in the middle, all of them staring at me.

"My vow?" I ask.

"To Ezkine." Father means to be informative but he can't hide his controlling sneer. Apparently this lava is making me silly.

Henna lightens the tension with a soft laugh, but it does nothing to alleviate the heat. Never before have I felt so hot, not even the one and only time I ventured to the surface.

"Do you, Syedahl, promise to serve the citizalus of Ezkine under the command of King Ezkun for all of your life?"

The lava flickers, answering for me. "I promise."

There isn't a moment to regret it. The initiators use their staffs to separate the lava into three glowing orbs. I jolt away, but Father seizes my arms and rams the first hot globe into my stomach. My cries cover whatever spell he utters, and I finally understand the meaning of the word *burn*. Every pore on my belly opens to the searing fire, and the substance escapes inside. I look down to see a stomach as pale as ever.

Henna is upon me, shoving the top of her staff between my eyes. The second orb of lava melts into them and I cry out in pain. When next I open my eyes, the orbs whirling around in their staffs seem brighter.

Dawein's staff is in my mouth, scorching my tongue and all of my delicate insides with the third globe.

It is over. The temple is dark.

The Teindahn comes in with lightfish and strings them to the apex of the ceiling. He opens his mouth, but another voice, one that is commanding and inspiring, drowns him out.

This new voice comes from inside my head.

I'm too afraid to listen. I block it out. I'm not strong enough.

"Syedahl?" the Teindahn probes. "Syedahl? What is your principle skill? Perform something for us."

The first ability comes as a natural inclination. Nearly all else is learned.

"May I?" I ask, looking at Henna.

She doesn't answer. The moment is small, but I know what

it means: a silent request to return the favor. I may have to lie for her, depending on what I find.

My hands are not my own as they reach awkwardly for her across the empty bowl. I feel a twinge of guilt as she jolts with the pain.

The experience is immediate. There is no searching. I'm transported to a rectangular gray room. In the distance someone says, "It's hilarious! Break into the Tribe of All Seas? I thought *I* was crazy. Yeah. It'll take one moon to get word. Yeah."

The lungs don't feel like mine as I take a soft breath and bite my right thumbnail. There are no other prisoners, just my—Henna's—uncle.

I worry that my plan won't work, that they'll come and tell me they've decided not to let me see him, but there he is, staring up at me with bright black eyes that are far from defeated. I search the gray room for his staff but don't see it.

The smells of blood and feces are strong. I gag and then whisper, "Hello, Uncle."

"Hi Henna."

Hasat pushes himself off the floor and hangs onto the bars. His arms are festering—green and pink and white. Blood rises from the gashes. I turn my head away but then feel bad for doing so.

He always told me Heas weaken when trapped, that we can do nothing except mind-reading without our staffs, that even telekinesis is taken from us, and now I believe.

"Where's your staff?" I ask.

"I don't know."

I wasn't prepared to go around killing. I'm not here to join him. I'm lucky Queen Tilas let me leave Tila, and I have every intention of returning. I'm not a traitor.

"How am I supposed to…?"

He looks angry with me. I don't have a choice. I rush back to the two guards and burn their fingers off with red orbs until they lead me to Hasat's staff. They hand it over with stubbed hands that I will not allow to fill me with remorse.

Blood flows into my mouth.

I freeze them both solid so they can't trouble me and then heal Hasat and give him his staff. He blasts the bars into bits of sand.

I unfreeze the guards and we flee. I hate the taste of this foreign sea and the taste of blood corrupting my breathing. I'm relieved I had the foresight to disguise myself. Now I'm wondering how Hasat could tell who I was.

"Your debt is paid," he says.

I am *me* again. Syedahl.

I remember Hasat's scars.

Henna tentatively opens her eyes. I'm exhilarated by the experience of reading her.

"Anything good?" the Teindahn asks.

Father and Henna exchange a look. She is frightened. He is accusatory.

I certainly owe her. "No. Just her...eating."

The Teindahn chuckles, sounding half his age. His black half-circle eyebrows venture farther up his bald head. The three Heas sense that I got something more, but the Teindahn is fooled. "Oh!" he squeals. "Well, was she breaking any rules?"

I give the room what it wants, what it needs to relax. "She did have a mixed dish."

Henna feigns embarrassment. The Teindahn shakes his head at her and points a crooked finger at me. "Well, there's a lot of room for improvement. You have to set an intention. Tell the Great Volcán what you need to know and he will show you."

I am apparently working backwards here. If that was the memory, then what was my intention?

The Great Volcán emerges from the layers of my conscience.

Leave Ezkine. Tonight. Leave.

The Teindahn says, "There is time for one lesson outside of your principle skill before we all dine with the king and the Band of Thrones. In what area would you like your training to begin?"

I shout, "Transformation!" Then I answer the Teindahn more quietly, "Transformation."

Father smiles with self-satisfaction, thinking that I want to help him recreate the magic that brought Joaviz to me.

"I must leave immediately for the Ch'tlan Court," Henna says.

I never thought I'd need lies to earn power. Only pure blood.

"But wait. Her staff," the Teindahn says.

I arch backwards, look up at the apex of the ceiling, stretch my arms wide and then slam them together. As I pull my hands apart, my staff forms between them.

"There is something that you will join together," Henna prophesizes.

15

Joaviz

I'M SO STUPID. I THOUGHT I should trust Syedahl and look where it got me. Stuck in a room. Trapped.

As if my life couldn't get any worse. Stuck in this body. Stuck underwater. Now I'm actually a prisoner.

Every time I swim the room I cut the corner with the light-fish. I don't want to get too close to it.

I've been circling this room all day. Finally tired, I move to the back and slump down against the wall.

Right below my belly button, my skin gets bumpy, morphing into red-orange scales.

That oval scar on my side pisses me off. I know I didn't have it before, so did I get it from the transformation? Or did something else happen to me?

I run my hands down my tail. It still feels foreign. If I couldn't feel my own touch, I wouldn't think this was my body.

The scales around my eyes are gold, that's what Syedahl told me. She said they start out dark gold and fade to a light shimmer at the edges. Their shape is sharp and triangular, spiky like the wisps at the tips of my flukes. Syedahl's eye scales make curlicues and her flukes are scalloped.

She says no two fluke patterns are the same. Only alas have eye scales, and they're also unique. I asked about the ridge fins I've noticed on every alee, and she explained that they are a masculine trait.

Alu breathing is not like that of fish or humans, but somewhere in between. We inhale through our mouths and exhale through our gills.

I see something out of the corner of my eye and jump up. I should have left after Syedahl untied me. I just didn't want to be alone, but it's better to be alone than stuck—or tortured.

"Hasat!" I say happily.

He's hanging on the black horizontal bars that block the opening, looking at me with his crazy, wide-set eyes.

I swim forward and grab his hands. "Get me out of here."

He nods. "All you have to do is get out of my way."

There's something about him I can see that Syedahl can't. She thinks he's irresponsible, but I just see an alee who gets what he wants.

When I move back a bit, he raises his hands in front of the bars and squeezes them shut. The bars burst open, disintegrating into tiny bits of sand.

I zoom out of the opening, forcing Hasat to dart back. "Whoa there, pup."

"Sorry. I'm not waiting for anybody to have a change of heart. I'm out of here."

I angle myself up and start kicking my flukes to go to the Realm of Court.

"Wait!"

The purple rock of the tunnel is rough. "What?"

"You…you should eat something. Come on."

"No way. I don't care. It's not worth it," I say in spite of the growling and grumbling that I know the vast empty ocean won't solve. "No."

"I'll tell you something you need to know…" he offers.

That's a reasonable proposal. "Fine."

I move my tail awkwardly in reverse motion. Cualt must have gone to the market or got a delivery because there are about twenty fish in the kitchen now, flapping around.

Anywhere else, I'd be able to *hear* them flail. Cualt has silence charms all over the house to keep him from getting distracted…from what I don't really want to know.

"When will they be back?" I ask, closing my eyes and grabbing a fish. It twists in my hands until Hasat graciously takes it and guts it for me. The smell is divine.

"Soon. Very soon."

"What!?" The smell of the fish is almost enough to placate me, but not quite. I have to get out of here. Now.

"Hear me out."

"Why?" It's not the fish that makes me turn back around. I don't want to be alone out there. Not ever again.

"Give Syedahl a chance. I have a gut feeling about this."

"Yeah, well I don't—not anymore. You obviously don't care if Cualt traps me again!"

He hands me some chunks of meat and I eat them greedily. "Helping you isn't my task."

"Then what is?"

He shrugs his huge shoulders, sending his white hair spinning. "You want to know?"

"Not if knowing will get me trapped again. Bye." I take more meat out of his hands and turn away.

"You could think of me as a spy. Find stuff out and tell it to whomever the Great Volcán wants me to."

I chew up the pieces. "What does he want you to tell me?"

"To trust me. I'll get you out of here, no matter what. I promise. Just give me a chance to see if Syedahl will go with you."

I talk over my shoulder, not facing him. "I don't want her to."

"Can't lie to me."

"I'm serious. I don't want her to come."

"But you want someone to go."

"Yeah, well, that's not the same thing."

"Maybe not. But she's your only option, so it kind of is, pup. It kind of is."

Water streams out of my gills and I bend in on myself.

Two weird disconnects are going on inside me. Need versus want. Getting out of here versus being patient. I couldn't say which is need and which is want, but I do know that nothing in my brain is getting along. "What do I have to do?"

"Just wait. Leave with Syedahl when you have an opening. If I'm wrong and she doesn't want to go, then take off on your own."

I nod my head, thinking. What if she doesn't come with me? What if she does? No one can help me either way.

Hasat cocks his head, listening.

"What?" My heart thumps even louder as I think of Cualt.

Maybe it's just because Hasat is clenching his fists and grumbling to himself, but I can sense Cualt. My skin tingles and my scales prickle up. Just the thought of him makes me want to fight whatever he did to me, to never go back to that empty place again.

Where I can't remember who I am.

Hasat jolts out of the opening and into the entrance room. When I follow, he's already gone.

I can't hear what's going on out there. I curse the silence charms and dart around the entrance room, wondering how I'm supposed to know if this is my opening.

Either way, I'm not waiting.

I move up out of the tunnel and into the Realm of Court,

where groaning and swimming sounds greet me but no sights other than the usual zapping lights all around the edges. I'm in the middle, in obscurity.

Can Cualt see me?

I have to find Syedahl, but I don't want to shout for her. "Graahhhh!" Hasat grunts. I swim towards a light.

Hasat and Cualt move into the green glow, not even touching each other but somehow connected. Hasat has one hand on his staff and the other clenched in front of him, making Cualt's head rattle and his eyes roll back.

I dodge them as Cualt goes still and his face returns to normal. His green eyes are brighter in the light and pierce right through me.

Hasat's arm is twisted weirdly but I have to leave him.

There she is across the court under a blue jelly, burying her face in her hands and sobbing.

I rush towards her. "Come on! Let's go!" Behind me Hasat and Cualt are still struggling, groaning, switching off between shouting in triumph and shouting in pain.

Syedahl lifts her head. I've never seen anyone look so guilty. "I'm a terrible daughter."

"No, Syedahl, no." I don't know what to say, but it doesn't matter because Hasat is zooming this way, flailing his arms and flukes to stop his unnatural momentum. It doesn't work. The water doesn't slow him. His eyes are huge as he screams, "Move!"

I yank on Syedahl's hands and dart away. Hasat's head smacks me in the shoulder, grinding my bones together. He hits the pole with his stomach, twists around it, and falls to the ground.

I shriek and cover my mouth.

Hasat is completely still.

"Syedahl, we have to go!"

I hold her hand and start to swim but she isn't moving. She's a dead stubborn weight that I can't carry. "Come on!"

When I turn towards her, Hasat winks at me. Cualt points his staff at Hasat's back and without taking his eyes off of him, turns his other hand towards me. I'm stuck.

Really, truly, seriously stuck in Cualt's command. As powerless as when he helped Syedahl wrap me up in seaweed the first time.

Only this time she's powerless too, and I don't know if she's on his side.

Hasat is mumbling. I hold on to the image of that wink and know he's up to something. I scream to take Cualt's attention from him.

Cualt reacts by forcing us to spin all the way around with an easy twist of his hand. Syedahl and I hover towards him, back into the light.

Just when I hear a mysterious swimming mass, Cualt's eyes widen and flash at Hasat, ready to punish him if only there were time.

Something brushes against me, but I don't even have the power to turn and look at it.

I can only move my eyes. A huge shadow comes over us and I stretch my eyeballs up as far as I can towards the gray whale belly.

Suddenly, my neck is turning towards an octopus and next to that there's a squid. I suck in water. Hasat is mumbling like a madman again. He's up off the floor and shouting with glee. I take Syedahl's hand. She's numb, just staring at all the animals around us.

Whales and sharks and schools of fat blue-silver fish fill the Realm of Court. I hear multitudes in the darkness. Cualt raises his staff and collects blue orbs to freeze them, but Hasat grabs his own staff off the ground and floods the

Realm of Court with green orbs.

Green light spills over us.

When the light is gone, every creature has burst into a hundred eels. Eels everywhere, slick and gray with snapping jaws.

They rush past all at once, rubbery skin sliding between my arms and against my neck.

Hasat shouts at us to leave.

I pull on Syedahl and get ready to escape by swimming straight up, but she's still a dead weight. Not stubborn. Just *sad*.

"Please, Syedahl!"

She watches as the eels surround her dad, turning him into a giant squirming ball like an evil anemone. With a wicked popping sound, an eel bursts open. Then another and another.

Syedahl squeezes my hand, finally coming alive.

"Go!" Hasat shouts repeatedly between squeals of mad glee. A flash of his yellow tail stands out beside the writhing mess.

16

Syedahl

WITH FATHER OVERWHELMED by the eels that Hasat set on him and my guilt reaching across the Court, Joaviz is the one to realize that now is our chance. But once I become aware, I take the lead and swim straight up. Towards the surface and everything I thought I wanted.

The siren sings a warning to the guards. When I believe that we're well out of view, I lead us westward. The castle buildings disappear, replaced with endless depth.

At the protection boundary, pain rips through my whole body. Joaviz relinquishes immediately and falls behind. I grab her hand and remind her of the kind of pain that could befall us if we don't continue.

We swim and swim and swim but stay stationary, suspended past the western edge of the foundation, helpless against a strong current that feels like tiny spikes.

Perhaps I created the Great Volcán's voice in my head.

Just when I think we won't make it, I hear Father call out in pain and the resistance stops. We jolt forward.

Is he dying? I almost turn back to help him, but something inside me yearns for any other kind of life, even if my new existence means betraying him.

17

Joaviz

"What I don't understand is, why you?" Syedahl floats on her back and looks at me sideways. The daylight makes the water glisten. I can't see the surface, but I know that it's there.

"What do you mean?"

"Why would someone choose to transform *you*, over all other humans? Are there others like you? Are you a princess? Are you a Hea?"

I laugh. "We don't have Heas and I'm not a princess." Though I'm sure my mom would disagree.

Mom. Lank brown hair, tired eyes.

"Other humans? I don't know." The thought of others like me down here makes me feel better, but I wouldn't wish this on anyone.

Yesterday we fought with some diving puffins for herring, which was really strange. I wanted them to snatch me with their beaks and lift me the heck out of here. I got emotional and Syedahl had to catch the fish.

Then I snapped out of it.

I'm in this whole other world, but seeing those diving birds reminded me that I'm still on planet earth.

"What makes you unique?" Syedahl asks me now.

"I don't know."

Seriously though, this sounds like the kind of question my therapist used to ask. What makes me special?

"Had you ever seen an alu before?"

I shake my head. "No. I didn't even think you existed!"

"Hmm...well, that's good, isn't it?" Her tone is removed, like she's a super sleuth and not my friend. But I guess I already know that.

"What's wrong?" she asks.

"Nothing. I-I don't know why this happened to me!" My voice comes out frustrated.

"Just calm down. Let's think about this."

I drop my head and look down at the deepening blue. It feels nice to be carried by the current. "Fine."

"Where were you before? What's the last thing you remember?"

I feel a blank spot deep inside me. Some kind of really bad pain erased. "Ummm..."

Syedahl waits.

I remember saying goodbye to my best friend Lily. I remember when I first went to Ezkine. In between? I think I used to know, but now I don't.

I barely remember the pain of trying to look for...

What was I looking for? Something in the air? Why would my parents be in the air? A plane crash, but that doesn't feel right. "I don't know."

Syedahl touches my shoulder. "It's okay. Just tell me the very last thing."

"I was saying goodbye to my best friend. She was watching our house for us."

Syedahl cocks her head. "So you were going somewhere?"

"Yeah."

"Do you live on land close to here? Close to Ezkine?"

I think of the long, warm, sunny beach by my house, where I used to walk and listen to my iPod and drink cheap beer with my friends. "No way. It's too cold here." Something hits me in the chest. A memory. "Wait. Wait." I try to focus.

Dad. He took us on our annual cruise! We were going early, because...*no*. "My dad is sick."

"Sick?"

"My dad is dying."

"I'm so sorry."

"We were going on vacation for him. For the last time. We were going to...We were on a ship." We always go on a cruise in July, but it was February. We had to go while Dad was still strong enough.

"A ship?"

The gradients of blue are whirring. I don't believe my own breaths. It's that same question: asking *why* breathing water is really breathing, and then hating breathing all over again. Syedahl grabs me and holds me close.

"Don't think about it right now," she says. "Just let me know if you remember anything else."

A shadow passes over us, a huge chunk of ice.

I ask her questions about alus, Heas, and magic.

All the things that Syedahl explains about magic are really for her own ears, not mine. When she talks about following the Great Volcán, she tries to justify her actions. Everything is about her. How she left.

Her power.

Her father.

And now she wants to find Alinx.

I should have got more information out of Hasat.

Time passes. It goes by slowly, every moment the same

shade of blue, and every moment forgotten now that it's night.

"We can't rest tonight," Syedahl says. "We have to get out of Ch'tlan."

She thinks Heas in other Seas won't care to send her back to Ezkine and I hope she's right.

"Do you hear that?" I ask.

"Yes. Excellent!" Syedahl says. She's just an invisible shape now, pressing against me.

The current surges. When I open my mouth to breathe, the water tastes different. Thick and sharp.

Something bumps into me.

"Was that you?" I ask.

Something slick. And something else sticky.

"Was *what* me?" Her voice is too far away. "Catch everything you can."

A light flashes in front of my face.

"What's wrong?" she asks.

I stammer. Try to speak. But slimy bodies and random flashes of light surround me.

Waves roar louder and louder overhead. I want to swim back up current but I go limp.

"What, Joaviz?" Syedahl's arms are around me trying to shake me to life. "What is it?"

"The Deep..."

"Yes. Deep sea creatures often come up to feed at night. Everything's alright."

A pulsating blue jellyfish zooms past her head, illuminating her white face and big black eyes.

A squid slides against me and sparks my heart into action.

"Slow down!"

The flashing lights, silvery and shimmery, surround my

body completely. The hundreds of pairs of black eyes.

Get me out of here.

I see too many eyes on one green face. Huge and mean. Slithering. Red hair like mine. The snake monster from my dream.

I swim fast and hard to get away. I don't want to know. I *can't* remember.

18

Syedahl

JOAVIZ AND I ARE SWIMMING at a moderate speed in the blue middle waters. Our bellies are full with the morning's catch.

I betrayed King Ezkun the very night I promised my life to him. I deserted my father without explanation and watched idly as Hasat attacked him. I am an escapee, a disgrace.

And yet Alinx occupies my mind the most.

How he's doing, whether he's made it home, if he knows I've left and if he hates me for it.

I also wonder if there are others like Hasat and me, other Heas who left their cities on the Great Volcán's orders. Or maybe I made up that voice. Maybe Hasat and I are just selfish.

The warnings of my forthcoming inability to love are as mysterious now as they were then. I still love Alinx. He's still the only friend I've ever had.

He moved to Ezkine when he was nine years old. His parents had been living in his mother's city in Heiste Sea, but decided to return to his father's city of birth. The parents of officers are supposed to both be of Ezkinian descent, but I suppose that since the father's lineage is always more important, it was easy for the citizalus to let someone as talented as Alinx slide past the usual requirement.

Alinx is the best at controlling the weapons that Father infuses with magic. Most alees can't concentrate enough to give the simultaneous tactile and thought cues, but Alinx is dexterous and focused.

He can spear a target so far out of vision's range that it takes significant exertion to swim out and check that it was successful.

Once, two moons ago, Alinx invited me to the training arena, an extension of the Ezkinian foundation that protrudes far beyond the city boundary. Three thick metal poles stretch horizontally outwards from the city and boast many kinds of targets and obstacles. Father can sense when anyone leaves or enters the boundary, so I told him I was going for a short swim and took off long after Alinx did.

Alinx brought fifteen lightfish and put on a great show for me, zooming through hoops and shooting at targets while spinning around. He used magical wrist darts and klys and even speared a shark that happened by.

That was one of the happiest times of my life, seeing him so happy. I laughed harder than I ever had before. Nothing since has been so much fun.

When Alinx first came to Ezkine, his father was invited to Court often, for he had traveled widely and had many stories to tell. He'd often bring Alinx with him, and I'd shy away from the young alee who was always so rambunctious and energetic. He was a mystery to me.

One day Alinx made a proposition I could not resist. His voice squeaked with excitement when he told me he was going below the lightline, and that I could come along if I wasn't scared.

The lightline is the boundary between alus and slinus.

Their territory is vastly more spacious, but ours is more resourceful. No alu city can be below the lightline, and no alu or slinu is supposed to cross. These were the terms at the end of the war one thousand years ago. The foundation of Ezkine was originally a slinu mound. King Ezkun kept some slinu slaves to build it higher, just above the lightline—temporarily breaking the treaty to ultimately uphold it.

We saw not one slinu, which greatly disappointed Alinx.

To make the journey more worthwhile, I told him a scary story about the Serpent Mistress, the fabled leader of the slinus during the war, but he shushed me and made me feel childish. "Myths don't scare me. What's scary is what's real," he said, running his hands along the foundation and searching for protrusions of bone.

As we began our ascent, a bright bobble came towards us, shining and mystical. We should have known better, but he was itching for danger and I wanted a friend, so we gave in to our curiosity and floated slowly towards it, reaching out to touch it.

Then the teeth snapped. We raced, pumping our tails to get back home. The anglerfish pursued, and Alinx pushed me above him so that he would be closer to it. He swam slowly so he wouldn't pass me.

Just as we reached the top of the foundation, Alinx let out a yelp and swam through the neighborhood, still screaming. An old alee emerged from his home, speared the angler, and took it back inside with him.

From that day on, I've never heard Alinx scream, nor have I ever seen him unarmed. He must have vowed to himself to always be calm and ready. He began to go hunting, bringing delicacies home to his mother, but he would not let me go with him. He didn't want me to get hurt.

For some reason Alinx and his father stopped coming to

court. I believe now that they may have been uninvited, but I really don't know. So I started going to Southern End to spend time in their tiny house with his plump mother. I'd wander the alleys of Ezkine with Alinx, making up stories as we went.

When we were little, he was jealous of the power I'd get someday. He wanted to be mighty. I was jealous of his freedom. Over time though, our emotions changed. We fell in love with the traits we once envied.

Power has changed me. The tingling hot sensation in the pit of my stomach has expanded my abilities. Interpersonal magic is my principle skill. I can read minds and memories— through touch only, for now. My quick lesson in transformation allows me to change an object's color. Like all new initiates, I possess the basic Hea skills of temperature magic and language magic, acquiring a new language just from the sound of one word.

Hiding my identity is essential. I can turn my staff into a tiny wand that's easily concealed in a closed fist.

But nothing has been removed from me—least of all my ability to love. If anything, the ache has expanded so much that I can't believe it would ever go away.

The only way I can make sense of that misconception is if it's true for others. It must be all the responsibility that supersedes emotion. I'm not burdened the way other Heas are. I have no one to train me or make demands.

Instead I am hyper-aware of myself, knowing that to consider the needs of Father and the king would be to give up before I've given Joaviz some semblance of safety. Before I've learned what my decision truly means for me.

I'd kill to know what Alinx thinks of me, now that I've left—if he even knows. It's been four days.

I pray he's still in Kalein.

What business did he have with the Ch'tlan Court? Father sent him away so I wouldn't be distracted during my first few days with power, but what did he have him do?

What will Father do if he catches me? I'm assuming he survived Hasat's attacks but I'm not certain.

I'm the most vulnerable Hea in all the Seas, the most sought after and the least able to protect myself.

I watch the sunlight glisten off of Joaviz's scales. She smiles at me and I smile back, even though I think her gesture is more mocking than friendly. It seems she'd rather gab all day, but I need my quiet moments. I used to hate all of my alone time, but now I see how essential it is.

Joaviz is beautiful when she smiles, dimples forming in her cheeks. Her smile grants me reprieve from those intense eyes.

I'm constantly squinting, unable to adjust to the brightness. Though it gives me a slight headache, I love it. The perfect blue of the upper middle waters. The way my light blue scales take on an iridescent sheen in the sunlight.

"What's that?" Joaviz asks, frantically searching the quickening current for the source of the grumbling sound.

"A storm," I reply. "Stay low. It will be calmer down here."

As we approach, the waves carry us backwards half as far as they carry us forwards. They pull and crash down on us, tiny bubbles tickling my skin amidst all the pressure and power.

There's a loud rushing sound that I don't recognize. It's made up of a thousand smaller sounds. "Let's go lower!" I shout to Joaviz.

She's limp, letting the aftermath of the waves overhead rock her this way and that. Her turquoise eyes light up and her unexpectedly brazen smile scares me. "Is that rain?" she asks.

I've heard stories of the mysterious current in the sky.

Joaviz swims straight up, arms outstretched. I kick my flukes to try and grab her but am too late. For a terrifying instant, I can't see her.

I ascend, feeling the motion of the waves get stronger. I don't want to go too far up, for fear of storm sickness.

The waves crash into me, sending me lower and then bringing me back up. The visibility is horrid because of the bubbles and my spinning and turning. I'm nauseous and dizzy. Water pulls away from me, exposing my gills to the air and the falling drops of water. I gasp for breath.

Waves bend over me and force me back down. I relish the moment of calm and take a deep gulp of water. Here the water is a lovely blue. I search for Joaviz and finally see a shock of red hair.

She's further down current. I shout to her but the noise of the rain and waves is too great.

Her body puts up no resistance to the waves. The water rocks her in my direction, showing me that her eyes are closed.

I try to swim towards her, but am pulled back. I curve awkwardly and flip, my flukes falling first and then my head.

I spin and crash twice more, my every little reactive movement stolen by the power of the waves. Again the water pulls back from me and my skin is exposed to the rain.

Rain is so fast, so heavy in the air. Water broken into tiny bits falling quicker than anything.

I'm rushed forward and I see a glimpse of shiny orange scales before I smack into Joaviz. She opens her eyes with a start. The ocean is calm where we sway, but all around us the two currents are fighting.

"Now!" I shout. "Swim down, now!"

Joaviz ignores me and brings both of her arms out of the

water. A big satisfied smile crawls across her face. The top of her head is out of the water, the surface coming down as far as her eyes.

The waves ahead roar and groan, and I know we'll be tossed into them soon. I feel myself being pulled backwards.

Joaviz works hard to stay where she is.

"Come on!" I shout.

But she's lost to the beauty of the rain. Even when a new wave claims both of our helpless bodies, she reaches her arms skyward, searching not for the safe depths but for the novelty of the water in the sky.

We are tossed around many more times and I lose sight of her again. Every organ in my body feels upside down, my chest raw with accidental breaths of air.

The water gets colder and less salty. Calm again. We are in a new current, straight from the fresh melting glaciers of the high north.

Still Joaviz works her flukes to keep her hands in the air. I reach her and do the same. The new, victorious current carries us farther from the rumbling war.

The raindrops overhead are light and pleasant now. Joaviz's smile is unchanged.

Then I realize.

Rain is not new to her.

She opens her eyes to look at me, and though her head lulls with nausea and her back is curled with cramps, her eyes are clear. *So clear.*

I believed her before, but now I understand. She wants to go home so badly that she's willing to put herself in danger. She'll do anything for a reminder of home, for something familiar.

I throw my arms around her and give her a tight hug. For a moment she's upset that I've pulled her hands back into the water, but she relaxes and allows me to hold her without hugging me back.

I pull away, clasp her shoulders, and look intensely into her bright eyes. "I promise to help you. Do you hear me? I promise that I will do whatever I can to get you home."

She nods but does not speak. I release her and she holds her hands up again, palms flat, enjoying.

19

Joaviz

"THE CITIZALUS MAY RECOGNIZE ME if I don't disguise myself. And you, with your coloring—oh, you'll stand out." Syedahl is biting her pouty bottom lip.

We swim away from the city, a dull brown smudge in the distance, so she can be sure the Hea there won't sense her magic.

"Citizalus? Recognize you?"

"Yes. I've been here before. Just once. The only time I ever—"

I've been trying to talk to her all day but now that she's willing, I don't want to hear it. She's avoiding the issues. I cut her off with "Citizalus, *Syedahl*?" My voice comes out sharp. I say a little nicer, "What is that?"

"It simply means alus who live in a city. It's a term of respect. By Tribe law, all alus are required to live in a city, to be protected. So really the terms are interchangeable."

"Oh." I had been picturing some giant, muscled mafia with huge ridge fins that would snatch us up and then torture us to confess to some crime we had never even heard of.

"We need a reason for coming to Kalein. How did you find Ezkine anyway? How did you know it was there?" Her eyes are wide and innocent but the question pisses me off.

She's trying to fabricate a new story. I doubt she's really interested in learning about me. "Why do you care?"

"Just tell me, Joaviz."

I raise an eyebrow before giving in. "I don't know. I just followed my gut. I didn't want to go deep because it freaked me out. But I just had this feeling. Instinct, I guess."

"Instinct." She nods. "Oh, I hope this works."

"I hope so, too," I say, actually hoping that Alinx isn't there and we leave right away. I saw the way they looked at each other. Love like that is majorly distracting. And I need Syedahl to focus on me.

"Is this going to hurt?" I ask, thinking of when she extracted the orbs from her mouth with her fingertips. It sure looked like it hurt her. Plus she couldn't do anything but sleep for half a day afterward.

Syedahl furrows her brow. "I don't think so." Golden orbs spew out of her staff and cover us, making us shine brighter than the sunlight above.

When the glow is gone, my tail is light pink and my hair dark brown. Syedahl's hair is lighter, and her scales have turned pale orange. "There!" she says. "We should pass for Tilan." The difference in the shades of our skin is less dramatic now.

"Let's just keep going," I say, grabbing her arm.

"We have to start searching somewhere."

"But you said we had to get out of Ch'tlan."

"It will be fine." She brandishes her staff. "I'm here to protect you."

"Can't you give us better disguises? We look the same."

Her head drops. I've hit a nerve. "I can't. This is all I had time to learn about transformation. The Teindahn only taught me coloring."

I shake my head. "It doesn't feel right."

Finally, she understands why I'm so worried. "Joaviz, do you think I wasn't being sincere? I made a promise and I intend to keep it. I left Ezkine for you, not for Alinx. I doubt he's still here. He would've taken a different current to get home. Most likely, we've missed him." Syedahl turns her staff into a tiny silver stick and closes it in her palm.

I want to believe her, but I can see how different she's acting—looking around furtively. She's anxious, nervous.

In love.

I know that feeling. So yeah, I'm worried. I don't trust that she has the willpower to keep her promise.

"Let me do the talking," Syedahl says.

The city is a ringed disc on the light, sloping sand. As we descend, I see that the rings are made of houses and alleys. The water is a mild blue. We swim low, our stomachs barely above the sand, towards a high wall. "Why do they have a wall?" I ask.

Syedahl grabs my hand and we swim to the left, looking for the opening. She whispers, "To anchor the city spells, like invisibility to humans and protection from predators. It also helps the citizalus to know how far protection extends."

"Ezkine didn't have a wall," I say. I hear some alus talking on the other side but can't tell what they're saying.

"The boundary of Ezkine was obvious," Syedahl says shortly. She stares as though waiting for the wall to break.

We swim to the side to get out of the way of a fat tail and its yawning owner.

"Hello," the guard says.

Syedahl stares at him but he doesn't say anything else, so we pass through the arch just beyond him. Looking left and right, the first row of buildings appears to be houses. No hustle. We go straight. I follow Syedahl through the canal that cuts to the center of the city.

We pass rings of houses and shops with citizalus talking and rushing past. I notice that no one is swimming above the buildings, just like in Ezkine. I guess it's an etiquette thing.

"Where are you going?"

Syedahl hushes me. She's swimming really fast. Some alus turn to watch us as we go by. "I'm not sure yet."

We come to the center of the city, the inner circle. Three layers of alus are all crowded around. There's space above, so we swim up and join in. We watch an ala send orbs dancing through the water. A green one morphs into a snake and I shiver.

A purple one becomes an anemone, making a little girl laugh.

Syedahl's flukes pulse rapidly and she yanks on my hair. "Ouch!"

The magician ala glares at me.

I follow Syedahl to the opposite edge of the city circle, past an alee shouting, "Rishan becomes the twenty-second city in a growing list of cities that have approved the Tribe of All Seas representative. This time next year, Rishan will include the representative in its city government. Rishan officials cite the growing population of humans on the shores of their territories, and the increasing number of human sightings, as the main reason for the decision to accept additional support. Queen Risha claims slinus had nothing to do with it."

All I really process are the words *humans* and *slinus*. Citizalus around me grumble in response. "Nasty creatures always getting in the way." "Filthy things." "Never have enough." "Never satisfied." "Can't stay where they belong." Somehow I know it's not slinus they're complaining about.

The pain in my scalp gradually subsides. "What was that for?" I ask.

"That's Henna," she says.

"Who?"

"One of my initiators." Syedahl covers her mouth and closes her eyes.

"Oh." My heart pounds. I shake her. "What should we do?"

Behind us, the crowd groans.

"That's all the time I have. I'm sorry," says a soft, sultry voice.

Syedahl snaps out of it and takes my hand.

The same voice says, "Wait."

For a moment I think Henna's making me turn, but then I realize there's just something about her that's intriguing. I face her all on my own. She has a silvery purple tail, tan skin—not orange-tan like mine, but brown-tan—and huge eyes.

"So this is what you decided?" Henna asks in a kind way.

Maybe Syedahl has been over-exaggerating about everyone caring that she left. It wouldn't surprise me. She does seem overly dramatic.

Syedahl gapes at Henna.

Henna narrows her big brown eyes. "It's not too late to change your mind. I doubt you understand what you're getting into."

They stare each other down. Finally, Henna reaches for Syedahl's head, but she backs away.

"Fine," Henna says. "Keep your thoughts to yourself."

Should I tell her *my* thoughts? She's older. About thirty, probably. *Way* more experienced.

Syedahl asks, "Why did you agree to lie for me? Whose side are you on?"

"What sides are there?" Henna's eyes snap to me. "And you…" I can't tell if that's supposed to be a question or what.

I don't know what to say. I don't want to trust anybody,

ever again. The last time I did, I ended up heartbroken for weeks. But Syedahl *loves* Alinx. She'll leave me for him.

"I…" I lean in and whisper, "I'm a human."

Henna actually laughs. "I already knew that. Cualt wanted Syedahl to deal with Ezkine while he dealt with you. But my uncle wouldn't have that." Henna glares at Syedahl's forehead, trying to eat her thoughts. "And apparently neither would you."

20

Syedahl

"IT'S NOT MY PLACE," Henna says to me. Her facial expression is unreadable. I want so badly to take hold of her head and read her reaction, just as she tried to do to me. Though her principle skill is healing, she does well with interpersonal magic. She would be able to block me, and I her, so we're left with the mundane faculty of speech and speech alone.

"How is it not?" I ask. My voice is a little loud, but Henna has cast a silence charm around us so the citizalus cannot hear. They stare at us, mystified by the silence, even though they know who she is.

"This is between you and your father and King Ezkun," Henna says.

I object to her statement. Surely this is the business of the Great Volcán first and foremost. I feel a little abandoned by him. I haven't heard his voice since my initiation.

Henna, of course is my second objection. "You involved yourself when you didn't tell them about my meeting with Hasat. Father knows already, but Dawein..." I don't continue the sentence because a thought strikes me. She could have at least tried to block me during my initiation, but I didn't feel any resistance. She gave me the memory of her saving Hasat. "Why did you want me to see that?"

Joaviz is wringing her hands, obviously upset that her big confession didn't have any effect on Henna.

"I wanted you to see how dangerous your decision was," Henna says. "That was the only way I could show you."

She also revealed that she'd owed some debt to him. *Your debt is paid.*

"What was Hasat doing at the Tribe of All Seas headquarters?" I ask.

She covers an unexpected smirk with her small hands. "Oh, that wasn't headquarters! That was a small holding facility, unprepared to deal with a Hea. Hasat was spying, gathering information as usual." Her tone is dismissive, as though Hasat was playing a silly game or doing some household chore like directing suckerfish to algae.

I am utterly perplexed by her. "Don't you respect him? Love him?"

"No. *Yes.* There is a familial bond between us. I owe him recognition of that. But…he is not as effective as he'd like to be. He spreads mad, groundless theories. What is respectable about that?"

I stare over Henna's shoulder at the citizalus swimming by.

Joaviz breaks the silence. "Can you help me?"

How can she still not believe in me, after everything I've done? I abandoned my city and the only life I knew! She knows nothing about Henna, except that she's more powerful than I am. If Henna had tried to capture her after that little confession, I might not have been able to defend her. Temperature magic comes naturally to all Heas, and it's the only form of attack I have. Surely Henna has learned some telekinesis.

*She's more powerful than I am…*It isn't that Joaviz doesn't trust me, but that she doesn't trust my abilities.

"I won't involve myself in this," Henna says in her whispery voice.

She doesn't want to admit she's already helping me. She left after my initiation, before the lesson in transformation magic, so she could come tell the Court that I completed my rite of passage but not be away from Tila for too long.

Something inside of me—an instinctual, familial connection—says that Father did survive Hasat's attacks and that he's alive. But even if I had doubts, Henna wouldn't be able to address them.

"Are you helping my father?" I ask.

"I serve no one but Queen Tilas." She whips her head around, towards children chasing each other and merchants selling their wares.

"What is it?" I ask, straining to hear what she hears, but I pick up only the usual city sounds.

"They're here. Ezkinian warriors, looking for you." Her sense of boundary is obviously keener than mine.

I acutely feel the inadequacy of my disguise. Our colors are different but we look exactly the same, and Kaleinian guards will be quick to point out that they've never seen us before.

"You must hurry and leave now. Go to the Lunata Coven in Akati. They may be able to assist you, but probably not in the way you hope. They meet at the next full moon. Goodbye." Henna turns swiftly away from us.

Joaviz opens her mouth as if to call after her, but when she catches my glare, she snaps her mouth shut and looks at me with feigned obedience.

Shouts of surprise fill our ears as citizalus burst out of the way of the pale, black-haired warriors who surge through the crowd.

If we try to get through, they will notice the commotion and spot us, but if we stay here they will reach us in moments.

I'm sinking.

My stomach grows hot with rage. Suddenly the Great Volcán's voice booms in my head, overwhelming me with joy. *Trust your power.*

All the voices around me are shrill in comparison to his.

Joaviz tugs on my hand and swims straight over the crowd. I want to pull her back down but it's too late. She's acted stupidly, but I haven't acted at all.

"There! There they are!" The Ezkinian accent is gruff compared to the voices around me.

I follow Joaviz, swimming straight over the crowd and up toward the yellowing surface. Growing louder and louder, the shouting follows us. I can feel them speeding up behind us. In between the rings of Kalein, every face is angled up.

Alinx. Is he among them?

I spin around to face our dozen pursuers. Their features and sizes are different, but all are pale-skinned, black-haired, and wearing criss-crossing dark green sashes.

White-vested Kaleinian guards rise from the alleys below. I search for Alinx. Where are those golden flukes and eyes?

Where is the alee I love so much? The alee I could explain everything to. He would tell me right away if I'm doing the right thing.

Thirty guards and warriors are suspended in front of us now, waiting for me to make the first move.

Joaviz's scream alerts me to the presence of even more Kaleinian guards. We're above the city, completely surrounded. Twenty of them slowly converge on us, weapons drawn.

I flick my little silver wand and it grows into my staff, swirling with orbs. Instinctively, I allow ten blue orbs to unite at the top of my staff. I send them spilling out over the collected guards and warriors, spinning in a circle to cover them all.

They freeze solid in various stages of fear or vengeful attack, their eyes wide, their lips pulled back, their wrists still releasing darts that aren't fast or close enough to pierce my skin.

I fight a sinking feeling when I see that Joaviz is frozen as well. The anger is already present in her numb face. I shout at the shocked crowds below, "Be still, or I will make you!" I use a trickle of red orbs to warm Joaviz, who shakes off what must surely be an awful feeling. She surprises me by not yelling.

"Be my lookout," I say. "Is Henna down there?"

Joaviz scans the city below, the rings of alleys, all the faces staring up. "I don't see her."

"Is she?" I ask.

Joaviz shrieks with desperation. "I don't know!"

"Okay. Just look out. Okay?" I rush towards the nearest warrior, an Ezkinian that I recognize as Alinx's rival for the officer position. I grab his head and close my eyes.

His memories and all the sensations of Ezkine come back. I feel the pressure of the deep water. I taste the heady dustiness. Visibility is a sphere that is tight around me. I see Alinx's face and feel a moment of happiness before the alee's jealous reaction overrides my own.

"Congratulations," I say in the warrior's deep, sneering voice.

"Thank you." Alinx's reply is confident, smooth.

"Where you headed?"

"Kalein. To meet the Court."

This time I see the uncertainty in Alinx's face and notice what I was too sad to see when he told me he was going to Kalein.

He was lying.

Does this warrior know more?

Intuitively, I release him. This was his last conversation with Alinx.

"Syedahl! Syedahl!" Joaviz screams in a way that tells me she's been shouting at me for some time.

I look down to see Henna rising slowly towards us with an expression of both menace and wariness.

At the start of our first breakup, after I told Alinx that we could no longer see each other, his best friend Gen came to me with a plea on Alinx's behalf. I scan the collected warriors until I find his pudgy face and blue eyes.

Henna swims up to us slowly, like a warning, giving me time. She raises her voice and says, "The Kaleinian Hea is coming. You need to leave now." Her tone still seems too soft and calm for my urgent situation.

I can't leave, not until I know.

Alinx, where are you?

I swim over to Gen, grasp his temples, and encounter a strong memory. Alinx and Gen at Southern End, seated, letting their flukes fall over the edge of the city foundation the way we used to do. Alinx leans in and whispers, "Cualt is actually sending me to the Tribe of All Seas."

"Get out of the boundary," Henna's voice breaks through Gen's memory. "Take the Northern Loop Pull and then cross it. Go into the third inlet after the point. You'll have no trouble finding Akati. It's a loud city."

We feel no pain as we pass over the wall. The Hea lets us go, putting up no resistance at the boundary. Could I have stayed long enough to see if Alinx told Gen where, specifically? But now it's too late.

There must be several Tribe offices. Did he mean headquarters?

And...should I find him? I did make a promise, after all.

21

Joanie

WHEN I WAKE UP THIS MORNING, it isn't hard to forget who I used to be. Instead of the usual watery, weightless delirium, I feel perfectly at home in the mellow current, the absence of everything.

I force myself to realize that the current is cold.

My name used to be something else. Joanne. Such an old-fashioned name. My grandma's middle name. When I was little, everyone called me Joey. It was a boy's name, but that was okay because I was a tomboy.

I loved to climb things. And play soccer.

Then I hit puberty and fell in love with makeup, clothes, and boys.

And my nickname changed. Who changed it? Oh yeah. My best friend Lily started calling me JoJo and we liked to go parties.

But my family kept calling me Joey.

Then my dad got sick and *everything* changed.

I went to parties still, but I got too drunk and I was *that girl*.

You know.

I can remember all that stuff, but it's on the outside. Stuff *about* me. Not *me*. Who am I? I'm not sure if I ever knew. I remember a few words my mom used to call me. "Selfish. Irresponsible. Impossible."

And I'd say, "No, Mom. I'm a teenager."

What did our house look like? I can't really remember, but I think we had colorful walls inside. Mint green maybe.

Well, it's been two days since we left Kalein and I'm still mad. I'm always mad. It's an emotion I like. I feel comfortable with it. Being mad makes me shake, see red, feel alive. I find it easier to fall asleep if I'm mad.

Why wasn't Henna at least fascinated by me? Why doesn't Syedahl ever ask me anything about land? I'm not a curiosity to them, just a burden.

Syedahl endangered both of us to find out where her boyfriend was. She's a psycho. We could have been killed!

I feel like an animal. Eating raw. Sleeping in the open sea. Swimming for so long. My stamina is pretty amazing, but I'm exhausted and vulnerable. Part of the food chain. I might hear freaky stuff coming, but what the hell would I do? Syedahl's damn slow with that staff. They should have given it to me.

The journey to Akati is at least half a moon. I have to be like this for half a moon! Getting woken up by waves and catching my own food. Ignoring Syedahl as much as she's ignoring me just to see how she likes it.

Whoever did this to me is going to pay!

Syedahl is lost in thought, but her eyes aren't dazed the way you'd expect. Every thought makes her nose twitch, or her eyes open wider, or her lips tighten.

She doesn't even register my existence.

"What are you thinking about?" I ask.

Syedahl furrows her brow and takes a bunch of breaths before answering. "I'm trying to figure out why Alinx would go meet with the Tribe of All Seas. Before he left, he said it was a personal mission for Father. No…did he say 'personal'? Now I'm not sure."

I groan. She's thinking of Alinx. Of course.

Tribe of All Seas. Sounds kind of dreamy.

"What is it anyways?"

She's swimming faster now. "Hmm…?"

I almost shout. "What is the *Tribe. Of. All. Seas?*"

"I don't know much because in Ezkine we do not deal with them. We don't involve ourselves in…"

She stops swimming. I'm glad to take a break. We let the current push us along.

"I forget that you don't know things," she says. "I'm sorry. I should have already explained. I know only what the Ezkinian historian told me…that the Tribe formed 150 years ago in response to limited resources and growing human interference. They set mandates on hunting and fishing to make sure no species is completely decimated. They oversee trade between Seas, making sure food is exchanged equally.

"They also set the law that no one can live outside of a Hea-protected city, to lessen the chance of humans seeing us. They track Hea genealogy and draw up contracts between our rulers for mating. As a check on their power, the Tribe isn't allowed to have Heas of their own. Heas protect citizalus only under the guidance of their ruler."

She wonders why Alinx would go to the Tribe of All Seas. Why *Alinx* would go there.

Well, I don't want to hear it. I don't care why he went. I want to know what it has to do with me.

She already broke her promise, spending all this time thinking about Alinx instead of trying to figure out who transformed me.

None of these alus care about me at all. I don't care about

them either.

Syedahl and I both slept last night, which was stupid. We don't know how long the warriors stayed frozen. We don't know when they set out after us.

I could still see when she froze me, which hurt really bad by the way, so I know the warriors saw which way we went.

"Tell me more about the ship," Syedahl says out of nowhere.

"What?" What the hell is she talking about?

"The one you were on with your family."

I wish I could stop moving completely but the current shoves me on. "What?"

"You...oh, Joaviz. Didn't you say...oh, nevermind. It's... it's nothing. I don't know where I got that idea! I don't even really know what they are. I've heard they skim the surface, but..."

I grab her shoulder and force her look to at me.

I remember being home, planning for something. A ship? Did I get on a ship?

We used to go on cruises every summer. Is it summer? Shit. Syedahl knows something I don't.

"What ship?" I shake her.

"Joaviz, please," she says firmly. "You said you were on a ship. You must have fallen off somehow and then someone transformed you. I didn't mean to upset you."

I remember it now. Hanging out with my family, going to see some Cirque Du Solei-type performance. How could I have forgotten?

Everything was fine. We were just hanging out like we do every summer. But it was cold this time. We were in the North.

"Joaviz, don't worry. This is all very difficult for you. I understand that. Please. I'm sorry. I shouldn't have brought it up."

"What? No. If you know something about me, I should know it too."

Her eyes go wide and she changes her mind just like that. "You're right. I'm sorry." She tries to give me a hug.

I push her away. I don't want her pity, and I definitely don't want to pretend. She'll leave me or try to hurt me just like the rest of them. She should stop acting concerned because I know she isn't. I know what I am to her.

She really left for Alinx. Hasat and I came along and *vóila*: a better reason.

I'm her excuse.

Both of us hear it at the same time. A school of fish headed straight for us, coming down the current. Thank god. Syedahl whispers, "Let's go down and wait for them. I can't tell what they are yet. Hope for herring. They're the easiest to catch."

I don't want to swim down. I want to stay close to the surface forever, but I'm hungry and she's the expert. Barely.

The water gets colder and bluer. We wait. The sound is closer. Jiving.

"Herring," Syedahl whispers.

Finally I see what must be a thousand of them. The silver gleaming mass is right above us. We swim up to catch them, but I stop short, hearing huge bodies coming from below us. I scream and my heart flutters. The fish look like a thousand knives.

Syedahl grabs my arm and pulls me backwards. The herring squirm above us.

I can't get enough water, not when I can hear the huge creatures down there. Help me. Get me out of here. Syedahl covers my mouth with her hand. "Stop," she says. "Just watch me."

Then I hear the mooing sound. I've heard it before. Squeaky boots. Crying zippers. Echoing smooches.

Holy…

Here they come.

Fifteen of them. So huge! Not just long but fat! And those violently sharp fins. Two of them are babies with orange spots instead of white.

The orcas' creepy wide smiles stretch towards their massive eyes.

They're going to eat me. I've seen that shit on TV. Where they toss the baby seals through the air until they die of whiplash, but then they keep going, throwing them around for like forty-five minutes.

Syedahl says, "It's okay."

I look down at their smooth backs.

Is she insane?

My insides want to crawl out of my face but I can't move. I can't hide.

One of them gets closer, sending all my organs into a back flip.

They're swimming up to the herring, circling around them, creating a vortex. I almost faint when they pass by. When I can see again, everything is blue. Only when they've totally surrounded the herring do the stupid fish catch on. They swim in every direction.

I want to get away but I don't want to go down lower. All I can do is stare up at the orcas as they swim around and around the frantic ball of fish.

Syedahl squeezes my hand so hard her pointy nails draw blood.

I watch it ooze out of my hand.

The orcas turn on their sides and flash their white under-bellies to the fish, surprising them into swimming inwards, the ball getting tighter. The fish are corralled. I hear a single moo-like call and all the orcas turn around, tails hovering above the ball of fish, white bellies just above me. They slap their tails down almost in unison.

Lots of the fish die on impact. The orcas call to each other again. Half of them corral the live fish and the other half catch the dead ones and hold them in their mouths.

Syedahl squeezes my hand again.

My vision is cloudy and my head is throbbing. I notice that my flukes are flapping madly. I try to stop them.

One really big whale feeds the babies.

A fish is falling down, right above me. The whales surround us now.

Not even thinking, just acting out of straight up hunger, I reach out and grab the fish. An orca zips up from below, his eyes as big as my head. I try not to scream as he passes me. His tail hits me and I'm falling towards another one whose back is shiny like obsidian.

Black like the Deep.

A mouth opens to soft pink gums and sharp teeth all spread out. The orca hides the teeth again and laughs. Cackling.

Syedahl lets go of my hand! My loudest possible scream doesn't scare the giant away. It rams into me with its nose and sends me soaring, cutting through the water, smacking into the flailing fish.

The orca comes up from below and tosses me again. I break the surface, fly through the air, and choke. Then I crash back down. The fish falls out of my grasp. I take a deep breath of water.

I can't see Syedahl anywhere. She blends in with all their white and black. I'm spinning.

The whale comes back with a fish in his mouth and stops right in front of me. I'm tiny next to its wide face.

What are you waiting for? Hit me again!

It stares at me, and I shiver.

"Take the fish!" Syedahl shouts from somewhere.

The fish is nothing but a toothpick sticking out of a huge grin.

The whale bobs his head up and down. So I reach out and he opens his mouth, teeth shining. As soon as I snatch the fish, the whale calls out, deafening me. But that's nothing compared to when they all answer. I cover my ears.

Together, they swim back down. Their black shapes get smaller and smaller in the blue. For an instant, I think they're beautiful.

All the fish are gone except the one in my hand.

I stare up at the surface that keeps me from the warm, aching air. Maybe the whale knows that's where I belong.

22

Syedahl

THE FIRST TIME FATHER TOOK me to the surface, he said we couldn't venture close to land because humans might see us. I asked why he couldn't make us invisible, as he does with the city. He explained that the invisibility surrounding Ezkine is immobile. It stays in place and we swim in and out of its charm. Heas haven't discovered how to put a bubble of invisibility around something that moves. A trip from the depths to the surface would have to suffice.

As we got close, the water became striped with shards of sunlight. Though my eyes burned, it was the most beautiful sight I'd ever seen. Father told me to swim as fast and hard as I could, and to jump out of the water so I could see the light blue air.

But I was paralyzed.

"Go on," he urged me with his slick voice. "Swim back down to gather momentum." He had seemed quite bored for the majority of our vertical ascent, but now that we were close to the surface, I could tell that my nervousness amused him. "Everything will be alright as long as you don't take a breath."

I plunged down into the water and hated how the temperature got instantly colder and the water turned darker shades of blue.

Swimming down made me realize that soon I would have to return to the depths of Ezkine. A fierce hatred of depth swelled inside me for the first time. I found myself aching for the green shade of sunlit waters.

I was happy to spin back around and face the golden green above me. Dreaming of air, of what I had heard about wind and how it feels like a current of nothing, of the strange legs of humans and the ugly metal contraptions they call boats, I powered my flukes faster than ever before. I had childlike speed then, the kind that can beat any adult but doesn't endure. The water became like white light, or clarity, or nothingness. I couldn't have imagined water so colorless, like father's staff when empty of orbs.

What's out there? Just then my forehead broke the surface.

At that moment I broke entirely free of the bonds of water. Even the tips of my flukes sensed the warm air. The blinding blue sky enveloped me. In it swam foamy objects swarming with white life. I spun around on my descent and saw the way water looks from the air: endless, repetitive ripples.

My gills throbbed. My body felt heavy and massive. I imagined that I was as large as a whale.

When the sea pulled me back in, I was startled by its iciness.

I wanted the experience to last longer. It wasn't enough. With my face angled up towards the sky and its bright white shoals, I sucked in air. The pain was horrible. I tossed my head back even farther to reach the water more quickly. Before my mouth could take a drink, I saw the burning face of the sun.

Though that was the most exciting part of my first and

heretofore only journey, the real reason for the trip was to be presented to the Ch'tlan Court. I'd been worried I'd have to pass some horrific test, but when I arrived in the majestic room and inverted myself in total submission to the eight judges, the only injustice I suffered was their soft, thin hands jerking my face this way and that, their eyes boring into me with such intensity that I couldn't be certain they were seeing me at all.

I remember how Father spent four days and nights strengthening the city spells. He was exhausted by the time we left, but couldn't rest, for fear the magic would crash along with him.

I didn't understand at the time, but I'm beginning to know magic now. The power within me is energy. Harvesting a few sets of orbs exhausts me. I can sleep in any circumstance, even daylight, when I'm done.

I can't believe Father was able to accomplish what he did. What is it like to do spells for a city? Will I ever learn? Will I ever return to do Ezkine's spells?

My grandmother died before her time, when I was three years old. She left Father alone to protect the city at a younger than usual age. He was so eager for my initiation, so anxious to not be solely responsible.

Henna's also very young to be left as the only Hea, because of her father's illness and because of Hasat.

Henna lied to the Ch'tlan Court at the beseeching of my father, so obviously she feels some sort of allegiance to him, perhaps only because he's older and more magically power-ful. Henna must hold more political power than Father, be-cause she resides in what is considered Ch'tlan's holy city. A population of beluga whales, a species revered in this Sea, frequents Tila every summer. The city's structures are made of pure ice, multifaceted towers and caves that plunge from the thick ice ceiling above into the quickening dark below. Her city alone places her status far above his, for the Court cares the least about Ezkinian affairs. Surely she needn't pay him any favors. Why would she lie for him?

Could it have been for me?

When we left, she promised to keep the Kaleinian Hea from unfreezing the guards for as long as possible. Why would she do that?

Perhaps Hasat once begged her to leave, and though she resisted, she sees some truth and validity to his decisions. Or maybe she believes that I'm selfish and that I place my desires before the good of alukind. Heas are above all else protectors of alus—from slinus, humans, and predators—and yet I've deserted five thousand Ezkinians for one human.

I hope that her action wasn't a sacrifice. Anyone who aids my escape puts themself in danger, so I'm thankful to her. Besides, I rather like her. She's thoughtful, slow to act like me, but has such flair. She's effortlessly articulate, and somehow makes me enjoy waiting for her to speak.

She said she wouldn't involve herself, yet she revealed what must be her biggest secret during my initiation. Henna wanted to show me how dangerous this life is, but I distinctly heard the Great Volcán tell me to leave. He wants me to protect Joaviz. Danger or no.

Henna knows that Joaviz is a human and that my father wants to uncover the key to High Transformation. What else does she know?

Something that I don't?

It hurts so much that Alinx's last memory of me is when I told him I could no longer risk meeting with him. And before that, he knew only of my angst and unhappiness. Sometimes he could break through it and make me laugh, but he knew it wouldn't last. Does he remember the child who used to follow him everywhere?

We were always thrill seekers, and now we're both exploring the surface on our separate missions. When we next meet, will life have changed our bond? Will he be so entwined in Ezkinian affairs that he'll resent me? Does he consider me a traitor?

I've never before heard of Ezkinian officials, or any Ezkinian for that matter, contacting the Tribe of All Seas. They always come to us, asking that we turn our city into a great metropolis and harvest the marvels of the Deep. But King Ezkun always refuses. He holds to the First King's most important principle for founding our city: self-reliance.

Father wanted to involve us in external affairs. I know that much, but not why or how. Will he be able to do any of this without me there?

What is King Ezkun's plan? Why did he permit that awful slinu play to be performed at Court?

With all these questions having seeped from my brain and no answers to replace them, I come back into the present and take in my surroundings. The night is upon us, we swim very slowly, and Joaviz groans. She seems to sense that I'm listening again, for she squeezes my hand.

"Why can't you bring animals to us the way Hasat did when he fought your dad? Not all of those, but maybe just some fish?"

She was horrified for days after the feeding frenzy incident, and again after the orca played with her. So, her question surprises me. "I don't know that kind of magic."

She makes a low moaning sound. "Why not?"

Now that she's pulled me out of my distant worries, I remember our most imminent problem: acquiring food. "I wasn't trained."

"How long does it take to get trained?" Often when Joaviz

asks questions, I sense some latent anger, but this time she sounds genuinely intrigued.

I reward her with a sincere answer. "A lifetime."

"Are you mad you didn't get to learn more?"

"Not mad. No. I'm concerned. Eventually I have to find someone to teach me." I decide against mentioning that my other option is to go home.

"Maybe Hasat." Joaviz's voice is weak, without urgency.

"Hasat wants nothing to do with me."

"That's not true."

"Yes it is. He left us. He changed my life and then he left." She groans again.

"It's not your fate to die of starvation," I say.

She grips my hand tighter and stops swimming.

"Look at me," I say. Although it's dark and I can't see her, I imagine that the color of her eyes is subdued and that her lips are drawn. "We'll be all right. I can feel it."

"But you can't see the future."

"No Hea can, but I'm intuitive." With that last word I feel an inkling, a warning. "Joaviz, how are you?" I ask.

"What do you mean?"

Though we spend all our time together, we're wrapped in our own solitudes. It's mostly my fault, for I'm not one for talking. I vow to make an effort. "Are you sad? Do you miss your family?"

Joaviz says nothing. I clasp her hand. Her skin burns hot despite the cool water, so I know something's wrong. "Tell me," I urge.

"I'm mad." Joaviz emits a squeal that quickly morphs into shaking sobs. "I can't do this anymore."

I hold her tightly and flick my flukes every so often to propel us along with the current as her sobs soften.

Though her voice in my ear is quiet, her intensity makes

me want to pull away. "I can't go to Akati. This isn't the way it's supposed to be. I was supposed to be with him until the end, to say goodbye. To share the time he had left. You have to stop taking me to these places. I don't want to be dragged around."

I almost let go of her but then realize that she means it in a figurative sense. She clutches tighter and rambles on, "I hate her. I hate her for changing me. And he—"

"Her? He? Who do you mean?"

Suddenly Joaviz wriggles out of my grasp. "I hear something!" Her body is alive.

I grip her arm firmly. "Joaviz, you must let me read your mind. Who is *she*? Who?"

"I can't let you."

"There could be answers! We have more of a connection now, and I'm good at this. I could get something important from your memories, something that could help you."

I hear it finally, a single pair of flukes gliding through the water. "You must let me. You know something. Let me discover it."

"No!" she screams.

Whoever's behind us knows that something is very wrong.

"Hello. How are you tonight?" The voice is slick and nasally, like mucus and algae. The voice of a young alee.

"Fine," I say.

"Are you two alright?"

"Everything is fine."

It bothers me immensely that I can't see him, but a lifetime of near total darkness has taught me how to judge by sound alone. Even though my mind may be torn, my heart's resolved to never again live in endless night.

"Can I ask you a question?" he says.

"Umm…I guess so," Joaviz says with her usual haughtiness. She appears to have recovered from her breakdown.

"What would you do if you were separated from your family and you wanted to get back to them?" he asks.

I'm mute with disbelief, but Joaviz is quick to answer. "I would find a way to get back."

"But what if you couldn't?"

I hear in his voice that he's ugly. The sound of it hints at poor symmetry, a nose squished in on one side, squinty black eyes, and boils on his skin.

"Well, why can't you?" I hear Joaviz take a large gulp of water, but otherwise her voice is steady, concerned.

"They're dead."

"I'm sorry," she whispers.

My hands clench into fists. "Is there something that you need?" I ask.

The alee ignores my rudeness and asks, "Are you hungry?"

"Yes!" Joaviz squeals. I'm appalled by her interest in him, even if she is starving.

I hear him pass her one of his bags. I smell the old fish it contains, but can't place what kind it is. I fight the urge to grab the bag from her and feel its weight, to know how much he gave her.

"Slinus ate my family."

Joaviz pushes against me and I hold her firmly. The alee's voice grows louder. With every word, Joaviz twitches. "They came into my house one night," he says. "Four of them. They had red eyes and giant fangs. My father tried to protect us. He killed one of them and then two others bit his throat. His blood filled the room. I breathed it in! They killed my sister and my mother and ate them right in front of me. But they didn't kill me."

Visions of the play come back to me. The slinus, so near and so real. Alinx's arms.

"They let me live just to be cruel. Just to leave me damaged."

Joaviz mumbles, "Stop it stop it stop stop stop stop it stop it!" The sound morphs into a roar, and this morphs into a shrill plea. "Stop stop stop stop stop!"

The alee is quiet now, taking sharp pulls of water and listening to Joaviz shout to herself.

I hold her close even though she's screaming in my ear. I can't hear my voice when I ask the alee to leave. The thin stream of water from his gills wars with my own as he leans in to whisper, "I'm telling you the truth."

I shove him away with so much anger that my little silver wand morphs into my staff.

He shouts in surprise, then his voice drops again, full of fear and reverie. "You're a Hea."

"Leave! Go!" I roar, lifting my staff before me with one hand and holding onto Joaviz's shivering frame with the other. He speeds up, continuing down the current. "Not that way! Get out of the current. I don't want to see you again." My words and the tone of my voice come from somewhere deep inside of me, a place I'm still ashamed of.

He says something I can't hear even though Joaviz's screams have subsided. "I don't want to remember," she says.

I hold my staff against my side. Joaviz is still clutching onto the bag of fish, enough for two meals each. Her head drops onto my shoulder and she falls into a deep sleep, active and thrashing.

There's something greater than fear that consumes her.

23

Joaviz

A RUMBLE OF VOICES SPEWS from Akati, but we can't see a single thing in the dark night.

I wish my best friend Lily could be with me. I try so hard to remember things we used to do together, but no flashes come, just blurry images of lights.

I hear laughter, shouting, and maybe even music. I listen to the sounds of the city while Syedahl barfs up orbs.

Syedahl pulls ten little balls of colored light out of her mouth, one for each fingertip, and then taps them into the staff, where they expand and swirl, lighting nothing but seaweed.

Syedahl gives us different disguises this time, but again just changes our coloring. She makes my skin tan like Henna's, my tail gold, and my hair dark brown. She gives herself pink flukes, light brown hair, and pale skin. Not her freaky white skin. Just regular pale.

That scar on my left side is still there.

Today we saw lots of seaweed and seals and lobsters and crabs.

I can't guess where we are in human terms. It isn't nearly as cold as Ezkine. Aren't there lots of crabs and lobsters in

New England?

"You're not going to be able to understand anyone," Sye-dahl says.

"What?"

"We're in a new Sea now. They speak Sa'ari here."

"But you told me you can do language spells."

"Yes, but…"

"Then why can't you make me speak Sa'ari?"

I wonder if it was because she didn't have the orbs for long enough. She was too exhausted from traveling to harvest them before. Interpersonal magic and telekenesis don't use orbs at all, but almost all other types of spells grow stronger from dancing around in a staff for a while.

"We don't know enough about the Sea to pose as natives," she answers, "so we'll have to be travelers. It isn't believable that two travelers would be able to speak their language." She conceals her staff, leaving me in darkness again without warning.

I sigh. "No way. Let's pretend to be sisters." I'm desperate here.

I can't see Syedahl but I'm sure her eyebrows are raised.

"We could say our mom is from this Sea. What's another city here? And that we moved to Ch'tlan when we were lit-tle."

I hear Syedahl shaking her head.

"Please," I say. "You don't know what it was like. I don't want to be that confused ever again. C'mon!"

"Alright, alright. Calm down. We'll have to go into the city and then come back out. I have to hear them speak in order to learn the language."

But we don't have to go into the city after all. An ala and an alee pass by us, talking. They're both holding yellow-hued flashlights. Flashlights! The yellow light shines on a slice of eel.

I scream.

Syedahl's staff reappears in response to the shock.

"Be quiet," Syedahl hisses. I can feel her thinking. "Got it," she finally says.

"They didn't even notice you're a Hea," I say, tracking the dancing orbs.

"You're right. They should recognize the Hea of their city. They should have thought I was intruding."

I shrug it off, but Syedahl keeps rambling about how strange it all is.

"Okay, get over it," I say. "We'll go in. Maybe we'll get some answers, you know...*inside*."

"Perhaps the Lunata Coven meeting is somewhat popular and the citizalus know about it and are expecting to see other Heas."

I roll my eyes, not even caring that she'll see me in the colorful glow from her staff. "Yeah, perhaps. Now, c'mon."

Syedahl takes a deep breath to prepare. A flurry of yellow orbs shimmies to the top of her staff and zooms to my throat.

It doesn't hurt this time, I guess because my speech organs are developed now. All these new words swirl in my head. *Haazna. Ikenna. Aldaa. Feiplal.* "Wait," I say in my soft, pretty new language, working hard to stay afloat and not touch the seaweed below me, which is home to I-don't-know-how-many-eels.

"Excellent," Syedahl replies in Sa'ari. The orbs in her staff flash blindingly before the whole thing disappears back into the tiny wand. With the glow gone, I can't see her anymore. Then a second triangle of yellow light bounces towards us.

"Is someone there?" An alee's voice calls. He sounds young.

Syedahl says nothing.

"Over here!" I shout, relieved that Syedahl concealed her staff just in time.

Syedahl's invisible gaze burns me. The alee comes over and tells us he's going for a little swim. He says his name is Enkirik and asks for ours.

Oh no. We didn't even have time to make up names. Luckily, Syedahl is talking fast. "I'm Solora and this is Kormi."

Kormi?

Enkirik lowers his flashlight so it stops blinding me and bows. He is muscled, chiseled, dark-haired hunkiness. Usually I like 'em hipster-boy skinny, but I'll venture out of my type for this one. Then I catch a glimpse of fluke and cringe. There's no getting used to it.

I really want to ask him, among other things, how the hell that flashlight works. I know it's not purely a human one. Tiny yellow light wrapped around a crowbar with wire. But I can't ask because that would give us away.

"Are you here for the Still Fest?" he asks, shining the light up at himself so I can see his smile. He has intense green eyes. The concept of being attracted to someone with scales is so wrong.

"What?" I ask at the same time Syedahl says, "We most certainly are."

He laughs and tells us to come with him to his favorite club because it's the best place to celebrate Still Fest. He doesn't even ask where we're from, just babbles on about how Akati has more festivals than any other city. There's two per moon, one for the lowest tide and one for the highest. When I ask why they celebrate tides so much, he says it's a matter of pride. They are the city closest to the Death Stretch, which has the biggest change in tides in the entire world.

He sounds like a tour guide. A very charming one.

Normally I would hate it if a guy talked this much, but right now I like it because there's so little I can safely say.

I'm done blurting out my secret.

We swim over seaweed that twists and spins in the light of his flashlight. Though critters live in its slimy strands, swimming above it is much less creepy than swimming over massive depths.

We come to the city wall, and as Enkirik swims over it, Syedahl gasps in shock.

"Are you from Ch'tlan?" he asks.

"Yes, but not originally."

Not swimming over walls must be a Ch'tlan thing. I hope the same is true of swimming over houses. That whole etiquette thing is just silly.

There are colored lights on every wall, illuminating every surface and angle, casting shadows of many shapes. The laughter and singing are sounds without bodies.

Attached to a few walls are propellers and blades from boats, fans, and even blenders. It's all I can do not to shout out their names. This place is powered!

Enkirik leads us down a hall of blue lights and into a very crowded room. Everyone is my age or a little older.

Thank the Great Somebody we got out of Ezkine.

No one stops us or asks for our ages as we swim between the layer of alus dancing wildly below and the layer of alus hanging from holdings.

When we get to the bar—a wall of bottles and squares cut from plastic bags—Syedahl says, "I don't think this is such a good idea."

Enkirik laughs. He has a gorgeous smile. His confidence is striking.

He's hotter than Alinx. I'm not going to lie, Syedahl can pick 'em, but Alinx is bad-boy hot. I like to be the bad girl who corrupts good boys. Enkirik is pretty-boy hot.

"You honestly believe puffer fish juice is poisonous?" Enkirik asks, making me realize I was spacing out on his sexiness and not paying attention to the conversation. It's pretty common for me to not pay attention, but right now I have a good excuse.

I mimic his sneer at Syedahl.

She actually rolls her eyes. Never seen her do that before.

"What are you, five?" he asks.

He and I share a look that says Syedahl is a loser. If everyone else is drinking it, it must be fine.

In the end Enkirik orders just two. When the bartender hands one to me, I almost faint. On the tied-up plastic, I can make out red block letters, "THA." It must have said, "Thank you."

I stare at it.

Enkirik says, "Just tear a hole with your teeth and suck on it."

I hit him lightly with it. "I know that."

He holds me around the waist. It feels so good to be held by someone male and sexy and strong. Hmmm…

If only Lily could be here to party with me.

But I can't think things like that. Enkirik leans in and touches my bottom lip with his thumb, then sucks on his bag.

Wait, *isn't* it really poisonous? Maybe it's different for alus. Oh well. I don't want to look stupid. Not in front of him.

Syedahl pointedly won't watch.

I take the plastic corner in my mouth and tear a piece. The stuff is disgusting. Sour, burning, like spiky hot death. I force it down.

The effect is immediate. I feel extremely comfortable and blissed out. Enkirik's green eyes shine like the Sa'ari Sea in sunlight. He grabs my hand and leads me in between the lower and upper crowds again. Syedahl follows.

I'm sorry she's the third wheel, but mostly happy that it isn't me.

We pass by the band. Two alees bang on something and turn knobs to create a beat that bobs and weaves, becoming something else just when I think I've gotten it down.

I take a second to notice all the different shades of skin. Even I know the sun causes color, but it still surprises me, especially since Syedahl said alus hardly migrate. Shows how much she knows. Here there is every shade of skin, and some tails are even bright, like mine.

Enkirik leads us up to a break in the ceiling. We discover a room full of young alus who shout out when they see him.

Enkirik is holding my hand while he introduces us. Everyone says something polite and then goes back to talking. One ala with curly blonde hair and pink flukes gives me a dirty look.

Her voice is loud and shrill. "I can't believe you're not going! We're old enough now, and it's our responsibility," she says to the alee next to her.

"Going to what?" Syedahl asks.

Enkirik touches the small of my back, right above my scales. "Some political meeting. Not for you two to worry about." He taps my nose.

I draw back. That is not okay. I hate all that cutesy stuff.

Somehow he catches on and says in a deep voice, "You're here to have fun." Syedahl rolls her eyes a second time.

The room is lit with dizzying red light. Enkirik kisses me before leaving to get more drinks. Syedahl still won't have one, so he gives the third to the blonde ala, which kind of pisses me off.

"My name is Zeekitanai," she squeaks. Her eye scales are

like bright fuchsia flames, in contrast with her pale hair.

Enkirik whispers, "Just call her Zeeki."

She gives him the stink eye. She has slight features, nothing remarkable or special about her.

"I'm *Kormi*," I say with a cringe.

"Friends of Enkirik are friends of mine, though he does seem to befriend every lost foreigner at every fest."

Lost. The word hits me almost as hard as the nasty fish juice I'm sucking on. I *am* lost—more than this fake, whiny-voiced "friend" could imagine. And more *foreign* too.

"Good to know," I say, eyeing the dark gray ridge of fins down Enkirik's back.

Zeeki stares at me a few seconds too long. What's her deal?

Something in my stomach feels heavy. I sink a little. Enkirik grabs me. He puts both hands around my waist and lifts me up.

His flukes slap against mine.

He guides my hands to some holdings above us. I can't see anything in this vibrating red light with these hazy eyes. I hold on for dear life.

"You were saying?" Zeeki asks.

But she's talking to a different alee. Everyone has their arms inside these metal casings that stick out from the wall, their flukes hanging lazily. There are about twelve of us here.

Zeeki sneaks a look at me.

I get it now. She's jealous! The little green-eyed skeeze. Oh well. Any harm I do isn't my fault, because my head is spinning and I can't really see anything. Syedahl keeps whispering in my ear, but I turn away.

Enkirik is fuzzy and red. Where does this light come from? It feels like a stoplight. *Stop* laughing.

Someone says my name. I hold my fingers in front of my

face. "Five," I say. Did they ask me a question?

Then Enkirik is back and he's holding more bags and there's a picture of a carrot on one of them.

He puts his hand behind my head and leans in, "Do you want to go somewhere after?"

The water from his gills rushes against me in a funny, tickling way. I feel my scales get hot and prickly.

I narrow my eyes and he leans in to kiss me, his lips hovering just in front of mine. I move forward. Our lips part and our tongues meet each other. I notice the water in our mouths. Everyone around us makes a *woooo* noise.

Still kissing Enkirik, still prickling and tingling, I hear Zeeki ask Syedahl, "So you've never heard of the Death Stretch? Where'd you say you're from, *Ezkine*?"

The resulting laughter grows small in my head. I know I should be listening to the conversation. Zeeki is asking Syedahl too many questions.

But I feel warm, ready.

"Why do you care?" Zeeki asks. Her voice is distant but it squeezes between Enkirik and me, making me pull away.

"I'm just interested," Syedahl says, trying to sound nonchalant.

Enkirik's eyes glow red in the light. One hand holds the circle sticking out from the ceiling while the other clutches my waist. I run a hand down the fin on his back.

I feel my scales begin to part. I've never felt this way before. Not in this body.

Warm and soft. A part of me that wasn't there before, now alive. I want to kiss him again, but my eyes are wide open and horrified.

Enkirik laughs, proud and arrogant.

Everybody notices, looks at me. They're all laughing too. Different types of laughter. Zeeki is disgusted, crinkling her nose.

The room is red.

I'm so ashamed.

What do I do? I don't want to look down. Don't look down. But I do.

The scaly flaps are parted, open.

Finally they close and I'm getting a headache behind my eyes. Syedahl grabs my hand and leads me out of there.

Zeeki calls, "See you in a couple of days."

24

Syedahl

"IF ZEEKI'S HIS COUSIN, why did she care?" Joaviz asks suddenly, loud enough to be heard by the neighboring rooms in the inn.

Joaviz has hardly said anything today. I can feel the shame still rippling off of her. Yesterday we spent the day resting and eating crab, salmon, and seaweed. As I ate, I looked around nervously, thinking I might get caught, but my food infractions are insignificant compared to what else I've done.

Today we wait for Zeeki. She should have been here by now.

I think about how to best word what Zeeki told me two nights ago, but decide there's no nice way to say it. "He's a flirt. He tries to woo everyone his age. Zeeki's tired of it because she wants him to court her friend."

"Why?" Joaviz asks, turning to face me. The brightness outside the opening darkens her features. "I don't pass my friends off to whores."

"She thinks it's time for him to settle down."

"But he's so young!"

I stare at her wide-eyed. "He is not. Cities certainly have different standards, but eighteen is an average marrying age."

Joaviz shakes her head. "Good luck to Zeeki with that one."

I sigh. I can't have them angry at each other. That would distract me from whatever I might learn at the meeting. Joaviz spent yesterday either sulking or deliberately ignoring me. "What were you thinking?" I ask. "Did you *want* to make love to him?"

Joaviz groans. "What? No! I was just having fun. Messing around. All we did was kiss." She turns her back and grabs a set of holdings, looking out at the opening that's too small to swim through.

I long to kiss Alinx again.

"What makes you think we're going to get anything out of this?" Joaviz asks.

"The Lunata Coven meeting is in two days, according to Henna. We have to be here anyway, so we might as well follow any lead we get." I'm daunted at having to be responsible for every decision.

If I knew enough transformation magic, I would have forged the resin-filled shells that are Sa'ari currency—even though it's illegal, by Tribe decree, for a Hea to forge money. But instead, to pay for this inn, I had to pretend to be an amateur magician and make unimpressive animal illusions out of orbs for coin. Joaviz was excellent at encouraging the citizalus to donate. She flirted. She begged and whined. I taught her to hum her appreciation, but it wasn't long before she was singing.

This was never an issue in Ezkine, where everything is trade based. We didn't even have inns. No need. I'm in a whole new world in Akati. Joaviz feels more at home here than I do.

"We might learn something," I continue.

Joaviz hangs her head a little lower.

"What?" I prompt.

"Nothing," she says. "It's just…embarrassing. I never…"

"You never…?"

She turns back around, her eyes the most vulnerable shade of blue. "Do you think he'll be there?"

"Zeeki said he wouldn't be."

"Good. I…well…it doesn't *show* for human females when we get…*excited*. You can't *tell*, so I've never…"

I try to mask my expression of shock. How could it not show? I don't understand what she means. Learning how to control our reactions is something all alus have to face. "Oh…I see."

"Yeah."

"Well, at least it isn't mating season."

"Mating season? When is mating season?" she asks.

"Quiet down!" Sometimes her ignorance is too much to endure. "After the plankton blooms. When the winds pick up. We don't have these markers in Ezkine, so the siren tracks it. One can sense it, as well. Alus can't couple for three moons, unless they hope to get pregnant."

"Three moons! That's just wrong. Have you ever…?" Joaviz's eyes are hopeful.

"No. Have you?"

She plays with the wrappings on her bedposts. "Yeah, but it was a mistake." A flush comes into her face, one of bitter anger, not shame.

"Oh, I'm sorry."

"So was I."

With that the conversation ends. I hope that Zeeki's uncle, whom she spoke of incessantly two nights ago, might be able to guess what Alinx is doing with the Tribe of All Seas.

Legends about the Two-Tailed Warrior flash into my mind. It's easy for me to slip into that silly fantasy. The Two-Tailed Warrior was the son of a Hea and a fighter, powerful not only magically but physically as well. He was supposedly born during the First War, centuries before it was illegal for Heas to mate outside of contract.

In Ezkine, I tried not to think of Alinx in *that* way. Although I always professed my love for him, I never let myself imagine such a bond between us. If I had, I would have given myself freely to him and been tied to him forever.

I'd still be his and would not have promised to protect Joaviz.

I miss him so much. I miss lying next to him and resting on his chest. It's there, nearest his heart, that I feel most at home. His sway over me is as natural as that.

Alinx didn't treat me differently because of my near-certain ascension to power. Nor did I put him below me.

He understood everything about me without trying. Once, when I was twelve and my growing breasts were hurting, an ala purposefully bumped into me. I clutched my chest and yelped with pain. All the alees were laughing, but not Alinx. For the moment he did nothing, understanding that I didn't want to make a scene. Then later, when we were alone after school, he said, "My body's changing too."

That was all he said. Embarrassed, we looked out into the darkness, both of us drifting, dizzy with all that we couldn't say.

When we were thirteen, it was clear to Alinx that he wanted to be a warrior and break the tradition of doing as your father does. If he'd followed that convention, he would have become a professor.

He was muscular and agile and good at every physical activity he tried. When Alinx's mother told us stories about her brothers who were warriors in the Hieste Sea, Alinx always beamed. He was ready to learn how to fight.

One day in school the teacher was discussing how the First

War of the Species brought Heas and alus together all across the globe, and how this sealed the relationship between Heas and cities.

An alee declared his approval of the fact that Heas never overthrew the monarchs. The eyes of the class turned to me, making me flush. I didn't understand what made me different, for I hadn't yet received power. Only the promise of it.

When the alas brought lunch that day, everyone paid even greater attention to my plain, unadorned food, and I watched with envy as they ate Ezkinian knots. These are strips of fish tied together, their flavors supposedly well paired. Alinx's mother may have even tied them, for she often passed by the school, hoping to sell her work.

I had cubed fish, and just one type per day. All Ezkinians are only permitted to eat food that can be caught within our greater waters, but as a Hea I couldn't even mix the restricted options.

The same alee asked me, "How does that taste?" and Alinx said quietly, "Boring." Everyone laughed.

After school, Alinx and the alee slapped flukes and went off to play together. This alee was of course later to become his competition, the one whose mind I read first in Kalein.

Alinx's friendship with the alee lasted four moons. During that time he didn't speak to me at all, not even at school. I was devastated but refused to grovel. Instead, I turned into a statue, ignoring him the way he ignored me.

They fought and the alee sliced Alinx across the stomach with his wrist sword. Alinx came to my home bleeding heavily, asking to be healed by Father.

He came back to me, and I was so grateful that I didn't even ask him to apologize. We went back to the way things were: eating lunch together, meeting every day after school, Alinx swimming beyond the boundary, trying to find something, anything in the Deep. His adventures were mostly un-successful and only served to make me wait, frightened for him.

My mind wanders to Joaviz. I had once thought humans similar to Heas, believing them to be magical. It's obvious from last night that she feels more at home in the presence of citizalus.

I vowed to protect her, and yet I seem destined to get her killed, or at least to frighten her into a state of shock.

She still refuses to let me read her mind.

Finally, Zeeki appears in the bright room. She and Joaviz make eye contact, smile weakly at each other, and face me.

"Sorry, Solora!" Zeeki says as she swims forward, takes my hand, and bows. "There was a delay! Forgive me."

I pull my hand away. "Of course." Although I know we kept our disguises, I glance down at Joaviz and myself. We look the same to Zeeki as we did two nights ago.

"Someone tipped off the Akatian guard so we had to move the meeting," Zeeki explains.

Joaviz glares at her with enough intensity to catch both of our attentions. "What kind of meeting is this?"

Zeeki looks at her sideways. "It isn't illegal. Just unwanted."

"Count me out," Joaviz says.

I politely ask Zeeki to leave the room. Joaviz and I conduct a whispered argument, in which she tells me that she doesn't trust Zeeki and I tell her that we need as much information as we can get. Finally I deliver the blow: "Your embarrass-ment has gotten the better of you."

Joaviz says nothing. She turns her grimace into a curt smile.

We leave the inn. Swimming over buildings still makes me feel like a spy, subversive somehow. Or at the very least, rude.

Joaviz seizes onto the little triumph of my unease. "See! Told you this city makes sense."

Zeeki leads us into an alley with whirling silver blades that power the lights and food processors. I feel as though I'm from some barbaric, backwards place, and then remind myself that I am. Ezkine is separate and simple, without science or human trash.

We come to a squat, cube-shaped brown structure with bars over the entrance. The silver wand in my hand vibrates, wanting to morph into my staff.

Zeeki peers into the bright alley. "Keep a look out."

Alus pass us by and we pretend to be waiting for someone. When we both say it's clear, Zeeki removes a bar and darts inside. We follow her into a pitch-black tunnel.

Zeeki stirs up dirt and murk into my face and lungs, with Joaviz groaning behind me. Blue lights adorn the tunnel in between tiny, barred rooms. Dungeons or prison cells. I shudder, knowing exactly who lived in this place. Soon other voices drown out Joaviz's complaints. We come to a vast empty space with five tunnels leading from it.

Twenty or so alus, all middle-aged, wait anxiously. Furtive glances and hushed voices.

Here we find shackles and chains, the dead white shells of crabs, and strange bones that are knobby like alu bones but longer and thicker. The tall, angular bones of shark fins are scattered this way and that.

"I don't like it down here. What is this place?" Joaviz asks.

Luckily, the group doesn't hear, but Zeeki eyes her suspiciously. "Can't you tell?"

The blue light illuminates Joaviz's blank stare.

Zeeki explains, "This is where the slinu slaves lived. The ones who built the original city? Before the war...before the truce."

Joaviz, realizing her mistake, smiles and nods emphatically. "Right! Of course! I never payed much attention in history…"

Zeeki furrows her brow, but my worry over her suspicion sinks into another type of worry. Enkirik enters the room from one of the other tunnels leading here. He swims over to Joaviz and whispers, "Wasn't expecting to see you again."

She turns her shoulder to him. "Wasn't wanting to."

"Why not?" he asks with a smirk.

"You got me drunk."

A few alus turn to look at us, stifling their laughter.

A masculine voice shouts at everyone to be quiet. The gathered group backs against the wall, hovering horizontally to give this alee the center. Zeeki and Enkirik hover below Joaviz and me.

"That's my uncle," Zeeki says, looking up. Pride brightens her expression, but then she narrows her eyes, calculating, summing me up.

He has the short hair, silvery scars, and muscles of a warrior, but no weapon bands adorn his arms. His flukes are red-brown and his eyes a stormy gray. He tells us that his name is Macluin but we may call him Mac.

Mac spins slowly about the room as he speaks. His eyes always circle back to me, lingering for a while. His mischievous smirk doesn't match the seriousness of his words. "In three days there will be a council meeting about whether or not to accept the Tribe of All Seas representative."

Everyone nods. It's a neutral opening, a fact they can trust. "The opposition will tell you why the city should deny the Rep, but they won't tell you the real reason. They'll cover it up with all this political nonsense about trade." Something about his tone makes the alus chuckle.

Zeeki is silent and attentive.

"I'll tell you the real reasons. That's why we're all here."

He smiles at the group's anticipation.

The ala to the right of me jokes, "The Akatian warrior reject is at it again."

Beneath me, Zeeki glares up at the ala but keeps her mouth tightly shut.

Joaviz can't stop peeking at the piles of bones mounded up against the walls as if they might come to life.

"The proponents are spreading lies about the slinus, saying they're attacking at random. But the slinus aren't attacking at all. They haven't attacked us in 1000 years and nothing's changed," Mac says.

"Oh, they're not?" says the ala hovering next to me. "Everyone says they are. Even citizalus who have no business with the Tribe."

Half of the crowd mumbles in agreement.

Mac nods. "Yes, you're right about that. Some of these alus are hired. Some are just telling tales."

"Why are we here?" Joaviz whispers.

I hush her and wave my hand to catch Mac's attention.

He smiles at the interruption. "Yes?"

"I met someone who claimed that slinus ate his family. He was lying."

"How could you tell?"

"I just knew it," I say.

As sure then as I am now that Mac knows something about me. The satisfied inclination of his head...the unbroken eye contact...

"The Tribe wants even more control than they have now," Mac continues. "They don't want to be *between* the Seas, they want to be *within* them. Within our cities even!" Here he pauses, regains an even tone. "They blame the slinus to make us afraid. So we'll be willing to do anything they say."

Mac twists rapidly to one side, body horizontal, arms solid at his sides—ready to attack with sword bands that aren't there.

I hear the movement too. Three Akatian guards enter from the tunnel across the room, scattering the crowd. I hold Joaviz back against the wall as the guards chase the citizalus into the other tunnels.

My sigh of relief is met by the sound of more approaching flukes. Joaviz and I cross the room and dart into the tunnel from which the three guards emerged.

Joaviz cries out before I've made it very far.

A guard holds his wrist sword up to her throat. My staff engorges, ready to cast a freezing spell, but I'm now surrounded by a different sort of bluish light. Involuntarily, I spin around to face a Hea whose staff spreads the light around my body. Slowly it fades and I'm his captive.

Joaviz and I are led out of the tunnel. My eyes are locked on the Hea in front of me. He pulls us up over the city for all to see, then brings us down to five conical towers in a square created by a wrap-around building boasting murals of colored sand. The alus swimming around the towers are all in a rush.

It's impossible to breathe. I think of Joaviz that first night we wrapped her up in Ezkine, and now understand why she thought she was a captive and not a guest. The Hea lets go momentarily so we can take a breath, then overpowers us again.

I'm dragged along, carried through an opening—the mouth of a giant, faded eel.

The Hea allows us another breath, and I find myself able to track the turns we've made. Left after the opening. Right at a split in the hallway. The second left. Another right. Soon the Hea stops and forces me through an opening. He follows me into the room.

Inside is a table with straps to hold someone down, another table with sickles and knives, a large black cage with parallel bars and an empty net. Light comes in from three tiny openings high on the wall in front of us. Metal spikes consume the entire wall to the right.

The Hea smiles cruelly at my bluing face, then relaxes his hold just long enough for me to take a breath.

Joaviz and the guard come into the room. He has her by the arm, no longer threatening her throat with his weapon.

With a stubby key around his wrist, the guard twists the square lock and throws Joaviz inside. Water slows her momentum and she crashes softly to the rusty iron floor.

The Hea relinquishes control over me. "Grab her staff," he says to the guard.

I let it drop from my hands before he's even near.

"Now will you go inside?" the Hea asks.

I nod weakly and swim inside the cage, avoiding Joaviz's murderous gaze.

The Hea elongates the net on the wall. He places my staff inside as the guard locks us in, and swims off with the key.

The Hea watches me with something like fascination. My eyes follow the few sets of orbs that collide in my staff. The longer I look at them, the quicker they move. They spin around and around each other, fighting their way to the top. They've nearly emerged. I curse the pain in my eyes. The Hea laughs. He leaves. I slow my breathing and the orbs come to a halt.

25

Joaviz

"I TOLD YOU NOT TO TRUST HER!" I shout at Syedahl. We're stuck in an old lion's cage with rust and crusty green stuff all over it.

Syedahl doesn't seem to care. She's lying on the nasty floor. I'm trying not to touch anything.

I'm going to die for nothing. Stupid Tribe of All Seas has nothing to do with *me*.

"Listen to me!" I shout.

"Joaviz, please. I'm thinking."

"Ugh!" I say, turning away from her. I want to grab the bars and bang my head against them but the disgusting rust keeps me away.

"This isn't Zeeki's fault."

"Well it sure isn't mine."

Syedahl opens her eyes. Her lavender irises are paler than usual. "What could Zeeki have done?"

"Something. *You* could have done something."

Syedahl slowly turns her head away towards the opening. "You don't like her only because of Enkirik."

"Not true! I don't get why you like her."

"And I don't understand why *you* like Enkirik."

"I don't! I don't want to see him again, ever."

Three openings above us torture me with a glimpse of open water. Too small to fit through, they let in a bunch of yellow sunlight. I'm dying to be free. This has nothing to do with Enkirik.

"I'm sure you won't," Syedahl says.

"You've said that already. Wait." I think of the blade against my throat. "What's that supposed to mean?"

Syedahl shakes the thought away. "I don't really know." She stretches her arms over her head, still leaning against the bumpy bars.

I sneak over to her. "What did you see?"

"Nothing. I can't see the future. No Hea can. Forget it. I don't want to worry you."

I throw my hands up and dart away from her. "Worry me? Worry? Me? Don't I look a little worried to you?"

"Joaviz, calm down. I need to think of a plan."

I want to smack her, but instead I just stare and grit my teeth, arms crossed. "Think of a plan? Haven't you *thought* enough? What are we gonna *do*?"

"Tell me why you're really upset." Syedahl settles down onto the floor of the cage. "Is this because of what happened with Enkirik?"

"Oh my god no. I told you—*no!*"

"Okay, well I thought…"

"Thought what? That you could give me some alee advice, based on all your experience with *Alinx*?" I spit out his name.

Syedahl's eyes light up and her lips part. "Of course not…"

I stay on the other side of the cage, as far from her as possible. "You can't get him out of your mind. Alinx this and Alinx that. What is Alinx doing? Where is Alinx?"

Syedahl drops her head. "I told you already. I had a feeling the Tribe had something to do with your transformation."

I'm not stupid. "A *feeling*...So it just happens to be the place where Alinx is? We didn't go and get caught because of Alinx? Really, because...I think we did."

"It just happens to be the place," she repeats. And then her voice is a whisper. "I'm doing everything I can, but you aren't."

"What?"

She props herself up on her hands and winces, speaking abnormally fast. "You're keeping things from me." Her eyes dart back and forth between my face and my raised hand.

I lower it, burning inside. "You put me in danger for him. Again!"

Syedahl reaches out to touch my shoulder, but I bat her hand away.

"Let me read your mind," she pleads. "There could be a memory of the transformation. I could find it."

"Your dad couldn't."

"Interpersonal magic is his weakness, but it's my strength. Let me try."

I shake my head when Syedahl lifts her tentative fingers. "I said no. Besides, how could you make me remember something that I don't remember?" Mid-question, the vulnerability in my voice makes me wish I hadn't asked.

Syedahl peers around the room and her face drops exactly in the direction of those knives on the table. "Listen to me. There is something there. I understand that your memories frighten you."

"How do you know that?"

"Remember the alee whose parents were...the one we met on the way here?"

I think of his awful story and his oily voice.

"He reminded you of something, someone, an experience.

You started screaming. You practically had a seizure."

"What if this is pointless?" I cling to my little bit of resistance, though by this point even I'm aware it's my resistance that's pointless.

Syedahl holds me with her gaze. "Then at least we'll have ruled it out. At least we'll have done everything possible."

She doesn't get it. That's what I'm afraid of. If we do everything, then what's left? "You know what? Fine," I say, shrugging. "Then maybe you'll leave me alone." As soon as I hear myself say it, a big rush of water comes out of my gills. My heart feels better, but my stomach is sick.

Syedahl grabs my head. She's not about to let me to change my mind.

My breath and my heartbeat are loudly out of rhythm.

Syedahl's hands are so much kinder than her dad's. My eyelids close gently. My breathing slows down, calmer than normal.

Her thumbs graze my temples. Gentle pushes. The last few weeks go by in a flash. Swimming, sleeping, not understanding why even my mind doesn't feel the same.

I raise my head above water to find the ship. That's how I got here. On some kind of ship. Now I'm choking on air.

Daddy, please wait for me. I want to say goodbye. If saying goodbye is all I can do for you, then at least I need to do that.

Now I'm leaning over the railing, in the dark. I'm all by myself, in my sweats and rain boots. A tentacle slams against the deck and nearly tips the ship.

My scream freezes on the icy air and hangs there, useless, with all the other noises of surprise. Clanging metal and shouts of fear spatter the sky. The tentacle wraps around me and pulls me into the black ocean.

The cold water pierces my lungs. Beams and orbs of light

blind me into a teeth-rattling headache. She sings to me. I'm sleeping now but I can still see her fifteen eyes.

The most powerful alee of all time pierced the sixteenth, she's showing me. A Hea and a warrior combined. The one who would rule with her. Rule the Deep and all the Seas.

Her voice is leagues and fathoms, ripples and layers of vibrations wrapping around me. Tighter. Tighter.

You'll be mine.

There's a plan for each of us, but mine is the most special. I'll never be the same.

Pain bursts on my forehead, expands above my eye. Over and over.

"Stop, Joaviz no!"

Bang my forehead. Cut my eye. Grab the bars. Slam my head again and again. Smell the blood. Syedahl grabs my shoulders and pulls me back. I shake her off me and start again.

All of a sudden I stop.

I spin around while blood twirls in front of my eyes like red smoke, obscuring my view of an old ala. Her Hea staff is pointed at me.

Her face is swaying off her skull.

Syedahl slides near me and whispers, "Now you have to be calm."

26

Syedahl

TWO GUARDS FOLLOW the old Hea into the room. I try my best to comfort Joaviz, whispering in her ear that every-thing will be all right. Watching her shake and groan, I'm reminded of when she tried to fight off Hasat's language spell. I wish that she would break through and shout happily now as she did then.

Joaviz crouches on the floor of the cage, the peeling iron making little cuts in her tail as she shivers.

The pace and size of my heart both seem to have doubled. It slams against my ribcage relentlessly.

The Hea is old, possibly the oldest alu I've ever seen. Her eyes are cold black dots in the loose lines of her face. Her lips are nonexistent, her nose grown huge. Her straggly hair snakes around her head and her tail is nearly black.

She takes slow, exaggerated breaths, shawl-covered chest rising unevenly and weak flukes kicking without rhythm.

As soon as we hear the lock click open, Joaviz collapses, folds in on herself, and heaves desperately.

"Where are you taking us?" I ask.

"You're the little Ezkinian brat," she croaks. "What do they call you?"

I lower my eyes. She's my elder, and she loathes me for my selfishness. I abandoned Ezkine, my king, and my father. "Syedahl."

She holds her staff aloft, revealing its slow-moving orbs, and asks, "Will you come without force?"

I nod my head. Joaviz turns away as if ignoring her could make her disappear. I lean in and whisper, "Trust me," even though I do not trust myself.

The Hea prods me out of the room with her staff. When I turn my head to see if Joaviz is coming, she grabs my face in her ancient hands and pushes my head back into place, but not before I see Joaviz flanked by the two guards.

I can hear the difficulty with which the old Hea breathes and swims. It isn't hard to see that her power will soon be granted to the next heir of King Akat's choosing—with the Sa'ari Court's approval—in another city within the Sea. This will keep the balance of power always changing within the Seas but stagnant between them.

It's something I don't often think of, but now as I'm pushed down the white halls, I wonder who before Sarta burned with this very same power—and who will have it after I'm gone. Will I leave an imprint on this orb of lava, or will my use of it be erased?

I hear my own ragged breathing. We dip into a poorly lit hall and then swim completely inverted down a tunnel. Three guards hover in front of what appears to be a dead end. They all make themselves as thin as possible against the wall so we can pass.

The old Hea leans in close and whispers something to the gray stone, causing it to crumble into tiny particles of sand. We pass through and enter a tall room. Thin slits let in light where the walls stretch above ground. Elaborate classical statues of alas adorn the walls. Jewels dance from marble shelves. King Akat hangs from pearl positioning sleeves that protrude from the far wall. He smiles grandly at us and says, "Welcome."

He waves the Akatian guards and the Hea away. The alees escape before the wall closes back up, but the Hea holds her ground. "Master, I'll stay."

"No. Thank you, Fairesa. Syedahl doesn't have her staff, does she?" He looks at me smugly, with all the privileged self-assurance of King Ezkun but none of the fat. His lodgings are majestic, but perhaps he abstains when it comes to food.

"No, she does not." Fairesa bows, her shawl swaying around her thin frame.

My father is treated as an equal by the king, so it shocks me to see her displays of subservience. Especially since she is probably sixty years older than he is.

King Akat ignores her and swims closer. "You're too tan for an Ezkinian. Was your mother dark or is this a disguise?"

"Disguise," I say.

He casts a command over his shoulder. "Do away with their disguises."

I feel the reluctance of the orbs in Fairesa's staff as they gather, and I know how taxing it must have been for her to harvest them. I hold Joaviz's hand as the tingling sensation washes over us, leaving our natural colors behind. King Akat smirks and narrows his eyes. "Not so good at transformation are you?"

I look down.

"Are you?"

"No."

"Well then, what can you do? What's your principle?"

I raise my head to meet his green eyes. They remind me of Father's eyes and I feel a twinge of guilt. "Interpersonal."

The king laughs loudly, a hollow sound. He turns to Fairesa and says, "Nothing to worry about. Out." He enunciates the last word to make it an insult. Fairesa leaves through the once-again crumbling stone. It seals behind her.

Does he really value Hea power so little? Or is this some sort of message to me?

"So, you're with Mac?"

Joaviz squeezes my hand tighter.

"Did you catch him?" I ask.

King Akat surveys me, wondering how to answer. "No, but I could have him taken to the Death Stretch if I so please. What I'm dying to know is are you a Rebel, or is your father only having you act as one? Are you on some mission for him, and all this nonsense about being an escapee is just a trick? Which is it?" As he eyes Joaviz up and down, a perverse smile forms on his lips.

I feel the power inside of me burning with rage, but I'm not sure what I can do without my staff. Am I skilled enough to utter a spell from within? Can I freeze him?

King Akat laughs. "Of course you won't answer. Who's your friend? She's obviously not Ezkinian."

I stare at him defiantly.

His laugh turns cold. "That's fine, Syedahl. One of my three very obedient Heas is a master at interpersonal, so she'll find out everything. And then I'll trade you to either King Ezkun or the Ch'tlan Court for…something that suits me." His gaze is even and relentlessly cruel. "So fine, don't speak."

He turns away from me and lifts Joaviz's chin with a gentle touch. "Exquisite. Exotic. You have the most unique coloring. And your eyes." His voice is smooth. "Your eyes tell a most mysterious tale. You shall be at Court tonight, by my side for the evening's festivities. How would you like that?"

Joaviz doesn't please him with a flirtatious answer, but instead shudders with disgust. I place myself between them.

"She won't attend."

"Don't be so sure." He smirks, then shouts, "Fairesa! Take them back." The stone crumbles to sand again and Fairesa reenters the room.

I'd like to transform the smile off his face, but all I can do is read his mind. What good is that against what he wants to do with Joaviz?

I imagine Joaviz in this very room with his sneer upon her, devouring her unwilling flesh. It makes the power grow hot inside of me.

"Get the guards and take them back," King Akat says.

Fairesa prostrates herself into a low bow, to the King's displeasure. "I can take them myself, Master."

"No, you're not capable."

"Yes, I am." Though she is an enemy to me, I hate to see one so powerful and aged be so demeaned.

"Take one of those guards, there," he says.

"I don't need to."

He exhales audibly.

"It displeases me that I have lost your trust." Her voice is sharp and grating, labored with the burden of breathing.

"You still want to prove your worth, I know, Fairesa. I know."

She turns her head to look at him sideways. "I told my son where to find them, didn't I?"

"You did," he says loudly so she can hear. Then he waves us away, saying softly, "Sometimes I look forward to that inevitable day when I will once again have only two Heas." A glance at Fairesa's smug face lets me know she didn't hear that he wishes her dead. He knows well the limits of her ears.

I get an odd impression of the old Hea. She's at once proud and uncontrollable yet meek and eager to please. I suppose that wanting to please is a trait all Heas share, myself most severely.

Perhaps being a Hea of Ezkine is more desirable than I realized. Father was like a second king. They were friends, always together. Nearly equals, it might have seemed.

Fairesa whispers something to the wall again, then moves back as it turns to dust, letting us pass.

It will take moons for King Akat to decide my fate, because he'll have to negotiate my ransom with either King Ezkun or the Ch'tlan Court. King Ezkun would have good reason to forgive and forget if he could convince the Court to stay out of it. But if the Court were to win King Akat's game, my power would surely be passed along to the next heir in Ch'tlan. No Hea survives extraction. This is many moons off still.

Whatever injustices will befall Joaviz could be committed tonight. I grab her hand again, but Fairesa shrieks out an order and I let go.

As Fairesa pushes and prods us to make the correct turns, I'm lost in my mind. All we gained from Mac is the knowledge that the Tribe of All Seas is spreading rumors about slinu attacks. Joaviz was right. It wasn't worth this.

My heart, hands, and every part of my being yearn for my staff. It calls for me. It sways in the net against the wall, trying in earnest to reach me. I swim into the room first, followed by Joaviz and then Fairesa.

Sick with defeat, I swim into the cage without being told. She's infinitely more experienced than I am.

The sound of quick motion surprises me. I look up from my wallowing to see Joaviz grab two knives from the stone table. She holds them out in front of her, shaking.

With Fairesa's attention directed at Joaviz, I swim over to my staff and yank it from the wall. I grasp it firmly, the netting strange beneath my fingers.

Fairesa works on collecting her dancing orbs. I send a

stream of pale blue. She gathers red orbs fast enough to block me. Ice and steam battle in a stream of light before we both let go. Fairesa breathes horridly with the exertion, but manages to envelop the cage with a haze of gold orbs before I have a moment to recover.

In an instant the cage doubles in size to surround me. Then it begins to shrink, slowly trapping me inside. The door is shut and locked now.

All I have to do is swim out before the bars get too close together, but Fairesa has stilled my muscles. I'm under her command. Her thin lips flap fiercely to hold me in place.

The bars continue to close in around me in agonizing slow motion. My eyes are locked on Fairesa, begging her for a breath.

Motion catches my eye. The long thin knives quiver in Joaviz's hands.

With a fierce cry, she rams them into Fairesa's gut. Blood billows out from her furiously churning gray shawl.

I gasp for water as Fairesa looks down in shock. As I regain use of my lungs and ready another ice spell, Fairesa heals herself, using a bubble of pink light to bring all the blood back into her body as if in reverse.

Fairesa catches my blue light with the tip of her staff and redirects it, freezing Joaviz in an icy scream.

Muttering fervently while raising her hands, Fairesa directs Joaviz's frozen body up off the floor.

She sends Joaviz gliding towards the back wall, where the spikes will shatter her to pieces.

The Great Volcán's voice booms in my head. I join it with a war cry.

Suddenly Joaviz halts and Fairesa slams against the front wall with audible force. Her black eyes harden with fear as her head hits the wall, cracking the rock. Her crumpled body falls forward.

Cutting through the bars with red orbs, I melt Joaviz, who winces with pain. Our hands throbbing and wild with nerves, we lift Fairesa onto the torture table and strap her down.

27

Joaviz

FAIRESA IS PASSED OUT on the table, barely breathing. Syedahl did it. I throw my arms around her. Finally, I can really trust her.

Then she ruins the moment. "We have to find Mac and Zeeki," she says.

All I want is to leave Akati. Lunata Coven be damned. "No, we don't."

So some alee and his niece think the Tribe of All Seas are like totalitarian rulers or something. Whatever.

"I can try. I can try to locate them. I haven't done it before but—"

"We have to get out of here! Stop doing this."

Fairesa groans.

Syedahl whispers, "This is for you."

"No, its not. It's for Alinx."

"No, don't you see?"

I shake my head. She doesn't care about my safety at all. "You don't even like me."

Syedahl hugs me again. "I love you."

I pull back. "Then get me out of here." I look around the room and then down at myself. "Out of this body."

"Please trust me."

I don't respond.

"Please." Syedahl takes my hand, guiding me back along the canal we came through. We don't see anybody.

"We're not even disguised."

Syedahl leads us through the monster-mouth-shaped opening and into the busy plaza. "We have to find them. I can feel Zeeki, feel her calling to me. She wants me to find her. She must know I'm a Hea, because it's working."

That really freaks me out. Maybe this is a trap, but Syedahl and I have come too far with each other to give up now. I need to let myself trust her. She made me remember the snake monster. Now I'll be scared of everything for the rest of my life. I can't trust my own judgment, so I have to trust hers.

"This is wrong," I say, despite myself. We swim over the city, looking down at all the pale buildings. It's not nearly as colorful as it is at night, but now we can see all the propellers and blades spinning on top of the roofs.

"Everyone can see us," I whisper.

"They're not looking. Now be quiet." When I guffaw, she says, "So I can focus." She closes her eyes.

"Don't close your eyes," I whine.

She glares at me, so I shut up. I follow her down into a much smaller plaza. In between two buildings opens the mouth of a tunnel, pitch black. I shake my head.

Syedahl says sorry and dives inside.

I follow, dodging the dead crab on the floor and keeping my eyes off the wobbly-barred prison cells.

"Akati enslaved slinus long after the war. They were taken out to work, then locked back in," Syedahl says.

The tunnel dips down lower, colder, darker.

My belly skims against sand. "Hurry!" The lower we go,

the more sand and the less water.

Syedahl kicks it up with her flukes. I cough and complain.

The light is just ahead, yellow-gray. Syedahl is silhouetted in front of the brightness. We emerge and the daylight blinds me. I breathe a little easier. I think of that creepy alee and don't feel sorry for the slinus who were enslaved here, not at all. Syedahl says he was lying about what happened to his family, but I don't think so. Why would he?

"Zeeki's calling to me. She must be…yes, this way!"

I don't hear anything.

We swim up a column in a cluster of tall white houses, then pass over a few roofs of varying heights. Syedahl dives into an opening. We find Zeeki inside the house, hanging onto circle holdings. She's saying Syedahl's name over and over with her eyes closed.

A fat ala is slumped on the floor crying while Mac circles the room, eyeing Zeeki and the ala. Zeeki's shoulders are hunched and her breathing is uneven.

They snap out of their heads and notice us. Zeeki smiles, the ala wails, and Mac looks even more worried. What do they know about us?

Syedahl goes down to him. I stay by the entrance, hovering vertically.

"I didn't know if it would work," Zeeki says.

"The close proximity…we were both trying…" Syedahl breathes deeply. "Listen, it doesn't matter. I battled Fairesa. They must be looking for us right now."

Mac's thick brown eyebrows bend up and he grabs her shoulder. "Let's go then."

"What do you mean 'let's'?" I ask. We're not disguised any more, so how do they know who we are? And how did Zeeki know Syedahl's real name?

Mac smirks at me. I cross my arms. "We're taking you with us," he says.

I stare at each of them in turn, dumbfounded.

The ala on the floor slumps down even more. She looks like she's praying. Zeeki swims over and holds her face. "I have to go, Mom."

"I'll never forgive you, Brother."

"This is good for her, Joisa," Mac says. "She deserves more."

With her fierce and unforgiving stare, I know Joisa does not agree. "Not like this," she says.

Zeeki's hair is a thick, curly blond halo. "Hug me, Mom. I have to go." Even in this tender moment, her voice strikes me as high and annoying.

"What's going on?" I ask.

"Later," Syedahl says.

I don't get how *she* even knows. Mac definitely wasn't there that night I got drunk, but apparently I was even drunker than I thought. This is usually the case.

Zeeki and her mom share the saddest hug I've ever seen and my heart sinks. Maybe it's harder to say goodbye than to just disappear, but I'd still rather get to say goodbye.

Their pain makes me remember.

Last year they sent him to see a doctor in San Francisco. I spent the whole week wailing for him, rocking in his favorite chair, the green one that smells like tea tree oil and old cigars, though he would never admit to using either. Mom told me that he would be back; he might even come home with good news. Mom said it wasn't over yet. I imagined that it was, and so sent myself into that spiral like when my cat died. She became every curled-up sweater and canvas bag.

To me it was like Dad had already died. I could imagine him all over the house. Slouching in the kitchen hoping Mom would make him something to eat. Pulling weeds around the back deck.

I could see and hear him everywhere, walking around with his heavy steps. I imagined him listening in on my phone conversations through the cracked door.

But he wasn't there. It was just the girls: my mother, my sister, and I, each with our own set of hurts. Mine was the loudest. I cried the entire time he was gone. Tessa was living under the strain of optimism. Mom was doing chores, errands. The last couple of days, she started to get angry with me. She wasn't ready to grieve. She still had hope. She told me to act my age. I was sixteen and didn't I understand the difference between death and a hospital visit? Don't act like your father is dead. I won't allow it, she said, as if it were just any other rule.

Finally he did appear in the doorway. I was sitting on the couch when he came in, which is a very good thing. Crying in his chair, smelling the squares of fabric that cover the arms, would have scared him. I was the first to get a hug from him. The little black hairs on his face rubbed against my forehead. His firm belly pressed into my flat one, and his shoulders, twice the width of mine, seemed to wrap all the way around me. He kissed the top of my head.

But there was no good news. He hadn't called because he wanted to tell us in person.

I have to get back to him. That's all that matters now.

We're leaving; I'm following them. Mac and Zeeki have cloth satchels. Syedahl has her concealed staff. I have nothing.

We swim straight over the city nonchalantly, as though we're going shopping. Three alas and their chaperone.

The city ends and the seaweed begins, swaying this way and that like a crowd at a concert. I see two seals swimming around each other, dancing along.

I sigh.

"Cute, huh?" Zeeki says.

Someone's coming after us. We all turn around to see a Hea with a vibrant purple tail. Mac says, "Let me handle this."

But Syedahl positions herself in front of us, her staff held out defensively. She has only one set of orbs, red ones for steam. Syedahl is holding it aggressively. She's bursting with confidence this time, though this Hea's staff is full like a lava lamp.

"Why did you almost kill my grandmother?" she asks.

"Because she tried to trap me," Syedahl says.

The ala looks past Syedahl. "Where are you taking her?"

"You know," Mac says.

She looks at Syedahl again. "Do you know what you're getting yourself into?"

"No."

The Hea laughs. She is lean and beautiful. "And you."

"Me?" I ask.

"Yes. You're the one the king has eyes for?"

"I...I..." I can't take my eyes off those spinning orbs.

Mac swims to Syedahl's side, "We have to go, Liada."

Liada's blond hair cascades and rises around her as she looks at Mac sideways and purses her lips. She even flutters her eyelashes.

Mac swims forward and kisses her on the mouth. "I'm glad you came to say goodbye." They kiss again, open-mouthed this time.

I realize she must have sensed that he was leaving the boundary.

Do all Heas have a thing for warriors?

"Come back," she says.

"I will." Mac kisses her cheek.

We turn away from her and swim south.

Syedahl's face is straight-up shocked. "Are you…?"

"Lovers?" Mac asks.

Zeeki shakes her head mockingly. "He's dangerous when-ever he can be, in every aspect of his life."

Neither of us can afford for Syedahl to get lost in her thoughts right now, imagining that she and Alinx could be like that too. "Where are we going?" I demand, yanking her back to the problem she shares with me.

"The Rebel Army Base," Mac answers. "Where else?"

28

Syedahl

WE WERE UNABLE TO ATTEND the Lunata Coven meeting that Henna told us about. I truly hope we didn't miss anything important.

We swim for half the night, then Mac lets the three of us sleep while he keeps watch. No alu sleeps all that well in the open, but in our case, it's still best to have one of us completely aware. I'm concerned about this half moon of travel because I know how much swimming in the open ocean upsets Joaviz.

In order to optimize our speed, we all stay silent. Joaviz seems to have benefitted from silence. She's calm, reserved.

The clear blue water, along with memories of Joisa and Zeeki hugging, make me wonder if my own mother lives in waters this beautiful. I consider asking Mac if it's possible to find the records of Hea matings, but decide against it for now.

I picture my mother with dark hair and tan skin, a beautiful warm smile, and kind lavender eyes that match my own. She'd take me in her arms and immediately understand everything about me.

The thought of shattering my image of her is frightening.

Besides, one task at a time.

Yesterday, before we fell asleep, we all took time to get better acquainted. Zeeki wants to be a spy. She must have some experience. She did after all link my weak traveler's lie to news of the escapee Hea. This is how she knew my name. She's going to the Rebel Army with hopes of becoming one of their spies. She's been ready for some time and only recently convinced her mother that it was her choice to make. She's 19, which surprises me. She was born the spring before I was. I feel so much older, though. I can't tell if she has genuine passion for the Rebel cause, or if she merely wants to please her uncle.

Joaviz and I swim behind Mac and Zeeki. The current is mild and the waters warm. The temperature increases a little bit every day that we swim south.

I feel an immediate appreciation for the clarity and calm motion of the middle waters. I fully understand why most alu cities, like Akati and Kalein, are built at this level.

"Can I talk to you?" Joaviz whispers, casting a weary glance at our partners ahead.

"Sure."

"No, like in private."

At this, Zeeki raises a curious eyebrow before facing forward again.

"We'll catch up to you!" I shout. I'm actually grateful for the break. But my muscles clench and tighten as soon as I stop swimming, so I sway my flukes lazily to keep from cramping up.

"Why do you trust them?" Joaviz asks after checking to see that Mac and Zeeki are out of earshot.

They keep a few stretches ahead, politely waiting.

"That night that you…" I stop and start again. "I got on well with Zeeki. Mostly she made fun of me, for not knowing what the Death Stretch was. I learned that when the Akatians were done with the slinus, their Heas cast an invisibility charm around the Death Stretch, which is apparently the place with the most severe sea-level change *in the world*. The tide takes—"

"Okay." Joaviz raises her hands to make me stop. "So you like her. Fine. You trust them. Whatever. But you risked our safety and told her who—"

"No," I say, happy to be the one to interrupt for once. "I didn't tell her. Because I hated swimming over other alu's heads and because Enkirik joked that I didn't want to swim over the city wall, they knew I was from Ch'tlan and that I was not an experienced traveler as we had claimed. When I didn't know what the Death Stretch was, Zeeki joked that I was from Ezkine, because Ezkine is famous for not studying anything but our own history and geography."

Joaviz's eyes have a semi-dazed look, so I make an effort to hurry my explanation. My excuses only ever raise her snarl higher.

"She had heard about the escapee, about me. When I went to the meeting, I could tell that both of them knew who I was."

Joaviz raises her hands and splays her fingers. "Okay, fine. But...where the hell are we going?"

"To the Rebel Army Base."

Her eyes narrow, flash wide, and flicker back into anger. I know she's trying to think of how this connects to Alinx, always convinced that I'm trying to find him instead of helping her. The less she trusts me, the more I wish her accusations were true.

"And what do they have to do with me?"

"I'm not sure."

Joaviz groans.

"They can provide something that we need—safety," I say. "Perhaps they have information. Either way, we can stay there for a while." Her angry glare causes me to revise. "For a few days. So we can come up with a plan."

"Based on what?"

I lose my patience. "I don't know, Joaviz! Alright?"

She tries to hush me, looking nervously towards Mac and Zeeki. She's probably afraid to reveal a crack in our friend- ship that could later be used to pry the two of us apart. How did she become this paranoid?

"I need time to think," I say, regaining my calm. "Without having to worry about escaping. Just…time."

"Okay."

I give her my own nasty glare and she smoothes her gri- mace into a frown.

She concedes more sincerely this time. "Okay, we'll go. We're going."

We reach Mac and Zeeki and join ranks again. They say nothing.

I recall the things that have given Joaviz her strange sei- zures: the alee who said his family was eaten by slinus; the feeding frenzy; the time Father read her mind, the time I read her mind and evoked her memories of…what was it exactly? I saw only a very large tentacle and glowing eyes.

Glowing eyes. Sixteen of them. That's what I saw. How could Joaviz know that old myth?

Maybe the storytellers are right. No Hea can transform a human into an alu. The only creature more powerful than a Hea is the Serpent Mistress, a legend used to frighten chil- dren from going too deep, or wandering off alone.

I'll have to talk to Mac about what I saw, to see if those images could have been from a hallucination or a dream. But I can't with Joaviz around. I don't want to send her crashing back down into that lonely place where her body twitches and her eyes see another world entirely.

All of these thoughts occupy my mind only by force of will. Joaviz is right. What I truly want to know is this: How does Mac manage his love for that Hea?

He told me nothing about their relationship, but he did tell me a little about himself.

Mac was discharged from the Akatian army 17 years ago. After traveling around the Salamauro Sea to learn the arts of shark fighting, taming, and riding, he met the Commander of the Rebel Army and joined the cause. He returned to Akati to recruit Akatian youths and serve as envoy and liaison. He gave me no specific information about his duties.

In the distance we see a medley of fish feeding off of some floating human contraption that has acquired an impressive amount of algae. I snag as many as possible while Mac works near me, fetching them with his bag.

I hear Zeeki saying to Joaviz, "Sorry about how I treated you when we first met. I'm just protective of my cousin."

Yesterday Mac explained that Enkirik isn't his own son, but the son of his older brother. Mac never married or had children and claims the thought never crossed his mind until Liada.

Joaviz replies in a sharp but distant voice. "It's okay. I get it. Who would blame you?"

"No, I don't mean it that way. I'm like that with everyone because…"

I take advantage of Joaviz's distraction and ask Mac pointedly, "Why are you taking me to the Base?"

He smiles at my directness. "Why do you want to come?"

I whisper, "There's something wrong." A quick glance in Joaviz's direction gives Mac all the information he needs.

"And you hope we know how to help?"

I nod my head. I'm not sure if Joaviz realizes how she's been acting. Anyone could reasonably declare her mad. Her episodes are like seizures of the mind, of memory.

"You'll be disappointed, but you might learn something."

I stare at him incredulously.

He leans in closer, showing me the thin wrinkles forming around his bright eyes. "I know what she is."

I pull back. Joaviz looks at me sharply, but thankfully Zeeki rambles on about how excited she is to finally go to the Base. I can't tell whether or not Joaviz has heard.

"Wow, that's great." I'm sure an eye-roll accompanies Joaviz's sarcastic response, but I don't actually see it because I'm still focused on Mac.

Zeeki stops talking, so I can't ask Mac any more questions about Joaviz lest she hear and accuse me of invading her privacy. Suddenly, the question dearest to my heart bubbles up, "How do you manage to see Liada?"

Mac's mouth drops open and then closes in a big smile. "So that's why you left. I can't get my love to do it yet, but I'll convince her! Where is your lucky alee?"

I don't know how to answer. He obviously doesn't like the Tribe of All Seas, so if I mention that Alinx is with them right now, he may decide he can't trust me enough to take me to the Base.

"In Ezkine. He couldn't come with us. He's sworn in just like I was."

"Is he a warrior?"

"Yes."

Mac is even more skeptical. "A warrior who's more loyal to his king than to his ala. What kind of warrior is that?"

Now I understand why Mac was discharged.

"He would have come with me, but I didn't give him the chance. There wasn't time."

Mac grabs a small wrasse from the bag and chews on it whole, killing it with a decisive crunch. "Well, I'll tell you it's not an easy romance."

Joaviz hears us talking about love. "*So that's why you left Ezkine.* I knew it!" She swims off, the silence of her anger loud in the contortion of her face.

I follow her. "I left to protect you. And because the Great Volcán asked me to."

My attempts to convince her are half-hearted. I can't claim that I would refuse Alinx if he came to me now and asked me to give up on her to create a life with him.

The Great Volcán rarely speaks to me. Does that mean what I'm doing is right?

I still don't know what Alinx thinks of me, of what I've done. I wish his wasn't the only opinion that mattered.

29

Joaviz

MY DAD HAS HIS LEGS TIED together behind him and he's flapping them to get through the air in the living room. When he opens his mouth a bubble comes out, the soapy kind that's all shiny and iridescent.

The living room has no ceiling.

He's drawing a picture in the white glow of the moon. He's bent over his work, crouched on the carpet.

He draws with a pencil, but the lines don't show up.

He asks my mother for a pen. She has a huge stone bowl of them behind her, but she lies and says there aren't any. My sister Tessa comes into the room. She floats across the floor on her two feet, saying that she'll help Dad.

She draws big, thick black lines on the paper and says, "It's time for Joanne to rest now. She'll be the watcher now. She'll watch out for us from over there." She points towards the door, the direction we used to point at with our thumbs while shrugging and asking, "Do you want to go to the beach?"

Mom says it isn't time yet: it isn't time to let go of me. I will come back. She can't believe that Tessa could be so sure. Mom remembers when it was just the two of us for a while. Just Mom and me.

Dad stares at the paper, Tessa's lines now gone. The moon throws a bright spotlight on his blank page.

He wants to fill it with something, anything, but he doesn't know what yet.

I am a disembodied voice in the living room crying, "Wait for me."

I wake up screaming. Syedahl and Mac are talking about slinus but they stop right away. Syedahl gives me a guilty look.

I'm shivering. I can't take this anymore and I'm really serious this time. Does my family actually think I'm dead? Well, I'm not dead, even though I want to be.

Syedahl tries to hug me but I push her away. Just leave me alone.

My teeth are chattering and I'm pulling my hair out. It's so dark that I can't see anything, but the way their eyes glow tells me it isn't nighttime.

I can't be split in two anymore.

White hands come towards me. I yell, "NO!" over and over and over again.

"What's wrong with her? She's freaking out!" Zeeki doesn't understand what's happening.

"Let me try to help, Joaviz. I need to know what's going on," Syedahl commands. Those white hands come closer.

I won't let her. If she really cared—if she could stop getting sidetracked—maybe I'd be home by now.

"Don't let me go," someone whispers.

What I hate the most is that even *I* don't understand what's happening to me. I can't think. Everything is cloudy, hazy.

I don't want anyone touching me, but I don't want Syedahl to leave.

I realize that she holds me to this place. I just have to go. I can't wait anymore!

Kicking my flukes, I tear through the bubbled haze.

"Joaviz!" Syedahl shouts after me.

I just keep swimming.

"You're going the wrong way."

Everyone is going the wrong way. Not just me. I look down at my hands and at my stomach and see that circular scar.

When I touch it, no memories come. The shakes come though, but this time they don't hurt. I give in and let them have me. I don't fight or tighten up. My teeth chatter until my jaw aches. Images flash around, out of my control.

Wide-eyed faces with scales, peering in at me. Surrounding me.

Darkness.

Syedahl, stretching her fingers towards me. Always.

Mac, gliding in and out of a crowd of angry citizalus and finding my face every time.

Zeeki. There. Just there. Right in front of me.

Blue.

Everyone so concerned, worried for me. The blue sea gone black, but not really. It's more like a dream. Or like when you're outside in the sun and then you go back inside, and your eyes haven't adjusted yet.

Syedahl catches me and takes my hand. Something clicks, changes. I clasp her hand gratefully. She's all I've got here. She's my only friend.

The seaweed shines golden, all spindly and leafy with pockets of air. The stuff just floats. No roots or anything, but perfectly alive. A floating world out here in the middle of nowhere. Trash bags and colored plastic.

"It's okay," Syedahl says. "We'll keep going, just come this way."

We swim hand in hand for a long time, with me in control of my body but not my eyes. They flick around, looking for something I didn't ask them to.

The seaweed scatters across my back. I push away a piece of wood with nails sticking out. Something reacts—a striped fish with little brown dots, knobby like the seaweed. Camouflaged just for this place.

I don't want to adapt.

Syedahl hasn't let go of my hand. "They're only little fish," she says.

When I bump into more seaweed, baby eels explode around me. They squiggle against my face.

I don't scream because I don't want them in my mouth. The shakes come back. My eyes open like crazy.

Sunlight. Seaweed.

Turtle beak.

A big swordfish with a sail on its back that closes, sending the fish soaring *zoom!* across the blue.

I shudder and can't move. The open ocean. No current. Shiny black bubbles of oil appear among floating seaweed, trash, and fish.

The oil pollutes an unexpected place for life. Slippery and disgusting. The smell makes me cough and throw up.

I wave the barf away from my face, swim away from it. My stomach is sore.

Trash and fish. Humans and alus. Which one am I? I wish the current would move again and separate my two worlds and force me to decide.

When the shakes stop, I'm looking straight down, watching the blue deepen.

"What is it?" Syedahl asks.

I nestle into her arms. "Something!"

"What?"

I look down harder. I don't see it. I feel it. Something slimy that lives down deep, far away from this floating world, and comes here just to eat.

Mac says, "I've seen this reaction before. At the Base."

Half of me is terrified and the other half angry, but there's another little part of me that is resigned to stop fighting and just go a little insane.

30

Syedahl

THE REEF IS A MOUNTAIN that stretches beyond the surface. We swim halfway around it to the other side. Fantastically colored fish, octopi, and eels are whirling and dancing across this coral reef for my pleasure, but I can't enjoy them. In these aquamarine waters I have a new sense of clarity. I see what I couldn't in the darkness of Ezkine: agreeing to care for Joaviz was a mistake.

Of course I didn't mean to offer her my help. Initially I only wanted to protect her from my father and take her from the city, but then when we encountered that storm and she worshipped the rain, I felt pity for her and made a promise that I simply can't keep.

How could I have been so confident? I'm the youngest Hea in all the Seas, and I thought I could perform the mystery of transformation that none of my kind has ever, in thousands of years, been able to master?

It's shameful really.

I wish I could focus on the beauty of this place, let it soothe my weary mind, but instead I dissect those brief flashes that I read from Joaviz. Sixteen glowing eyes. I have nothing but myths for insight.

I have to tell Joaviz that our journey is futile, but how can I when she goes insane whenever the Deep is mentioned? If she knew she must stay an ala forever, there would be no hope left. She might have one of her seizures and never stop.

Or perhaps she could accept and heal.

For my own sake, I need a leader. I don't want to be like Hasat. His mission was to get Joaviz and me safely out of Ezkine, which he did, and I thank him for it. But the Great Volcán has led me toward an impossible task—one that I can't accomplish alone. He never even asked me to help Joaviz. That I promised on my own. All he asked was that I leave. I've let my own vanity get the best of me. Solve a mystery no Hea ever could?

The Great Volcán hasn't spoken to me much at all, but according to Hasat, many Heas never hear him. He has only commanded me during the most trying times. Perhaps he led Joaviz to me just to lead me to the Rebel Army Base. If only I hadn't made that promise…

Alinx could help me decide if I'm doing the right thing. He can council me better than anyone, can tell me what my subconscious is too quiet to get across.

"Ah!" Joaviz gasps, bringing my focus to the deepening blue below. I hadn't even realized that we had begun to swim down the mountain.

"What is it?"

Mac responds in a strained voice, his tail a muddy blur against the bright hues behind him. "All of you stay calm."

I look to my right and see in the distance a shark twice my length. Fish dart in and out of the coral and she catches them easily. I know immediately, instinctually, that this shark is the type that attacks alus. There's something about her intelligence and speed that tells me she finds it fun.

Joaviz, Zeeki, and I are absolutely still, locked in place,

inverted awkwardly in descent. Mac kicks his flukes to continue downwards.

"No!" Joaviz says.

Mac flips right side up and looks at the shark, his strong arms crossed over his smooth, muscled chest. "She's usually very shy."

"She? Shy?" Zeeki squeals.

Mac nods his head. "We don't have a Hea here. These waters are free of protection magic, except for the Base's invisibility. Greizjo set that up for us. But you're going to have to get used to predators."

One of the three Akatian Heas must have been good at animal magic and kept fearsome species outside the city. I guess Zeeki isn't used to dealing with sharks the way I am—only because Father was so inept at animal magic.

The look in Mac's eyes as he watches the striped shark is the same as when he saw his Hea lover brandishing her staff. He has an appetite for dangerous beauty.

In Ezkine I never had the luxury of forgetting about predators, granted the unwanted visits were uncommon. Still, there's something about this shark that unnerves me even more than usual. Her elegance, the ease with which she corners the fish and plucks them one by one with the razors in her mouth.

Without any intention, my staff enlarges to its clear and colorfully buzzing state.

Mac turns swiftly and shakes his head as if I'd tried to kill the creature.

"What do we do?" Joaviz whispers. Her stiffness doesn't surprise me. Only the Deep causes those horrible convulsions.

"We keep going," Mac says.

The shark turns towards us, wagging the high spikes of her

fins. She moves slowly, methodically closer. Joaviz opens her mouth to emit the tiniest shriek.

Mac's tone changes a little but his words remain calm. "She wants to say hello."

Joaviz's and Zeeki's eyes are as wide as the shark's, but not nearly as beautiful. I've never seen eyes like these—round and soft, sensual and intelligent, the whites so pure and the blacks so perfectly deep.

As the shark draws near, I curve to float horizontally. Zeeki does the same, but Joaviz is as still as if I'd frozen her. The only thing moving is her long hair.

The shark quickens its speed, coming towards us decisively now. I raise my staff but Mac commands me to stop just as the shark hits Joaviz's stomach and pushes her into the reef wall.

Red flows from her body. I didn't even see teeth. Water fills my lungs in tiny, desperate gulps. I hold onto her as the shark turns briefly away. I know no healing spells.

But Joaviz is laughing, a sharp and crazy sound, her heart hammering fully alive against my cheek. She exhales gushes of water, her red hair dancing.

The shark continues to feed, moving farther away from us.

Mac chuckles and hits Joaviz on the back. He narrows his deep gray eyes, crinkling the tan, worn skin around them. "Good thing you didn't cut yourself on the coral. She wouldn't have been able to resist."

I sigh in Mac's direction. He courts danger. Can I?

31

Joaviz

SUNSET-COLORED CORAL, in some places sprawling and in others dense, clings to the rocks. It is pink brains, fuzzy red antlers, purple discs and trees.

I squeal when I see some tiny neon fish.

We descend down the mountain face, which breaks the surface at the top. We arrived at some Caribbean island! I can't believe I've swum this far.

On second thought, considering how my tail and abs are rock solid and not even sore anymore, I guess I do believe it.

I do a somersault and let all the colors whirl together.

I see an orange octopus stuck to the wall of coral, and a school of yellow fish. Lots of weird, spiky anemone things. And then a black, angular shadow passes over us.

"It's okay," Mac says.

A giant manta ray turns and swims under Mac, who grabs onto its white horns. "He's always here. He's our friend."

The three of us watch Mac and the manta ray zoom through the open water. Mac lets go and waves goodbye to his buddy. Together we work our way down the mountain, pointing out our favorite fish and coral. I freak out when I see a long gray shark lying on a flat rock. I relax a little when

Mac says it's harmless.

As we descend lower, two wooden poles stick up towards us, with round platforms wrapped around them. Is it really...? My heart stops.

Lookout decks! A sunken ship!

The ship leans against the wall past where the coral ends on the mountain. As we get closer, I see a ledge just wide enough to support it.

We pass guards on our way down, their bored faces suddenly lighting up. Mac must look pretty weird bringing three young alas here.

I beg to see the front of the ship before we go in. Sure enough, there is a mermaid carving. Her nose is broken off and so is some of her wavy hair, but the curve of her tail is totally intact.

Syedahl is dumbfounded.

Mac explains, "This comes from a time when humans knew about us."

I study the ship. It reminds me of movies about the discovery of the New World. "This thing must be so old!"

Everyone stares at me. I get the sense they're waiting for me to say something more about it, but I don't know anything.

They think humans are all magical Heas because we make metal contraptions. They also think we're greedy and should leave their territory alone. I don't blame them for either of those thoughts. We have so much stuff while they live simply.

We swim back out towards the open water and enter the ship through a big gaping hole. The guard there is happy to see Mac. Regardless, we still have to state our names and business.

We swim into the front room. It was once three stories,

but now there are gaping holes everywhere, so you can see all the way through to the bottom. Algae and crusty creatures coat the walls.

Mac leads us onto the deck where a bunch of young warriors are putting on their wrist swords. Mac explains that they are new recruits leaving for training. I ask about wrist and arm swords and he says that often in battle, warriors just keep moving, dodging and slicing as they swim by.

I'd flirt with the recruits individually, but all of them looking at us at the same time is intimidating.

After a short wait, I spot the Commander. He's not wearing a sash or jewelry or anything. It's the way he holds himself that tells me who he is.

His green tail and eyes are bright against his dark skin. He looks just a little older than Mac. He shows a row of gleaming pointed teeth when he smiles. They look sharper than mine feel.

He speaks a different language to Syedahl and she catches on right away. Then they switch back to Sa'ari. Mac introduces Zeeki, who bows with her hand upturned. The Commander puts his hand on hers and bows too.

Then it's my turn. I'm glad Zeeki went first or I wouldn't know what to do.

Syedahl blurts out something to the Commander in the other language, but he raises one massive hand to stop her.

In Sa'ari, he says, "Mac, why don't you take Zeeki. Get her started right away. Very nice to meet you, Zeekitanai."

"Likewise, Commander." Zeeki gives another little bow. Then Mac and Zeeki swim down through a hole in the deck.

An older alee shouts to all the warriors and they head off towards the open ocean, making it impossible for me to hear what Syedahl and the Commander are saying.

He turns to me. His curly black hair is pulled into a low

ponytail. "Joaviz, I need to talk to Syedahl alone. There are some..." he takes a deep breath, "other humans that were transformed, two that we've intercepted. Would you like to meet them?"

My stomach sinks. I feel duped, embarrassed. What are we really doing here? If there are humans here, then these Rebels can't help us at all. "Yeah. Sure. Of course."

He explains that the humans speak Kai and asks if it would be okay for Syedahl to teach it to me. We both comply. I wonder if my brain can handle it.

The Commander watches with calm admiration as Syedahl bathes me in light.

New words swim around in my head, opening notes to a crescendo. My headache lasts only moments. I'm left feeling numb.

We follow him across the pitted deck, through the damaged walls of the room at the other end of the ship, and then through a tunnel that goes straight into the mountain.

Tiny holes have been cut into the creamy rock above and around us, letting in natural light.

We don't make it far before jaws snap. I scream, and the Commander shoos the moray eel down the tunnel. "This is their home too," he says.

We make a left at a split and then another left into a wide, low, bright room.

Inside we find one ala my age, a middle-aged ala, and a middle-aged alee.

My heart pounds so fast. These are humans. I feel my eyes start to cross and I think I'll faint. The Commander says, "I need to take Syedahl and speak with her alone. Is that alright?"

I nod my head. I'm left alone with these strangers.

"Are you human too?" I ask the young ala.

"No. I—"

The alee interjects. "She's our nanny," he says with a smile. What does he have to smile about? "I'm Peetare, and this is Heleina."

I can guess what their real names are, and wonder if they could guess mine. "I'm Joaviz."

"So how long have you been transformed?" he asks.

"Almost two moons too long."

Heleina is seated on a stone stool, her right cheek touching her right shoulder. Not even looking at me, she says, "I've been like this for four moons."

"I'm sorry."

Peetare explains that Heleina is from London and that she has a son and a husband there. He's from the Canary Islands off the coast of Morocco. He says that after a lot of effort, what with the vastly different place names, he and the Commander discovered that they grew up pretty close to each other.

I tell them I'm from LA and that my friend is a Hea. "She's trying to find out how to turn me back."

Heleina laughs bitterly and turns to face me with dead blue eyes. Her voice is like puffer fish juice. "The Heas don't have a clue how to fix us. There's one, Greizjo, who comes to check on us once a moon, but he understands nothing about us."

"My friend will find out," I say, a pit in my stomach weakening my words.

"I don't want to go back. There's nothing for me on land, no one waiting," Peetare says.

I never thought of not going back. I can't. I need to see my dad.

Heleina curls back in on herself again like a clam. "Besides, the Commanders are probably trying to get Syedahl to join them right now. They don't have their own Hea. Greizjo won't leave his city."

"Commanders?"

"There are three. The one you met is the First. The main one. The other two, we just call by their names."

Like a wrist sword slice to the chest. Three of them. One of me. Who will Syedahl pick? I hold my head with my hands, feel my hair dance all over my fingers.

Peetare says, "Your friend won't leave you."

Heleina makes a loud noise, a cross between a grunt and a sigh.

Syedahl won't leave me. But if the Commanders give her some valiant task that she can't refuse, then maybe...

I ask them how they got transformed, but they ignore the question. I can't remember at all. I was just a girl in LA who got bad grades and hung out downtown smoking cigarettes in a long-stem holder. I don't know how I got to Ezkine, just that I was on a cruise. My family took cruises every summer, no big deal. But this time it was February, because Dad was sick. It couldn't wait.

Searching their torsos for scars like mine gets me nothing.

"Why us?" I ask.

"The Commanders think it's random," Peetare says.

No new piece to the puzzle.

Just temptation for Syedahl.

I drop to the floor and cry—no tears, just a headache and loud sobs. With what was left of my hope now gone, a memory creeps in, slowly at first. My own voice screaming.

And then. I remember *her*, if only for a second.

Heleina says, "All they do here is teach us to forget."

32

Syedahl

THE COMMANDER LEADS ME BACK down the brightly lit hall of ancient coral. We come to a simple, small room with a stone table in the center. On the table is a crumbling tablet and a skull that I instantly know to be human.

"Please," the Commander says, motioning to a set of holdings and then clasping a pair himself. I'm grateful. It's been a very long journey.

My skin crawls and my scales prickle. I'm nervous, not about him, but about me, about how I'll answer whatever he might ask.

Just as he tells me that we're waiting for the other two Commanders to join us, an alee comes in. I release my holdings and we bow to each other, layering our hands. His tail is the color of a storm. The Commander seems even larger next to his thin frame.

"Syedahl, this is Tasapi," the Commander says, watching our encounter intently.

Tasapi smiles weakly at me and takes a pair of holdings. "How was your journey?" he asks.

"Tiresome, yet rewarding," I respond, instantly sensing

that my presence here irks him for some reason.

A third alee squeezes into the room, breathing unevenly. His dark brown hair is thinning and cropped close to his round head. His eyebrows seem permanently lifted in curiosity. We bow. The Commander introduces him as Rew and explains that they're to be called by their names, or Second and Third Commander respectively. I nod, full of anticipation.

The Commander apologizes for the fact that nothing I tell them can be trusted, not until the Hea Greizjo can interview me in a half moon's time.

"Mac said you didn't have a Hea," I interject.

Tasapi inhales noisily towards the ceiling. The Commander smiles and drops his gaze before bringing it back to me. "Greizjo is the Hea of the nearest city, Dorma. He comes to us once a moon, but his king doesn't know."

Tasapi is restless, adjusting his grip on the holdings, shrugging away the blond hair that searches out his face. "Commander, may I?"

With a sigh, the Commander nods.

Rew's fat frame bulges from the holdings. He appears pleased and relaxed, as if this conversation is a much-needed break.

"Are you on Ezkinian business?" Tasapi says.

I reply as calmly as I can. "No. I'm in danger of death. If I'm ever caught, King Ezkun would most likely be forced to turn me over to the Ch'tlan Court." I try not to be offended by the question, but my voice no doubt betrays me.

The Commander and Tasapi share a look.

"What's your business then?" the Commander asks.

"I…" Here I falter, not wanting to show them just how torn I am about my own motivations. "…To save my friend."

"The human?" Tasapi asks.

I nod, thinking I gave the wrong answer. Their shared looks and nods are too much for me to understand. "My father was trying to experiment on her. I had only just met her, but I knew I needed to keep her from him. She's my responsibility and…"

I don't know where to stop, or how much to tell them. If they're questioning whether or not they can trust me, then how can I be so certain that I can trust them?

"About that," the Commander begins, "About your father. Do *you* know why he was so interested in her?" The way he asks this makes me believe that he already knows the answer.

"Because he wants to learn High Transformation, at any cost. He got carried away, I suppose," I say.

This time it's Rew who guffaws, but when I cast a glance at him, he returns an endearing smile.

"Well, we know it's more than that," the Commander says.

I wait for him to continue.

"He wants to align himself with the Tribe of All Seas."

"How can he?" I ask. "He's completely devoted to Ezkine." I let go of a holding and touch my chest, trying to show that for my father, serving Ezkine is more than a duty or promise.

"He and King Ezkun have plans to increase Ezkine's power, to involve themselves in the Tribe of All Seas. The Serpent Mistress has been transforming humans. How many, we don't know, but since the ones we've encountered have been in different stages of…mental unrest, we get the sense that she's trying to perfect the technique."

"I'm sorry," I say. "I don't…I…What?"

The Commander waits, giving me time to digest this.

Someone has to tell Joaviz that transforming her back is impossible, and it has to be me. If the Serpent Mistress did this, then she's the only one who can undo it. And to face the most powerful creature in all the Seas is to face death itself.

The Serpent Mistress! I can't believe that *I believe* she exists. I keep trying to deny it, but what else can that gigantic stretch of scaly skin in Joaviz's memory be? If Heas can't transform humans into alus, who else can?

The Serpent Mistress, like each of the Great Serpents before her, is the guardian of the power of the Deep, the mythical myst gem. Only one Great Serpent lives at a time. For millions of years there was only deep green magic—the power of fear and the unknown. When the Great Volcán created alus out of lava, he left some lava power in the first four hundred to bring balance back to the Seas. Heas have always been the protectors of alukind, guarding them from humans, slinus, and other dangerous creatures. We're meant to use our power.

It's common belief that the Great Serpents were never meant to use the myst gem, but only to protect it and prevent it from being used. By whom, I'm not sure. Alutian knowledge of slinus decreased so heavily after the war that we're unsure if they can make use of the magic. We don't even know what form the power of the Deep takes.

The Serpent Mistress is said to have organized the slinus against us. She's the only Great Serpent who ever meddled in the affairs of other species, and the first to use the gem. One thousand years ago she intervened in slinu slavery, working with krakens and dessas to free them from their nightly duties and daytime imprisonment. Slinus and krakens slaughtered alus for fifty years and then fled to depths impenetrable to us.

Hundreds of thousands of alus were slain, our cities rendered unsteady, and our work force destroyed. Some cities, such as Ezkine and Akati, enslaved slinus after the war, but only in much smaller numbers and only temporarily.

Hundreds of years have passed since then. I think back to the play, and to that alee claiming that slinus had killed his family. Are they attacking again? Mac says they aren't.

I never even believed the Serpent Mistress existed, and now I'm beginning to wonder if she's still alive, one thousand years later.

But the myst gem and the Great Serpents are merely myths; stories told to children to encourage their respect of the Deep. *Be careful little ones, the Great Serpent has died. The creatures of the Deep no longer have help protecting their gems. They've become even nastier. I wouldn't go down there if I were you.*

Joaviz tells me that humans use symbols to communicate. There are some Seas with writings on stones, and some Heas who use inscribing tools, but we mostly share knowledge orally. Our stories are all we have, so it's widely accepted that myth and history can't be separated. Two creatures that many believe never existed are said to be the opposing leaders of the war, and this is perfectly acceptable.

The Two-Tailed Warrior killed the Serpent Mistress. *A king may mistreat the slinus if he so desires, for the Mistress is dead. But he should be careful, for all our sakes. We never know when the next Great Serpent will arise.*

Does this mean that the Two-Tailed Warrior, that child born of a Hea and a warrior, is real also? A massive alu with two tails, physical prowess, strength, knowledge of battle logistics, and magical power?

That huge tentacle in Joaviz's memory…a kraken?

Our myth and folklore suddenly real?

"How many humans have you intercepted?" I ask.

Tasapi intakes water audibly, causing the Commander to raise his eyebrows. Tasapi counters with a little shake of his head. The Commander juts his chin out thoughtfully and lifts only one eyebrow, as if telling a little joke. Tasapi concedes with a smile.

Rew watches on.

"Fifteen," the Commander says.

I gasp for water.

"Your friend Joaviz is the sixteenth." The Commander looks intently into my eyes while I search for whatever meaning I'm supposed to glean from those numbers. Then I understand. The Serpent Mistress has fifteen black eyes, and the sixteenth atop them glows silver. It's the eye that can seek out the power of the Deep. For Joaviz to be the sixteenth is undeniably eerie, for it is this eye through which the Two-Tailed Warrior was said to have pierced the Mistress's skull with his staff-kly.

"Do you know if any of them are still with her?" I ask.

"From the pattern, we think not. She seems to be experimenting, unsure of how to get them to stay...sane. But of course," he flexes his hands, "we can't really know what goes on in the Deep."

"So, my father..." I begin.

"Wants to give the Tribe of All Seas a human army, an expendable resource so they can go after slinus and the Serpent Mistress. The Tribe wouldn't have to commission warriors from city rulers. They would have their own army to match hers."

"But that's against the agreement," I say.

"Yes," Tasapi says wearily.

"If my father could discover the magic, he could be their Hea while leaving me to watch over Ezkine. That's why he rushed my initiation." I look around the room but am mostly speaking to myself. "So when I brought Joaviz home, he couldn't contain himself. He wanted to get all the answers he could from her."

I look into each of their eyes now, hoping they can see that I'm sincere, that they need not fear me, that I'm not yet masterful at interpersonal and can't force thoughts into their heads. That I'm telling the truth.

I want no part of my father's actions.

The fact is, alus loathe humans. They plunge deeper and farther into our Seas, extracting our resources. We do without, always monitoring and sacrificing to protect ourselves. Humans with their contraptions and machines are no smarter than we are, no more advanced. They're simply lost, searching for more, going into places they can't understand. We find them despicable.

But Joaviz has changed all of that for me. She's stubborn and haughty to be sure, but real and loveable too. Relatable even.

"How many would he want to transform?" I hear the anger in my voice.

It's Rew who says, "Thousands."

"So has my father found out yet? How does the Serpent Mistress do it? Does anyone know? Is there really such a thing as a myst gem?"

All these thoughts of the Deep cause me to blink away the brightness of the room. Memories of near-permanent darkness enfold me. Home. Could I have been closer to the answer there?

"We don't know," the Commander says. "The deep creatures come up at night, but we can't ever go down. We don't communicate with the slinus. We don't have a single deep informant. The deep creatures are always so loyal, beyond loyal."

"Well, then," I say. "We have to…"

Tasapi spits out, "What?" His tone surprises everyone. "Go ask the Serpent Mistress how to do the spell?" He chuckles and rolls his eyes.

"We can't let them do this. Humans don't belong here," I say.

"We have to take care of our own," Tasapi says. "The Tribe is going to tighten control on trade, travel, Heas…and you want to go to the Deep and implode?"

I ignore his incredulity even though it pierces me to the core, and instead focus on Joaviz. I can hear her crying out. Soon I'll rush to her, but not yet. "Were the other humans able to speak?"

"Yes," Tasapi says, drawing the word out into a question. When I don't explain my curiosity, he continues, "Mostly Sa'ari or Kai. One Salamauro. A couple Raisgan."

"Where are they?"

"We keep them here for a while, until they've worked through their fears," the Commander says. "Then we place them with families—the moms, sisters, or wives of our warriors—so they can adapt to alu life." The Commander's tone is honest, defeated.

It's not the best remedy, but what else is there? Will Joaviz remain here now, to be placed with someone? No. I'm her protector. She'll stay with me.

"So…" the Commander begins, stopping for the approval of Rew and the chagrin of Tasapi. "Syedahl, would you like to be the one and only official Hea of the Rebel Army?"

The Commander isn't smiling now. He's waiting, expecting, even hoping, yet still acknowledging the tribulations that will follow.

"I…" The sound of Joaviz's cries make me feel exposed and torn, even more confused than when I left Ezkine. I know Alinx and I can never be together, but I can still be Joaviz's best friend.

"You have much to learn," the Commander says. "You

haven't been trained. We'll need to make sure you get along with Greizjo, that you trust each other and can work together. There is an Annual Hea Convention." The Commander stops to see if I already know about it, but I only stare back blankly. "It's in Ertra, not far from here...four days from now. You should go and meet Greizjo there, present yourself. They're mostly elders from cities with another Hea to stay at home, and also Heas from here in Kai Sea. See how they receive you. Be among your equals. It may help you decide."

I thought we were lonely, solitary creatures. "What do they do?"

"Share the year's progress, newly learned magic, insight for training new Heas..."

My ears perk up, causing Tasapi's eyes to roll and Rew to look at me proudly. Who are these alee that I feel I already know so well?

"I'll go for myself and for Joaviz." I shake my head slightly, fully aware that this dedication is silly and futile. "To see if they know anything. Will you watch her while I'm gone?

"I won't give up on her. I broke my promise to Ezkine, because it was forced upon me, but Joaviz...helping her was my choice." The words spill out of me, clearer than I realized.

"I commend that," the Commander says.

Tasapi smiles tiredly. "We all do."

With a thankful bow to each of them, I rush out of the room and find her. I hold on tightly to my only friend.

33

Joaviz

"THAT'S GREAT!" I SAY. Peetare and Heleina may have given up, but not me.

Never.

Syedahl doesn't look so happy though. She keeps wrapping some seaweed from the bed poles around and around her hand. We're in our plain little dorm.

"When do we leave?" I ask.

"Well…"

"What?" I ask.

Those big eyes look up at me all sad. Oh no. "What?" I ask again.

"I'm going to bring Mac with me."

The silences grows and grows and…oh. I get it. I know why she's worried about bringing me. But what am I supposed to say?

It's like a mood swing on crack. I get so scared, and then something comes over me. The episodes aren't just caused by fear, though. Something's wrong inside.

Like I can't handle these two different worlds. Every time I form a new memory, some other one from home emerges and takes over my mind. It's like I get close to remembering the transformation, then I block it with something else, and then I've lost them both.

The only thing I'm working hard to hold onto is Dad.

I consider him my real dad, but he's technically my step-dad. My biological dad tried to kill my mom. That's why she left. If he hadn't done something that crazy, she would have stuck with him forever. I have no idea where he is.

I think there's something bad inside me, too. Why do I act scary just like him? Get so outside of myself that I don't care whether it's sunrise or sunset? I'm mean and selfish and I never do anything for other people.

Bad girl. Bad ala. That's me. Flunk every class. Get drunk every other day. Smoke cigarettes constantly. Cuss a lot. Go clubbing. Sounds like pretty basic teenager stuff, but having a homicidal father makes it…telling.

Like when Nicolai said he didn't want to be with me any-more, I totally flipped. We had just had sex two nights before. It was my first time.

We were sitting on the floor in my dad's study. Nicolai was a college freshman and was doing some research on global-ization. Dad—who has a ridiculous number of books—said he could borrow whatever he wanted. He had pointed out the informal anthropology section before leaving for his weekly poker game.

Well, we were sitting there. I was just having a grand old time flipping though all this boring stuff when he said, "I have to break up with you."

"What?"

I was so glad no one was home.

I didn't cry. I got really angry. "We just had sex! *Will you still love me tomorrow?* Is that what this was? Take what you want and leave?"

He smirked at my stupid oldies song line. I grabbed a brass candlestick from a shelf.

"No. No," he said, finally registering the look in my eyes. "I met someone."

"Someone?"

"At school." His black hair slid across his face. A skinny Russian hipster. With an accent. So hot.

She was a college girl. No curfew. No dad at home. Damn. "When?"

Nicolai couldn't hide his smile with his shrugging timidity and false uncertainty. Yeah, right. He was pleased with himself. Oh so pleased. "A week ago?"

"A week ago??" I had the candlestick over my head.

He was staring at it. "I wasn't sure. I've been trying to decide between the two of you."

"So you had sex with me? And what, I *failed?*"

"No. I shouldn't have. I'm sorry. But you were ready and I…" he raised his hands like whoopsy-daisy-what-can-I-say-I'm-a-stud.

That did it.

Joanne in the study with the candlestick. Like a game of *Clue.*

I flung it at him. He caught it. And left.

While my family was out having fun, being sweet and normal and nice, I was trying to hurt the boy I shouldn't have slept with.

My mind circles back to the present. I need Syedahl. I just can't let her go. "Did they ask you to join them?"

"I told them I'm going to try and help you first."

One word cuts me. "Try?" I ask.

"Yes, Joaviz. *Try.* My very best. But with the information I'm getting, it's very unlikely that—"

"Then why is Mac coming?" I unwrap myself from my

sleep wrappings, sick of staying still.

"To protect me."

"You don't need protecting," I say, sure that Mac is really going along to encourage her to find out whatever *they* want to know. Mac is going to direct her. But I'm not going to let that happen. I need to call the shots.

"I'm going too."

"Joaviz…" she says.

"I'm going."

She shakes her head. "You need to stay here."

"Why?" I ask. I know full well why, but I want to hear her say that I'm nuts. I dare her to say it. I'm not even embarrassed. I just want to know what she thinks is wrong with me.

"You're unwell."

Unwell? It's worse than I thought. So vague and all-encompassing. *Unwell.* "What's that supposed to mean?"

She takes a big gulp of water and lets it rush out in a stream of bubbles. She looks at me pleadingly. I don't care. I just glare back at her. I've got all day.

"You've been acting…strangely. You know that, don't you?"

"Yeah. I know."

"It isn't safe for you to come with me. Those Heas might disagree with my actions and try to capture me themselves. They might try to give my power back to the Ch'tlan Court. I don't know how they'll receive me."

"So?"

All I hear is Syedahl going blah blah blah worrying about this and that like she always does. I want her to go, take me with her, and find out how to change me. Why is she making everything so complicated?

I need it to be simple.

"*So*," she says, her head tilted away, afraid to look at me. She handles her words like they're slippery things. "If you get upset, it could endanger us both. I have to protect myself."

So it's my fault that something is wrong with me? I don't want to be stuck with these crazy humans. I have to push her, remind her to help me. "You promised."

"Yes, I did, but keeping both of us safe is *not* in defiance of that promise."

Wow. That's the most certain and confident I've ever heard her sound. "I'll just follow you," I say.

"I'll leave when you're sleeping."

I laugh at this. "Then I won't sleep."

"We're not leaving for two days. You'll need to sleep. You can stay here and get to know—"

"I'm coming with you." I don't know what does it but my stubbornness crumbles and my voice cracks. She could leave me here if she really wanted to. "What's happening to me?" I ask.

"It's not just you. It's all the humans. There must be something wrong with the spell, or maybe transformation is simply too straining on the mind."

I nod my head, whimpering softly. But she doesn't know. There's something evil and dark inside of me. My biological father was an alcoholic. He snapped. I don't know how or why, but he stabbed my mom.

Then he was in jail. And now? Who knows.

Syedahl doesn't know that I'm a bad person.

If Mac is going, then so am I. If the Rebel Army is going to pull on her heartstrings, then I'll pull harder. "I'm coming with you," I say.

Syedahl finally meets my gaze. "I know. I know you are."

34

Syedahl

WITH MY EYES AT LONG LAST adjusted, the aquamarine waters of the tropics are just as beautiful, but a little less achingly so. Mac, Joaviz, and I are journeying alongside the drop-off of another, larger island. Every few stretches of sea, the pale sand and turquoise water plunge into dark blue cavernous ravines. Joaviz doesn't enjoy the changes; she bears them with gritted teeth. We swim where the current is strongest.

Mac clenched his fists when I told him Joaviz was coming with us. I know I could have tried harder to leave her behind, but I didn't want her to feel abandoned. Like this was the end.

"We'll talk more in depth once you're okay with how you've served Joaviz," the Commander had said before I left the meeting with the three of them. That's exactly how he said it—not once I've *helped* Joaviz—but once I'm okay with what I have and haven't done. No one believes I can help her, except Joaviz herself, because she doesn't know how to give up.

Her lips are tight and her eyes fixed straight ahead. She notices me looking. Her bright irises match the gorgeous color that surrounds us. A little smile turns up the corners of her lips and I recognize that emotion that scares me and makes me proud: hope.

Having her near makes me certain of why I left Ezkine.

We pass over another dark ravine. An awful pain clenches my stomach. Much like the sudden sickness after I secretly tasted a bit of puffer fish juice in Akati.

I groan and hold my stomach, folding in on my pain. My eyes burn in my skull. All the thoughts I consciously daily work to forget suddenly collide: My father is a terrible, immoral Hea...I can never meet my mother...Alinx hates me for not saying goodbye...I've devoted myself to a mission I can never achieve...I hate the choices I've made...I don't have a home...I don't believe in myself...

I've made promises I can't keep.

The water is dark blue and cold. Joaviz is screaming and thrashing. With every sound she makes, I become tinier, weaker.

My heart has been excavated. I don't even move. It's Mac who holds her.

She kicks her flukes madly. Not trying to get to shallow waters up ahead, but trying to swim down into the mysteries below.

She's frantic in Mac's strong grip. He focuses all his energy on holding her, letting the current carry them towards clarity and light.

She won't stop. But he's stronger and they make it past the deep ravine.

Now I'm here alone. How could Heas possibly have power to rival that of the Serpent Mistress? What do I expect to gain?

Limply, I let the current take me towards them.

I'm not hopeful. I feel her pain and only want to save her.

To save her is to save myself. To make it right—what I've done. That's what I want, but I don't know what I need. I keep on *feeling*. Escaping. All the while disbelieving that there is a place in the world for me.

35

Joaviz

IT'S GETTING DARK. This inn room has nothing but four bedpoles with ropes. Syedahl left for the meeting a while ago. Mac left to do I-don't-know-what and I'm supposed to wait here until they get back.

The innkeeper downstairs won't stop wailing and it's driving me crazy. Not *really* crazy, just annoyed.

Ertra's city wall is falling to pieces, like everything else here. The buildings are in crumbles. There are high archways that have collapsed. Spires that have been cut short. Openings that lead nowhere. Very few alus live here and most of them are old. *Darktails,* they say—the slang for those with that marker of old age. We've only seen two middle-aged alas, the innkeeper and the one we bought fish from in the empty square. No one my age. No children. No see-through babies.

The mood here is worse than in Ezkine. Ezkinians were emotionless, blank. These alus have the long faces of mourning, maybe for the ones who left or died and turned this place into a ghost town.

I go down the hall and ignore the ala's cries from below me. What does she have to cry about? Nothing that any of these alus have been through—even Syedahl—compares to my problems.

I'll probably be an ala forever, following Syedahl around. Her little side-kick.

Not even Peetare and Heleina know how I feel. They've given up completely. I try to give up hope but can't quite do it. Even though it hurts.

It would be easier if I could move on like Peetare or simply be depressed like Heleina. Hope is much harder to maintain.

It struggles with itself inside me.

Once outside the inn, I see two Heas swimming by with staffs, late to the party I suppose. I swim over the buildings and accidentally kick the top of a house, making dust swirl up. Whoever is inside yells. I kick the house again and move on, coming to the dull brown square where Mac bought us fish.

No one is here.

You'd think they'd send the Heas somewhere nice, like a vacation for all their hard work.

I hear three alus coming towards me.

"Hey, you're the…" says an alee's voice in Ch'tlan.

Hmm…an alee. I spin around. Then I choke on a breath of water. Two alees with black hair and white skin hover back while one with brown hair comes closer to me. "You're the human," he whispers. The two alees behind him look gleeful, relieved.

Alinx.

"Excuse me?" I ask.

"You're the one she left with! I knew Syedahl would be here." Alinx turns around and says to the two alees, "This is almost over." They slap flukes.

Oh shit. If she sees him, she'll ditch me for sure. He can talk her into anything.

Even the Rebel Army would be better for me than *Alinx*.

Alinx means Ezkine. And Ezkine means Cualt.

"She isn't here," I say, sneering, trying to make him feel ridiculous.

He buys it. "What?"

"I'm here with someone else." My voice cracks. I used to be such a good liar.

Alinx crosses his arms and looks around the deserted square. "Who?"

"Another Hea." I think of the one that the commanders told Syedahl to find. "Greizjo."

"At the meeting?" he asks.

"Yes. He's at the meeting." We stare each other down. "How did you know about it?"

"I found out," he says. "I knew Syedahl would come here if she found out about it too." His golden eyes are so challenging, and he's hot, scruffy-hot, but I won't let myself be swayed. He does not hold over me whatever it is he holds over Syedahl.

I focus on his too-wide face and prominent brow. Not a soft spot on him.

"Yeah? Well, she didn't. Sorry. She...pushed me off to another Hea. She didn't want to help me anymore."

Alinx nods once. "Syedahl left you? Guess we have something in common."

"Yeah, guess so. She's pretty flimsy, that one. Why are you even here?" My curiosity gets the better of me.

Alinx's tough expression hardens even more. He lets out a cold laugh. "I'm here to bring her home. To let her know that her father and King Ezkun want her back." His smugness makes me want to slap him—and not on the flukes.

"I'm pretty sure she already knows that."

"They've decided to let us be together." He really couldn't look at me any more intensely.

I try to hide my absolute panic. "Sorry to disappoint you then."

He smiles and nods to his cronies. The three of them swim back in the direction they came from. I have to find her first.

36

Syedahl

FOLLOWING THE PALPABLE PULL of a multitude of staffs, I swim along the alleys of Ertra, passing a few darktails gathered outside the decaying homes.

I only want someone to tell me that I did the right thing, that anyone would protect an innocent stranger from the clutches of her desperate father. I only tried to listen to my instincts and to the Great Volcán. What else could I have done?

Will one of the Heas understand, maybe even agree? They've left their secondary Heas in charge of their cities while traveling, so they must enjoy a greater level of autonomy than my father has known. Perhaps they'll deem my actions courageous.

The glow of a Hea staff emanates from around the next corner.

Its owner is an old alee. I want to speak with him, make a friend before I even go inside. "Hello," I say.

He turns around, waits for me to catch up, and introduces himself. When I say in Ch'tlan that I'm from Ezkine, he cocks his head as if trying to remember something. It comes to him—a rumor of me no doubt—and he swims on without another word.

I follow behind him, not seeing another Hea until we travel through a very narrow alley. He catches up to an ala in front of him. I sense someone behind me and feel the heat from his staff. A short tunnel leads us beneath the city into a massive, low-ceilinged room buzzing with the glowing staffs of seventy Heas. I heard nothing from the outside, but now I find myself in the middle of social commotion.

All the words I want to say catch in my throat as some of the Heas turn to see who has just entered. The Heas in front of and behind me are all well received with greetings, hugs, and kisses on the cheek—a custom wholly new to me.

Everyone chats calmly while floating vertically in groups of three or four. Along the walls are glass cabinets lined with jars full of beads, bones, and ooze—boons for magic that I don't understand. My principle skill requires only my brain and my hands. All else would come with the training I may never receive.

It's an embarrassment really, to have been a Hea for moons and still only be able to heat and freeze.

I force myself to approach a group of three Heas, middle-aged alas and an alee who looks slightly older than me. When I introduce myself, they go deadly silent. My skin tingles.

I ask the question that will make me appear naïve and silly, as well as fulfill my task. "Is anyone presenting new information on High Transformation?"

The alas raise their eyebrows and pucker their lips. One responds, "I don't think so." They excuse themselves and swim off to a table with platters of sliced meat held in place with nets. The smell of the food sickens me even more than the look of empathetic embarrassment on the alee's face.

"You're Syedahl?" he asks. "I've heard about you."

Another green-tailed alee, stereotypically controlling and

reprimanding. He reminds me instantly of Father and the Commander, two very different versions of the same form.

"Yes," I say, lowering my eyes and trying to look blank and innocent. When I catch his eye he smirks in a way that tells me I'm failing. "And who are you?" I ask.

"I'm Greizjo."

This is the Hea the Commander was talking about. I flush.

"I'm surprised you're here." His skin is not as dark as the natives of Kai, so I assume one of his parents was from Heiste, maybe even Ch'tlan.

I lean in closer and whisper, "The Commander recommended that I come."

His pale brown eyes open wide, friendly and sincere. "You met him?"

Maybe I've finally found a Hea I can relate to. I nod weakly, feeling proud of his incredulity.

"Are you their...?"

"I haven't decided."

Disappointment washes over his face and even though it makes no sense that he should invest anything in a stranger's decision, I want to make him smile again. "But I want to. I can't go back home."

"Are you sure about that?"

I imagine myself bowing to the king's will, hiding from Alinx, eating only the plainest foods, never again seeing the sun's power over water. "I'm sure."

He laughs, his long brown ponytail swirling up around him. His hair is a shade lighter than his skin.

"I was supposed to ask you something," I say.

"What's that?"

I look around to be sure no one is listening. "Would you be able to train me...whenever you have time, if possible...?"

A loud shriek interrupts us. The crowds are parting for an angry wrinkled face surrounded by wiry white hair. "Out! Out!" Fairesa screams, as if I were a pest, an eel in a cave.

Greizjo moves in front of me and says quite calmly, "We've never turned a Hea away before."

Fairesa waves a hand in his face, as if he were a pest too, but he doesn't move or even flinch. Her words are slow and calm, but every syllable is articulated with pure hatred. "This is different."

"How different?" Greizjo asks. He must think he already knows why she's upset, but this isn't about my betrayal of Ezkine.

All the Heas in the room—about ninety now—are looking at the three of us. The collective lava power, the magical gazes, are searing me. My cold-adapted body is sickly hot.

"What's the problem?" I ask in my sweetest voice. I round my eyes and pout my lips just barely.

Fairesa looks past Greizjo at me, black eyes shinning deadlier than that elegant shark. Then she dismisses me with a grunt and says to him, "I have an idea."

Fairesa explains that while no Hea has ever been turned away, I've done something that is similarly unprecedented in the history of the convention. Since its beginning, Heas have been tied to rulers, to cities.

No one who has left has ever been allowed among them. I only know of myself and Hasat, but there must have been others, years and years ago or maybe even right now.

Fairesa doesn't mention the attack or King Akat or anything that might taint her reluctance with the scent of vegence. Instead she suggests that my fate be put to a vote.

I know that at best I'll be forced to leave the convention; at worst I'll be dragged to the Ch'tlan Court. I turn away, my eyes and throat burning. Greizjo catches me by the shoulder.

"Where are you going?" he asks, then casts such a fierce look around us that everyone in the room turns back, awkwardly and forcibly, to their own conversations.

"I have to leave," I say.

"No. You were either brave or stupid to come here. Let's go with brave. Stay."

I search his face for signs that he wants to see me cornered, trapped, tied up, and pulled back to Ezkine, but there's only concern in his eyes and pride in his voice.

"Follow through."

I nod my head and retreat to the back wall. I lean against it for support, ignoring any attention directed at me. There are now at least a hundred Heas. I will speak after Fairesa, so though I try to plan my words, I know they will change according to her accusations. One thing is sure: I must keep up this act. I am young, confused, and simply trying to do what's best. It isn't so far from the truth.

Finally Fairesa declares that everyone expected is present, casting an evil look at me to show that I was most certainly not invited. "Some of you have heard about a young Hea who left her city on the night of her initiation." Many Heas stare at me, still astonished that the rumor has dared come into their midst. "But some of you are only hearing this now. Syedahl never had any intention of serving King Ezkun or the citizalus of Ezkine. She manipulated her father and the Ch'tlan Court into believing that she would serve them, when in fact she planned to leave. She took power that does not belong to her.

"There is no other heir in Ezkine, and her father will be left to guide the city alone until he produces another child. If something should happen to him…well…we dare not even think of the consequences."

Then Fairesa gestures to me. It would be so easy to swim

over the heads of the Heas to the front of the room, but I dare not. Instead I brave it through the crowd, through their shoulders and flukes.

As I speak, I look into Greizjo's eyes. His and only his. There isn't much that I can say for myself without endangering the human I care about. "I didn't plan what happened. I've always been an obedient daughter." I speak in my quietest, sweetest, and least confrontational voice. "The night of my initiation, the Great Volcán told me to leave."

I finally look away from Greizjo's face, seeking understanding in the others but finding only judgment. I come back to the solace of his eyes. "I didn't understand why he should ask me this, but his words were clear. He told me to leave over and over again. I wasn't sure what to do. Listen to my king or my creator? I had met a foreign ala a few days before who…" What can I say about Joaviz? The excuse that I couldn't understand her won't work now because I understand all languages.

A thought occurs to me, a memory of that creepy alee and his terrible story. "…Whose family was attacked by slinus. Father wanted me to find out more from her. He tried to read her mind. She was so terrified. She didn't want to remember what had happened to her." I pause.

Greizjo nods in encouragement and I continue. "She was horrified by the Deep, traumatized. So when the Great Volcán told me to leave, I took it to mean that I should protect her and help her find a new family." These words sting deeply, because I know this is the best thing I could do for Joaviz: help her belong in my world, the one I don't belong to.

"I only want to serve the Great Volcán. He's all merciful and all powerful. Father didn't listen to him. But I hear him, and I listen."

For a moment the room is silent, and I feel that lovely, healing thing called hope. I enjoy the warmth and gorgeous glow of all the staffs. Different colored orbs bounce and dance, lighting up their owners.

Fairesa cackles, breaking the spell. She demands a vote to send me back to the Ch'tlan Court, where I'd be killed and my power given to an initiate in another city. I ask to be allowed to stay at the meeting.

Greizjo swims through the crowd and then up to the ceiling. "This isn't a fair vote. The options are too extreme."

Many voices approve, and my heart begins to beat again. The heat is weakening me now. Greizjo is hovering on the other side of Fairesa, too far away.

"The best and most obvious compromise is to turn Syedahl away," he says. "Many of us have heard the Great Volcán speak. Sometimes his voice falls in line with the wishes of our parents and rulers. Sometimes—often—not. We've all faced this difficult choice. We can't say that Syedahl made a bad decision. Maybe the Great Volcán still has work for her. I do admit that she is hard to trust." Many Heas voice their agreement, a temporary release of tension. "Also hard to condemn. If she goes home willingly and soon, she could still be forgiven. I for one, couldn't live with myself if this respectable group sentenced her to death. I say that we let her leave and ask the Great Volcán to lead her back to Ezkine. All in favor?" he asks.

Seventy-five staffs rise—an indisputable majority. With forced good nature, Fairesa turns, looks at me, and waits.

Everyone is waiting.

Her white hair spins around her head, blocking my view of Greizjo. I can't see his eyes, can't give him my silent thanks.

I swim up and out of the tunnel and collapse in the narrow alley.

Great Volcán, why don't you speak to me now?

37

Joaviz

FISH SKELETONS FLOAT FROM OLD STALLS in the markets. Darktails appear like slow shadows. Everything is quiet. Empty. I don't hear *anything* that sounds like a convention. They must have done one of those silence charms on the meeting.

Brown building after brown building.

Those damned Heas are hiding somewhere and I'm sick of trying to find them! Alinx knows more about Heas than I do, but I don't know if that will help him. Please, no.

I've looked everywhere. Twice.

My only hope is that when it's over Syedahl comes right back to the inn.

Stupid Alinx.

Mac better be back in his room, I swear. I need someone to distract me and calm me down. Plus, when Syedahl comes back we won't have time to wait for him. We'll have to leave right away.

I'm starving, but haven't seen anything that looks fresh. Why are all the fish already dead?

The coral outside the city is dead too—sad, pale, lifeless, empty. Nothing like the Base.

Dad would have loved the Base, a scuba diver's paradise. Dad, keep fighting. Don't give up.

With that useless thought, encouragement he'll never hear in the language of another species, I swim back to the hotel.

In the entrance there's a hole in the floor that leads to the innkeeper's room. The sound of her sadness travels up with bright white light.

"Hello?" she calls.

Ugh.

I really don't want to deal with her. I want to sleep. "Yeah?"

"You're the ala? With the red hair?"

"Yeah."

"Come down here." Her voice is gentle and cooing but after hearing her sob all day I can't brush off an icky feeling. She *needs* me.

Well, I've got needs of my own. Unfortunately one of these is food.

I dive into the hole. In each corner are bright white lights. She's arranging little stone figurines of alas on a table.

"Hi," I say.

Her eyes bulge out of her face. She's frail and skinny everywhere. "Are you enjoying your stay?" she asks.

"I..."

She laughs. It's a perverse sound, like she's laughing at the act of laughing. "Of course you're not."

I float horizontally, feeling awkward because the only space is directly above her bed.

"No one who visits ever comes back. Everybody is always leaving."

"Oh," I say, wanting to leave.

"Except the Heas. They come back. But they don't help. This place can't ever be helped." Her dark skin has a grayish tone.

All I want to do is sleep, but a part of me does wonder what's going on. "Why not?"

She smiles, showing her gray gums. The fish in her hands is sickly white. It's obviously been dead for a while. "Do you want some?"

I'm starving, but... "No thank you."

"Oh, don't be shy. You're hungry."

"Yeah, but..."

She turns away from me and starts butchering it. Hopefully she cuts out any weird parts. I bet it won't make me sick, but it probably won't taste good either.

What choice do I have? It looks better than anything else I've seen. That fish we bought earlier was worse—funky and old. It tasted like death.

She hands me a gray bowl with netting on top. I take the plunge and pop a piece of fish into my mouth before there's time to change my mind. It tastes musty, but it's edible. I get it down and go for another piece.

"No one knows what happened here," she says, chewing slowly.

I furrow my brow. How could they not know?

"Some alus say it's because of that spot over there, up the current and a day's swim away. That spot gives me the creeps. But my Nana said that was nonsense. It's because of all the humans. They killed the coral and the spirit of our city."

I think of times on vacation when I accidentally stepped on coral with my plastic fins probably doing damage. I could have been swimming right past alu cities destroying their territory. I remember times being freaked out by a certain spot or just not wanting to go in a certain direction. Maybe the Hea's protection charm was keeping me away—but not far enough.

No one comes here to snorkel anymore I bet.

"My father thinks it's the Hea's fault," she continues. "He's good for nothing. We don't even have an heir!"

"Then what will happen when he dies?"

Her sharp shoulder blades shoot up to her ears. "Won't make much difference. The darktails will die. Maybe I'll finally leave. Everybody my age left." Her voice gets even quieter. "Why do I stay?"

I finish my fish, forcing down the last piece even though I can barely breathe.

I do feel achy and nauseous, but something tells me it's not the fish. "Thank you, but I..."

"Oh, I know. Get on."

"I'm just tired, that's all. I need some rest."

She nods. "I'll never see you again."

Then she holds her arms as though rocking a baby and looks into a face that isn't there. "Oh my sweet little ala," she cries.

I escape, go down the hall, and wrap myself up. But I can't sleep. Can't sleep at all. I'm sick with nerves—and with guilt.

Syedahl loves him.

38

Syedahl

AFTER A FEW SELF-INDULGENT MOMENTS of weeping, I decide I can't be here anymore. My embarrassment and shame are too great. I want to get out of this city and return to the Rebel Army Base, where I might be of value. Joaviz will have to accept a new life in the Seas.

Now that I've made this decision, I move quickly down the hall, anxious to tell Joaviz that our mission is over, anxious to get this off my chest and be done with it. I can't bear the suspense of wondering how she'll react when she realizes that I mean it. I stop when I notice how the light at the end of the alley is obscured.

A low, rich female voice groans, "I can't fit." The words are in Kai. Something about the voice is strange. It's gurgling and thick.

"Oh, hello!" she says. "I can't fit through there."

I get closer, but am reluctant to respond. She stops struggling and instead sweeps back out of my way, letting the wall lamps reveal her form.

I gulp water. I don't know if I should be afraid, disgusted, or intrigued.

All the tales I've ever heard of dessas flash through my

mind. Servants of the Serpent Mistress, caretakers of the creatures of the Deep, ladies in waiting, powerful and merciless killers during the war.

Should I turn back the other way and wait for her to leave? My staff pulsates.

I muster up enough courage to move into the wide alleyway. The dessa and I hover under the two lamps. "You're real," I mutter.

She giggles as I take in the sight of her terribly beautiful form, half-human and half-octopus. From her large breasts to her thick hips, her flesh looks like a tight-fitting black bodice, but in fact she's nude. The black fades to a color that's at once midnight blue and maroon. Her body splits into eight thick tentacles. At each tip, the color fades to an eerie, sunless white.

Her arms and face are that same strange blue-maroon. And her hair is not hair at all, but rather a bulbous sac atop her head, like the body of an octopus filled with all of its organs. From this bouncing sac two tendrils—tentacles—curl above her ears.

Giggling, a tiny black ink cloud escapes her thick purple lips. "I've been waiting here for so long. I have something to tell them, but I can't fit!"

I get the impression that she's trying to act playful. Perhaps in the Deep her flirty voice would be considered high-pitched, but to me she sounds more like a sultry alee.

"I sensed your struggle and came to meet you," I lie. For a moment I worry that the other Heas will hear her and come to investigate, but I assume that the silence charm is two-way.

"Oh good," she says. "Because I'd rather not go in there. What a good messenger you are. So you'll tell them for me?"

I nod my head, transfixed. She is monstrously large, each

tentacle the length of my body.

As soon as I have agreed, she grabs me with both of her tentacle-fingered hands, paralyzing me with fear and slime. Her voice is fierce. "You have to tell them."

I nod frantically. "Yes. Of course. I will."

"All of you Heas must leave immediately. You must go to the skench!" Her voice becomes a shriek.

"The *skench*?"

The dessa takes one hand off my shoulder and clutches her tiny waist, the only small part of her. She relaxes a little bit, regaining some of her throatiness. "Yes, yes. The skench! The slinu-built tower."

I instantly think of home, my own slinu-built tower so far away. I allow myself a moment to wonder how I got tangled up in this mythical mess. When I imagine Joaviz's face, I miss her.

Coming back to reality is a horrific exercise. I look away from the dessa's black eyes, which protrude out of their suckers to see me better.

"Where do I begin?" the dessa asks herself, a nervous ink cloud escaping. She covers her mouth with her other hand, leaving me gratefully free, but sore where she tore her tentacle-fingers off of me. "At the beginning, I suppose. My sister. Hmph. My sister oversaw the...*activity* at the skench. She was the overseer. The boss lady, you might say, for all these little..." she squiggles her fingers, "...slinus. She made sure they kept working."

"Working?"

She looks at me as if she doesn't want to clarify, then nods her head, flinging the sac forward. "Harvesting myst gems, the Serpent Mistress's external source of power. She has power inside too, of course." The dessa eyes my staff. "Much more than you. One must have power to use the myst gems. She has it deep inside, but it doesn't multiply. She can't harvest orbs the way you Heas can. The Deep creates gems for her. She doesn't do any of the hard work!"

My eyes grow wide. The dessa giggles at my intrigue and declares, "Yes. Yes. Enticing! The Deep only makes so many and only so often. The myst gems come from the trenches."

I gasp.

"Yes, from the very depths. The caverns and ravines. Slinus can go down there. And they do. They harvest them and bring them back up to their little skenches, you see. It is there that they crack them open, to be used by the Serpent Witch." The dessa speaks of her with a grimace.

"Why do they bring them up? Why do they build those towers?" I ask, hoping for the answer to a question that has plagued me all my life.

She nods her wobbly head. "The myst gems have hard protective casings. If they are opened too far down in the Deep, they sort of…die. And so those slinus are busy. Build build *build* a flat foundation on a seamount. A foundation for the hard work of cracking them open. It's just what they do."

I furrow my brow. "Why are you telling me this?"

When the dessa grips my shoulders again, I regret that I asked. Her eyes reach farther towards me, the suckers searching, deciding. "You'll be a good little messenger and tell the Heas?"

I nod again. "Yes, of course."

"Well. The Serpent Witch killed my sister because she used one of the gems. We dessas have power too, you see, though of a different nature." The dessa peels one hand off of me and unfurls it, blowing into it a burst of ink that solidifies and brightens into a starfish. She tosses the thing over her shoulder. "The slinus can't use them. We dessas can, but we aren't allowed. The Witch keeps them all for herself!"

This conversation tosses me around. I don't want to accept her words, don't want to know. And yet I must. I'm curious but oh so afraid.

"My sister…" She begins wistfully, a fat bead of black sludge squeezing from each of her eyes, "…was a silly thing, always wishing and dreaming, wanting to see the light. She used the gem to transform herself into an ala and back. Several times. If you use a gem to do something, you can do that same spell again and again with your own power. But the Mistress needs a new gem every time. The Great Serpents were only meant to seek them out. Never to use them, you see! Well, the evil little slinu brats told on my poor sister. And so the Mistress killed her in front of all her subjects. Oh, the slinus were so pleased! Now they have a new boss." The tentacles on her hand mold together into a point that she directs at herself. "But I want my revenge."

I simply stare at her, transfixed.

How many spells could the Serpent Mistress need?

"You and all your Heas will go to that skench. I won't stop you. You will steal her gems. To do so you may have to slay a few slinus." The dessa's wide nose flattens with displeasure.

I wonder if all deep creatures are loyal to the Deep, as the Commander said, but then I recall some of the stories about the dessas who fought on the alu side. "Where is this skench?"

She smiles, happy that I'll take part in her plan. "A day and a half's swim up the current. Follow your uneasy feeling."

I jerk back, remembering the place that made me feel so worthless, that would have drawn in Joaviz had Mac not been there to stop her. "Why is that place so unsettling?" I ask.

"The gem is a very powerful thing. Your lava power is light and masculine, easy to obey, but you alus are so afraid of the mysteries of life. You think darkness is evil, that the color black is bad, but it only signifies the feminine energy. Don't fear feminine power. Embrace it."

I feel as though she knows I was taken from my mother, and yet until now I didn't even believe in her existence. Many creatures of the Deep can rise up at night, but alus can only venture down so far. "How deep is it?"

She turns away, her sac nearing my face. I dodge it, just as she whips back around. "Very deep. You'll have to be fast. Now go and tell them! Get all the gems you can."

"Won't she kill you if she finds out what you've done?"

She dismisses the question with her swirly hand. "Oh, I'm just so sick of that bossy Serpent." Nonchalance gives way to apprehension, and she looks at me with eyes that are half closed in crescents of sadness.

"Will the Serpent Mistress be there?" I ask.

The black eyes snap open, drop, and then lift up again in laughter. "No! The Mistress never oversees the harvest. She finds it extremely boring. Thank Dreku it only happens twice a year!"

The dessa pauses momentarily, becoming a fantastical statue in my disbelieving mind. If only she really were a statue and none of these old legends were real.

Apparently deciding that she has told me everything necessary, the dessa comes alive again. "I must go. Tell them!" She glides off, her tentacles gripping the alley floor and then coiling to release.

I'm dying to leave the alley, but I force myself to wait, not wanting to invite the dessa's return. The news of the myst gem is frightening enough to keep me in place.

Once the water no longer ripples and I'm certain she's gone, my skin and scales relax. I turn towards the entrance to the convention, ready to tell the assembled Heas what I've heard and ask for their assistance.

If they know the truth, they'll know why I *had* to leave. They'll understand. Together, we'll be able to fight off the slinus and acquire the gems. Joaviz will be saved.

I hear a voice. The words are muffled but the language is clear.

An alee, speaking Ch'tlan. The sound of my native tongue frightens me. My past and present cannot—should not—collide.

I rush forward, out into the wide canal.

Was it him? Did I only imagine it?

The first thing I see is his eyes in the glow of my staff. I throw my arms around him. He holds me. These arms. This strong chest. The smell of him. The embrace I know so well.

He pulls away. But I lean in again, wanting to stay in his arms for as long as I can.

He whispers in my ear, "We're going home."

With these words, all the emotions of the evening veer off their course of sadness and desperation. I hear myself declare, "I'm not going home."

There's no point in denying what I must do.

39

Joaviz

I'M LYING IN THE INN, wrapped up in seaweed braids.

"I'm sorry but there isn't time to talk about this. I promise that we will soon." Syedahl's agitated voice enters the room before she does. I look up to see her trailed by Alinx and the other two alees.

He found her. This makes me feel like a loser, like I lost our little race, and by lying to him, I also lost my loyalty to Syedahl.

"Syedahl," Alinx says calmly, way calmer than her tone. "You're not even listening to me."

"Where is Mac? He wasn't in his room," Syedahl says.

Alinx gives me a self-satisfied smile that Syedahl doesn't catch. I can't get enough water. I need to throw up. Or die. Or at least get out of here. I say, "I don't know."

Her eyes grow wide. "You don't know?"

I shake my head.

"All you have to do is bring her with you," Alinx says.

"What?" Syedahl shrieks.

Alinx eyes me with a little bit of guilt. Shocking. I guess we'll both sacrifice each other to have her.

"That's the deal. Bring her home, and we can be together."

"Alinx, you don't understand what that means. I..." Syedahl closes her eyes. "I don't even want to go home!"

"So what happened?" I ask. "Did the Heas know anything?"

The two warriors in the room watch the three of us like we're actors in a play.

"No," Syedahl answers.

The word is so big it fills the room. My heart sinks.

"But..." she begins.

Whew.

"But someone else did."

Alinx grabs Syedahl by the shoulders and turns her to face him. "You made a mistake. Your father understands it. The king understands that the power affected you in a strange way. The Teindahn says it's happened before. It can be fixed. With more training." Alinx takes one hand off of her. "You need more training."

"I know," Syedhal says. She is weak from his touch. Then she asks softly, "Fixed?"

I want to ask how he found her, if he followed me to the inn or discovered her meeting place, but then she'd realize that I already knew he was here.

I watch him slowly swim forward. He gently backs her into the wall. "It's okay. You can come home, where we can be together."

"Alinx," she breathes. "No."

"It *is* what you want. Of course it is."

"But so much has changed..."

Alinx pulls away from her like her skin is poison.

I want to interject but I'm afraid he'll tell on me, call me a bad friend and a liar.

Syedahl demands that the warriors leave. She doesn't know

how to magically seal them from the conversation. Alinx tells them to go to the square. They leave without a word—or a facial expression.

"What do you know? Who told you what?" I ask when Syedahl swims over to me.

"I might know something that could work…could turn you back."

I shiver all over and my stomach aches even more, cramping with guilt.

"It's going to be dangerous, but it might lead to the spell we need." Her voice is amped up, like she's actually ready for this.

I brighten and unwrap myself from the bed, but I don't feel ready for anything. "Well, let's go."

She looks uncertain.

"Go where?" Alinx asks. "We have the chance for a life together."

"Alinx, you aren't listening to me! You don't even know why I left, or why Joaviz is so important."

"I know more than you think." He smiles, showing off those pointy white teeth. So handsome. So charming. I almost feel myself being pulled under his spell. Almost.

"You wouldn't believe me," Syedahl whispers, as if to herself.

I almost interrupt again, but don't want to piss Alinx off. He may seem manipulating, but he does love her. He wants to be with her. She wants to be with him. I can see that they're perfect together. Syedahl needs to be directed.

Problem is, I want to be the one to do it.

"Alinx, Joaviz is human."

His eyes flick to me. "I know."

Then Syedahl remembers. Alinx might be on the wrong side of things. "Why did you go to the Tribe of All Seas?" she asks.

"To deliver a message."

"About what?"

Alinx glares at me triumphantly. He's going to talk her into this. The safe route. "To tell them that your father was making progress but needed more time, because there was a delay."

They're both looking at me now.

Delay. Our escape ruined all of Cualt's plans. Syedahl would have protected the city and Cualt would have tortured me.

"Alinx, listen to me," Syedahl says, backing away from both of us. It takes all her strength to say what she needs to. "Remember all those stories about the Serpent Mistress? Her power?" Her eyes are closed. She's not waiting for him to nod. It's like she's talking to herself. "They're true. The Serpent Mistress transformed Joaviz. I need to get the object, a myst gem, that she used so that I can turn Joaviz back into a human."

I expect Alinx to be smirking or laughing, but he's just pissed off. "I follow you to the tropics for two moons to tell you that we can finally have what we've wanted for years… and you want to go chasing stories?"

I relax a little. She's choosing me.

Knowing that only makes my stomach hurt worse. She leaves behind everything she knows to help me, and I lie to the alee she loves.

"They aren't stories. Who else could have transformed Joaviz?"

"One of you," Alinx says, as though it's obvious. His arms are folded over his chest.

Syedahl shakes her head slightly. I can tell that his comment hurts her. *One of you.* One of the Heas. She and Alinx aren't of the same class. I can also tell that she doesn't like disagreeing with him.

Syedahl says, "Joaviz remembers the Serpent Mistress. She tries to fight the memories, but when they emerge—and I've seen them—they are strong and undeniably real."

Alinx looks at her like she's insane and then glances at me. Again. Smirking ever so slightly. I know what he's saying. That I'm not trustworthy. And not worth it.

But will he actually tell her that I already saw him? That I lied to him?

He hangs his head. "You're going to find the Serpent Mistress?"

"No, of course not. That would be suicide. She won't be there anyway. We only have to steal from her."

"How can you be sure?" he asks, but his tone is rude. He doesn't even think the Serpent Mistress exists.

Syedahl doesn't answer him.

I keep my eyes on the smooth floor. "What if she *is* there?"

"Then we'll die," Syedahl says. "There's no question about that. She's guarded the gems for thousands of years, and she'll continue. The gems are not a special form of magic for her. They are her power, just like my orbs."

Alinx smiles mischievously, reminding me of a younger Mac. "How deep is it going to be?"

"Very deep," Syedahl says.

"Will we explode?" I ask.

"Implode," Alinx corrects, not taking his eyes off of Syedahl. "Who *will* be there?"

Syedahl manages to turn a paler shade of white. "Slinus."

Just the word makes me start shivering, makes all the talk about the Serpent Mistress feel real. My teeth chatter and I start to lose control.

I can't face her mysterious power.

"Joaviz!" Syedahl says, coming to me in an instant, really caring about me.

I pull out of the fear long enough to say "I'm sorry" before I fall under the spell of a fit.

It doesn't last long, though. Instead I see my dad's face. The stubble on his chin, the lines on his forehead, and the flecks in his eyes are all drawn up so clearly.

The flash is gone, just like that.

I hold onto it in the darkness.

I remember. I remember. I remember.

And I care. I miss you so much.

When I open my eyes to the room again, Syedahl is still near me, hovering close yet drawing back at the same time.

"You're okay," she says.

"I…I…" My voice is weak. I don't want to say it. But I feel so bad. "I lied to Alinx."

There. It's out. Now she can leave me, and they can be happy. She doesn't need me and I don't deserve her.

I'm the worst friend in the whole world. The worst daughter, disobedient and wild. I suck at being a human. I can't be an ala. There's only one place I need to go and that's home, the place I never wanted to be.

40

Syedahl

ALINX IS READY TO SACRIFICE Joaviz to my father without even knowing what he'd do to her. Is this a testament to his love for me, or to a cowardice I never before noticed?

He came here believing that Hasat brainwashed me, that I reacted negatively to power, and that I can be fixed. Did he not consider, if only momentarily, that I could have had a good reason for leaving Ezkine?

I don't expect such thoughtfulness from Joaviz. I am *her* protector. It hurts a little, that she should keep Alinx from me, but if he told her any of the things he said to me, then I don't blame her. He needn't have said much to scare her.

I tell her over and over that it's okay and that I'm not upset with her, but still she's lamenting. I get the feeling that it's no longer me she's upset about.

The other warriors try to come back into the room, but I tell Alinx to send them away. I want none of this information traveling back to Ezkine.

I hover in the corner of the room, trying to process Father's ultimatum and Alinx's support of it.

"Syedahl," he begins. I used to love it when he said my name! Hearing it on his lips now only infuriates me more.

Alinx grabs my chin and tilts my face towards him. I keep my eyes closed but it doesn't help. I can feel his presence. Every breath seems deeper; every sound of movement in the room is lower, more drawn out.

I open my eyes and look at him.

"I'm coming with you," he says.

I don't know if I can trust him, but he's well trained and strong and able. He's a swift swimmer, with excellent reflexes and aim.

Joaviz is slumped against the wall. She meets my eyes and grants silent permission.

Just then Mac appears in the opening, parting the tight curtains. I can't contain myself, and surprise everyone by shouting, "What were you thinking leaving her alone? She's vulnerable! Anything could have happened."

Mac smiles at my confrontational reaction, notices Alinx, and then turns his gaze back to me. "I told you I had to do something for…" He looks at Alinx again. "Who is he?"

"This is the warrior I told you about. My friend, Alinx."

Mac crosses his arms over his chest. His biceps strain against their sword cuffs.

I fill the silence. "You have to trust him, Mac, because he's coming with us." I smile at Alinx, prompting him.

Boldly, Alinx comes forward to shake Mac's hand. "Sye-dahl's father sent me here to tell her that she could come home, that she and I could be together publicly. King Ezkun will—"

"Alinx, he can't understand you," I say in Ch'tlan, realizing that I'd been speaking Sa'ari. Mac and Alinx stare at each other in confusion. "I'll teach you Sa'ari," I say to Alinx.

"Great," he replies, and so I perform the spell. He restates what he said to Mac, this time with a dazed look on his face. "King Ezkun will allow us to be together."

Mac interrupts him. "That's quite a revelation," he mocks. "You'll change history with that." He playfully nudges my arm, but I'm not in the mood for his camaraderie or their competition.

Alinx smiles unpleasantly and says, "Her father knows that she's worth the battle with the Court and the possible repercussions. The city needs its heiress back."

Mac looks down momentarily, gathering even more confidence. "Repercussions like death?"

"Cualt is prepared to protect her from the Court," Alinx says, clipping his words. He has no problem expressing agitation in his new language. "I'm going to the skench to help her foremost, and give her a chance to prove herself."

To prove myself? He won't believe anything I say without physical proof? It's unsurprising, given his training, but hurts nonetheless.

I realize that Mac may not know what a skench is, but instead of getting clarification he asks, "And then?"

Alinx looks at me while he answers. "Maybe she'll come home where she belongs."

Mac swims towards Alinx, bringing their faces menacingly close together. "I doubt that." Mac turns away from him. "Syedahl?"

"Yes?"

"Do you want me to help you?"

"Yes."

"Then tell me what's going on."

In a whirlwind, I tell him all about the dessa. How she wanted to share her plot of revenge with the Heas but couldn't fit through the narrow alley. How I was on my way to tell the other Heas when Alinx approached me.

"They don't know?" Mac asks.

"I was going to tell them, but then I saw Alinx and forgot

all about that. All I wanted was to find the two of you."

"Good. We'll go on our own."

"But we don't know how many slinus—"

"It doesn't matter," Mac says with a certainty that seems absurd to me. He retreats, grabbing a pair of holdings. "We can't tell anyone else about the gems. Especially not Heas. The only one we can tell is Greizjo, but we can't get to him now and we shouldn't wait. I'll go with you, Syedahl."

I feel a huge sense of relief even though I never doubted that he would.

"But," he says, stopping my heart, "you have to get at least one gem for the Commander."

"The dessa says one must have power to use it."

"Then use it for him." Mac hangs nonchalantly, his tone and gaze level, his flukes draping limply. As if his request was obvious.

I suppose it is. Mac is here for the Commander. Joaviz's paranoia was not misplaced this time.

"You'll use it however he wants, and tell him everything you know about the power. Promise you'll do this and I'll go with you."

More responsibility. More promises. This time for a cause I don't understand.

In Ezkine, at least I knew I'd primarily be a protector.

If I do this, I don't know what I'll be.

Mac lifts my chin softly, unaware that he's using the exact maneuver Alinx used to sway me. "You know this is right."

All I know is that I can't go home. "I promise," I say.

Alinx slams his fist against the wall with a groan. Mac goes over to him again. "You want Syedahl to go home, but what does Syedahl want?"

Alinx's face is stone. He's upset with me for letting Mac up-stage him in their little battle for my heart, but I've grown beyond Alinx's games. I'm sure that his embarrassment doesn't compare to my pain. He's not even interested in listening to me.

This isn't the way I hoped to reunite.

Everything is so much easier when he and I are alone. Add someone else and we seem doomed to disagree.

Mac shakes Alinx's hand this time. "Then we will go," he says.

Joaviz lifts herself off the floor and swishes her flukes defiantly. "I'm going too."

"No." I shake my head once, firmly. "You can't come. You'll be too afraid. It's out of the question." Just the thought of bringing her is enough to tighten my stomach and send shivers down my spine. "I won't allow it."

Joaviz hovers. "I have to."

"Why do you have to?" I ask. "It will be worse there."

Mac interrupts. "It's her choice."

"No it isn't. She could endanger us, so it's *our* choice."

Alinx watches, on confused, but his stubbornness doesn't permit him to ask why we're all so worried about her. Oh, these prideful alees!

"Well," Mac says, "I choose to give *her* the choice."

"So do I," Alinx says, nodding to Mac, who smiles at him. I know he's only saying that to spite me.

"You have to let her go," Mac says. "She can take care of herself. She can make her own decisions."

"No, not this time."

Mac exhales deeply. "You're too involved."

"What?" My voice is dead, empty.

Joaviz half-hugs me and rests her head on my shoulder.

"I've done everything I could to be involved," I say.

Mac places one hand on my stomach and the other on my heart. "You're involved here. And here."

Alinx twists uncomfortably, but it's ridiculous for him to think I have something going on with an alee who is old enough to be my father. Part of me feels I don't know Alinx anymore. Mac is simply someone I trust. Why can't Alinx see that? "It's tearing you up inside," Mac says.

I draw back and look down at the places on my pale skin where he put his tan, rough hands. It's true. My obligation to Joaviz has made me shaky and unsettled.

"Help her as much as you can, but don't take on her pain," Mac says. "Don't make *her* problems *your* problems."

His words confuse me terribly, but I feel their truth. "What do you mean?"

"She's afraid of the Deep. You're taking that on. She's making you afraid too."

My throat constricts. "I *am* afraid of the Deep."

It is Alinx who speaks. "No, you're not. You never were. You were only afraid of what your father would do."

Mac continues. "*She's* afraid. *You're* curious." The way he points at her accusingly upsets me. "You want to know and understand the Serpent Mistress's power. We've all felt it, dark and mysterious. We all know it's there. It doesn't scare you. And it doesn't scare me." Mac nods towards Alinx. "Or him."

How could Mac know so much about us when he doesn't have the power I possess? I nod weakly, knowing that Mac is right, but having no idea how to do what he says.

"If she wants to face this, let her. Let her be afraid. But don't empathize so much that you feel that fear. You," he touches my chest again, "are ready to do this."

I nod, knowing but not understanding.

Mac continues, trying to push his lessons into my unyielding head, reminding me a little of Hasat. "Her journey is her journey. Yours is yours. Separate them. You have to. That fear will pull you down. It will rule you. Face this on your own and let her do the same."

"But go together?" I ask.

Mac nods. "Go together. But keep your energy and thoughts inside. Stop worrying about her."

I look at Joaviz and take both of her hands. For what feels like a long while, we just stare into each other's eyes. I see so much there, so much more than I've seen the whole time I've known her. I've only thought of her as an obligation, but what about all I've gained? She knows the home that she wants, and through that she's made it possible for me to search for mine.

What do I want?

Can I do this?

Am I curious?

I'm not ready to answer these questions. I'm too afraid of the power inside me. Perhaps the Deep affected Father's conscience and would do the same to me. If I were to find and steal the Serpent Mistress's power, wouldn't the greed I must have inherited from my father break free? Who's to say I would even change Joaviz back? Would I become power hungry like him? Would fear consume me?

Joaviz's clear turquoise eyes look deep into me. "You're not afraid."

"But I am."

"Don't be. You want to know," she says. "You're not your father."

I nod, somehow unsurprised that she knew my thoughts.

But isn't Father right? I am incapable of love. Alinx and I have done nothing but fight. Joaviz and I have been, up until now, mostly unable to understand or trust each other.

"That's my problem anyways," she says.

"What?" I ask.

"I'm scared of being like my father. That's my problem. Not yours."

I look at Mac, but all he does is arch an eyebrow at me. Alright. I've been too emotionally involved with Joaviz. "I don't want anything to happen to you," I say.

"I know, but I have to do this. I don't want to, but I have to."

I squeeze her hands tighter, so tight I think she'll pull away. But she doesn't. Finally I let her go and am left weak and empty. Alinx catches my eye. That golden gaze pulls me in. I drift towards him, needing his strength, needing someone to guide me.

"Our next adventure in the Deep," I say.

"The deepest yet."

We lean towards each other at the same time, but I pull away.

41

Joaviz

MAC AND SYEDAHL DECIDE it's too risky, with all the other Heas around, to try to find Greizjo. That means its one Hea, two warriors, and me...

After Alinx makes sure the other two warriors aren't going to follow us, we leave quickly, stopping to buy some nasty fish. We swim south for a while before going back east so the current doesn't slow us down. The sun rises, lighting up the insanity of what we're doing.

We swim through the day, resting only a little bit here and there. I fall deeply asleep every time we rest.

They all think it means I'm relaxed, and I don't tell them any different, but I know I'm getting pulled under. My dreams are vivid. I remember them for an instant and then they're gone.

I'm left with crescent moons, and clasping lobsters, and my dad turning yellower and yellower. In my dreams I'm not an ala or a girl. I'm more like an idea, some helpless wispy spirit.

When night falls, Syedahl takes over as watcher. I fall asleep right away. It's a deep, deep sleep. The sounds of the waves don't affect me at all. This time I don't recall my dreams. It's like I'm nowhere. Just gone.

I get shaken awake and the reality of what we're doing is the first thing I think about. Everything could be over. I don't let myself get my hopes up or worry about saying goodbye to Syedahl. All I can think about is right now. I don't have a future, because I don't know what it is.

It's dark, which means Syedahl didn't let us sleep long. The moon is bright, showing Mac's and Alinx's still groggy faces, so I'm guessing they slept too. Syedahl looks wild. Those lavender eyes are way too wide.

"You okay?" I ask.

"I keep having to separate you from them," she says. "You keep moving towards their weapons, trying to hurt yourself."

Their swords and spears glow in the moonlight.

"Sorry," I say. What am I supposed to say? I was suicidal in my sleep?

The darkness makes our decision feel more real. It seems less absurd and more necessary.

When the water grays, we all know we're getting closer. I'm tense, and that terrible feeling is back. Last time I was pulled down there, but now the magnet is reversed. I'm repelled.

I'm not strong enough to do this. I don't want to remember. I can't kill slinus. Syedahl would be safer without me.

The sun breaks fully into the water. Everything is beautiful turquoise again. This makes it worse. I should stay right here and wait for them to come back.

I can't face a slinu, or be surrounded by the power that did this to me.

I just want to go home.

I don't need to torture myself any further.

"Are you ready?" Syedahl asks.

I've followed them over the uneven outline of the drop-off. It's dark below us so suddenly. So cold.

Now I feel the pull. A silent song that hums to me. A lullaby maybe. Something chill. Like when you finally fall asleep. Like when you finally get over a terrible day. Like when you finally forgive someone. The Deep is as inevitable as any other impossible thing.

"Yes." Once I've decided, that's it. I'm the first to plunge downwards, leaving the light. They all follow behind me.

The ravine is craggy and jagged and totally barren of life. And so narrow that we have to follow it single file. I try not to kick up dust but I do.

Feeling itchy, anxious, I turn around to see puffs of silt.

And then…

A flash.

I went to sushi with Lily. We each got spicy tuna handrolls because they had the most seaweed. I learned to love seaweed from Lily's Chinese family. Fried seaweed chips…they were my favorite.

Then we got drunk at Lily's cousin's house and went with him and his friends to this gay club. Not because any of us were gay, but because it was our favorite place that we could get into. My fake ID was a piece of shit and Lily didn't have one. I could really only get away with buying cigarettes from old men at gas stations. But this place was 16 and up.

The gay club. We danced all night to techno pop and left at 3 am. Then went to Taco Bell, then crashed at the cousin's house. Lily had the least strict Chinese parents in the history of the universe.

My mom never tried to discipline me. It was always Dad. But when he got sick, he gave up. I figured he couldn't take it anymore. Maybe he was just letting me deal however I needed.

The ravine drops off completely into a cliff. I turn around to face everybody.

"Slow down!" Syedahl gasps. "You're going so fast!"

"I am?"

I look around. Dark blue. Freezing cold. Unnaturally cold. I freak out, I can't go down there! I don't even know what direction to go in. The icky feeling is everywhere. "No no no no no no no no no no *NO!*"

Syedahl holds me as my eyelids flutter open just long enough to see Mac's stern face.

I turn around and around frantically. "This can't be right! Where is the place? Shouldn't it be here?" The dark. The cold. Then where is the end? Of *this*? Of me in this body?

Syedahl shakes her head. "Look around. It's still light here."

"Light?"

"Relatively. It's not completely dark. I'm sure we have to go farther."

All I can focus on are the cracks and rocks in the cliff, which seems so far away but is right behind Syedahl. The rock wall is getting closer and farther at the same time. My head is pounding. "Farther?" I ask.

"Down," she says. "I'll lead the way."

I suck in water. "No. I can do it."

That memory with Lily was the weekend before I left for... what? I can't remember. LA to Ezkine. How did I get from one to the other?

I lead us down, straight down, but when the blue finally fades to black, I feel my body giving up. Syedahl holds my hand and we descend together.

Down and down and down we go, Mac and Alinx following.

Little outlier memories pop up. Packing. Looking at the calendar. Fighting with my mom. Kissing my car goodbye. Sitting in my dad's green chair before we left.

The pain in my eyes isn't sadness. They get sucked inside

my head as we go deeper, lower, trying to hit the back of my head. My breaths are never enough. My lungs can't hold much. I take tiny sip after tiny sip.

Total darkness. We can't go much farther. The pressure is coming from all around, trapping us. No escape.

Syedahl's staff is concealed now, so there's no light.

There's a killer in me too.

That night, with Lily, these stupid bitches walked up to us and one of them pulled the flower out of my hair. It wasn't some hippie flower. It was fluorescent pink silk. Anyways, I slapped the one who did it. And we shit-talked and pushed each other till a bunch of guys broke us up. I wanted to murder her. I saw some beer bottles and wanted to break one over her head. Lily was laughing, releasing the violence. Ready to have fun again.

But not me. It took all of my friends' stupid jokes and goofy-sexy dances to distract me. But still, when the girl and her posse left the place, I rushed out of there and punched her full on in the face. The bouncer broke us up.

Good thing too. I may be cute but I'm a killer. My biological dad passed it on to me.

That's why the Serpent Mistress chose me. I just didn't want to say it to Syedahl. The Serpent Mistress knew I was evil just like her.

I stop and hover horizontally. Can't go any farther.

"Sye—" but my words catch because I'm suddenly dazzled. Bright, colorful orbs spin in front of me, dancing inside eight different Hea staffs.

Like some trippy light show.

Like I could seriously do with an upper right now.

I look up at the colors, dumbfounded. They get closer, lighting us up.

Lighting up all the hungry faces surrounding us.

42

Syedahl

I STARE UP AT THE EIGHT spinning Hea staffs. The dessa must have told more Heas, after I left. And here they are, competitors for the myst gem power. Then the light goes out, the staffs now completely concealed in darkness.

I enlarge my staff, lighting up Joaviz's frightened face as she jumps back.

"It's okay. It's only me." Raising my voice, I call, "Who's there?"

Joaviz's teeth chatter. "I…it's the…Oh Syedahl! I'm so sorry." The immense pressure obscures and muffles the quivering sounds.

I challenge myself not to comfort her. "Be strong! You promised."

My emotions are so many and so conflicted that I find myself strangely calm and removed. I dart back to the edge of the skench and draw my staff across a section of it in a long sweeping motion, revealing faces.

Slinu faces. I can read from them a variety of emotions. They are shy, ashamed, perturbed, disrupted, intrigued, disgusted, excited, amused, embarrassed, shocked. I can't say that their faces are like those of alus. Not at all. The proportions are too different, the eyes too eerily large. But there is certainly thought and personality.

They all look the same, but show different expressions.

They don't look like me, but they can feel the same emotions that I can.

Another underwater half-human species.

Like me, but not.

I stop in front of a slinu who is only looking over the ledge from the eyes up. He pulls himself higher, rests on a pointy elbow, and reaches for my staff. I dart away and slam into Mac. I hadn't even realized he was following me.

Now I turn to see that Joaviz and Alinx are with me too, all of us staring at the creatures. These monsters are so manifest, so complex. What surprises me most is that they have yet to attack us. I imagine that all around the skench they are clutching, clinging. Absolutely silent. Waiting.

For what?

I look up, expecting to see the eight staffs again. My headache has begun to wear off, but somehow the act of looking upwards into the empty darkness brings it back with the added pain of a crick in my neck.

I've been so enthralled with the slinus, so in awe about meeting the species that is supposedly my opposite and my enemy that I forgot about the gem. The urgency of our mission returns to the forefront of my mind now. I zig-zag across the surface of the skench, holding my staff below me. My friends gather and we swim together, seeing metal tools, jagged sickles, bulky sledgehammers, and thin spikes of metal, all lit by my staff. Our movements disturb the silt. When I spot a lumpy brown rock, I continue on. I see another. And another.

Could they be?

So plain, so ugly. Could they be the source of magic that

was coveted in the First War, forgotten since, and only now—right now—rediscovered?

I'm doubtful. I move on, my friends following behind, looking for something worthy to be called myst gem.

And yet I feel a pull, not from the rocks behind me, but from something just ahead. A sound, a calling, a promise of healing muffled by movement.

Six frenzied slinus come forward as we near their edge of the skench. Dust swirls up and I wait for it to settle. Green dorsal and caudal fins are the first things I see.

The alu concept of their lower formation is absolutely untrue. Legs fused together by a thin green membrane? No. Their lower halves are like that of a shark, so that in their struggle to hide something from me, they sway from side to side, snarling at each other. "Let me!" one says.

I strain to understand more of their slurry whispering and am surprised when I succeed. "Get that one! Get that one!"

From above, their backs and shoulders look more like those of alus—except they are deep green. They are half-man half-shark, covered in smooth green skin from top to tip.

Another scoots over, but not before I see a faint beam of silver light cutting through the glow emitted by my own orbs.

"Move now!" I say, working my tongue in circles around the strange words. "If you don't, I will kill you."

They remain in place, but before I can repeat my demand, the eight Hea staffs alight again.

Now I see that they are not staffs at all. They slither and curl, coiling and uncoiling. The colors are not orbs, but flashes and stripes, a display I've heard of in a small creature called a cuttlefish.

The glowing tentacles press down on us. We all dart back and move towards the far edge of the skench.

The slinus rise, showing their see-through bellies, swaying side to side to create a wall around us. We are corralled.

Above, red, orange, and blue flashes of light ripple up the tentacles to the body. There's no escape.

"You weren't fast enough," says a deep, taunting voice.

It comes from above. From the kraken. Each of his writhing tentacles is a few times my size, and his body so much larger than that.

I'm instantly full of regret, an immediate sinking sensation that overrides my heightening fear. I'm at fault for bringing us all here.

The kraken angles towards me, showing me the wide fins of his head. His eyes are black and long, openings into the deep, dark sea. I steal a glance at my friends. Joaviz is to my left, Alinx left of her. And Mac left of him. All staring up with dread.

Taunting I can handle. Now is my time to assess him. "No, it would seem we weren't."

I briefly register that he's speaking Kai, the alu language of this region, not the tongue of the slinus. They whisper to each other, creating a chorus that scratches my pounding, protesting ears. They all want to know what we're saying.

"That dessa!" The kraken says with a laugh. Each of his syllables is punctuated with a sharp snap but I can't find his mouth. Only those long eyes.

With a shiver I remember that giant squids have a beak in the center of their tentacles surrounded by soft, oozing flesh.

"What about the dessa?" I ask.

Joaviz is still with fear. Mac and Alinx are pointing their spears at the kraken—tiny stingers next to the massive creature.

"She didn't tell you about me!" he says.

I stammer a reply.

"This is my territory," he shouts. Without warning, his stunning light displays stop. We're left in darkness with only my staff to illuminate a small space around me. I can't even see Joaviz. Only myself and three slinus behind me.

"This is your skench?" I ask.

"No. No. No." Each word comes with a snap. "This area. This was her skench. I...she smelled guilty when she came back. I made her tell me what she did. Many of you would come, she said. A feast of Heas? What a disappointing snack! There won't be enough to share."

The slinus spit out their protestations, presumably guessing by the tone of his Kai words and the insubstantial weight of our four bodies that they won't eat tonight.

I strain to make out the words of one of the slinus behind me. "But, Master! We've been here all day. Unable to scavenge!"

Something that the slinu says strikes me as untenable, but I don't have time to ponder it. My focus is drawn to the single tentacle lighting up Alinx's face, stricken with his need to be brave.

He hides four spears behind his back with one hand, and the fifth he holds feebly in front of his face.

The bright red tentacle winds around the spear and snaps it decisively in half. A whizzing, whirring sound shocks me out of my stupor and I notice what I was too overwhelmed to see before. In each sucker is a hook the length of my forearm and twice as thick, with a thin, pointed end—hard and white like a tooth, reflecting the kraken's light. Each hook spins, dangerously close to Alinx's chest.

With a gasp Alinx darts back, hitting the slinus behind him. They push him forward into the suckers and he groans in pain.

Mac rams a spear into the tentacle, and the kraken pulls it out. Alinx moans softly, the sound searing through me.

I gather red orbs in my staff and send the beam at the tentacle. The kraken groans as his seared flesh sizzles. My triumph is small though, because the spell has only affected the tip of one tentacle, which blackens and shrivels. Cast from his brightness, it falls out of view and thuds against the ground. Dust spirals up into his now blue glow.

I quickly count the orbs in my staff. Four more sets of red and two sets of blue. That's the most I've ever harvested all at once. How will I protect us when they're gone? Mind reading won't kill the kraken.

He is laughing now, confident that my magic is not enough.

"You're a young one," he says.

A tentacle comes towards me and the tip of a hook scrapes underneath my chin. The kraken is all aglow now.

The tentacle moves closer to Joaviz. Mac rushes up the side of the kraken's body, a tiny black shape against a massive, blue-glowing haze. Mac raises his spear, ready to lodge it in the kraken's eye, but he swiftly draws in his tentacles and propels himself backwards.

Then two massive tentacles slam Mac to the floor. He retreats, bleeding. The kraken laughs again.

"One left to taste before I decide who to eat first," he says, stretching to reveal his deadly purple beak.

I imagine myself being lifted into it, snapped into pieces and devoured. Joaviz's screams break my trance.

The kraken retracts. I can't see Joaviz, but I smell her blood. The slinus murmur desperately.

"I've tasted you before!" the kraken shouts. "I've tasted you before."

43

Joaviz

MY SCAR HAS BEEN RE-OPENED. I stifle the pain.
There's something inside of me that hurts even worse.

The kraken laughs. "Just as I remembered!" he booms.
"She thought you would be perfect. Are you? Or did you go
crazy too?"

That voice. That voice. Come to steal me away. *My scar.*

Sitting in my dad's green chair, crying and waiting for him
to get home from San Francisco. When he did, there was no
good news. No hope. So he planned one last cruise. I didn't
get it. Why be around all those people? It felt like evasion.

I would have wanted to be alone with my family.

But he wanted to celebrate his life. I was supposed to work
it around school, do all this stuff early. Instead I did even less.
Handed everything in late, if at all. Didn't show up for tests.
Smoked at the beach sometimes. Mostly I would head downtown to get away from the ocean. It was Dad's obsession. Sail-
ing, diving, surfing, boating all the time. All the photographs,
all the fresh-caught fish. I was done.

Dad couldn't handle it. He wanted us to be happy, celebrate the time we had with him.

I was left to die in the cold, dark sea alone.

Before that I remember crying in the cruise ship cabin. Muffling the sound in my pillow so Tessa wouldn't hear.

My dad. The glue. Our glue. The one who held Mom together. All her fragile pieces.

Please Daddy, don't go. I was so weak, but in that weakness there was madness. Anger. Frustration. All of it pent up. And now I had to hold it inside even more.

Cotton candy. Shirley Temples. Flirting for shots of rum. Swimming. Relaxing. Bundling up. Doing my make-up. All day my smile had been enforced. By all the smiling faces.

I cried it out. Tessa woke up. I quieted myself. I couldn't tell her how I felt.

Tessa could always cry all she wanted, but if I had, the cracks would have split open. I understood it. What would Mom do with me? Tessa was easy. She needed good food, nice clothes, and piano and gymnastics teachers. Throw in a stuffed animal or two and she'd be fine.

Mom was a vase, glued back together over and over again. All day she looked afraid that I would snap. Snap like my biological dad. He tried to kill her. I don't know the whole story. My aunt mentioned one time that it involved a knife. He had nothing but red wine for five days—not even sleep. Just red wine and red paint.

My hair is rich, bright red. Unnaturally so. Mom never drinks red wine, never wears red, can't stand the sight of blood. I was all of those things. Always intense. Too imaginative. Drawing. Always drawing.

Sketch after sketch. Dresses, blouses, shoes, tights.

I was a dreamer. Project Runway, here I come.

Above all: unpredictable.

Dad's diagnosis drew me closer to an edge I didn't know Mom had set. She was waiting for me to tumble. The car ride. The plane ride. Getting on the ship. Heading to sea. Settling in.

No one would comfort me. I had to be strong. Mom saw something bad in me. My biological father's eyes.

Dad's death would be the thing to do me in. Turn me into a psycho. Release it. Mom could never release. Refused to paint again. Just wanted to cook. Always the most elaborate presentation.

Creativity equals craziness. There was no line she could draw.

She only allowed herself to be a good wife with pretty dishes.

She wouldn't let Dad pay for design school. I'd have to do something real, practical.

Something healthy.

He would have paid for it anyways, but now that he'd be gone…

When Tessa woke up, I stepped out of the cabin and onto the deck. No one was out there. It surprised me.

It was like a gift.

I sighed, exhaled, but the tears were gone. Now that I could finally let them flow, there weren't any.

Dad is dying. I'm the strong one. Mom will fall apart. Life insurance policy. Mortgage. 401k. Investment. Direct deposit. All these words floated around in my head. Not the stuff I really cared about, not all the reasons I had to cry, but the things I would have to learn.

Harden. Just harden up.

A fat white tentacle slapped onto the deck. Horror-movie huge.

Thicker than me and three times as long. It curled over the rail. I screamed, scrambling back.

The ship tipped over and other people screamed too. Metal clanged and glass crashed.

There was nowhere to go. I wasn't fast enough. The tentacle wrapped around me, cutting only my side. It seemed deliberate.

I was paralyzed. Not even my voice worked. My eyes saw everything, darting with the fast pace of my heart. I was turned around and lifted into the cold air.

Covered in slime.

Brought slowly, cruelly over the railing.

And down.

Down into the water buzzing with colored lights. I was sick with amazement and fear.

Until the Mistress appeared and gave my thoughts a different tone.

I wasn't that bad. Never stole. Didn't lie very often. Just a regular teen.

I dealt the best way I knew how. I needed all my releases. I wasn't what Mom thought. I wasn't what she was afraid of.

I begged for mercy. Cried to be let go, but my voice was gone. I was only filling my lungs with water.

I wanted to live but knew I was dying. The colors of the giant squid. His long black eyes. And all of *her* black eyes. And her silver one—that eye was throbbing, oozing something silvery that came straight at me.

She wanted me to know I was her sixteenth try and that I'd be able to handle the sea. She didn't actually say any words, but somehow her thoughts went inside me.

I screamed and screamed and thrashed. Something cut into my side again.

The tentacle let me go and the Serpent—thicker than the kraken and endlessly long—spun around me.

Pain ripped through me as I drowned. Then I breathed, sucked in water and was sickened by the relief it gave me.

The Serpent's two huge fangs. Red hair down her body like a mane. Green scaly skin. Three clusters of five black eyes.

One silver eye on top.

Everything went black. The kraken wasn't lit up anymore. He was shouting, but I still didn't understand.

I was in hell. My heart was exploding.

I had been worried that Dad and I fought the last time I saw him or that I was bratty. But what really happened is actually worse than that. No wonder I forgot.

After the show, Tessa and I were outside on the deck. Dad and Mom walked past us, giggling, holding each other and stealing kisses. I remember thinking it was gross, but beneath that I was so happy to see them like that. As soon as I let myself feel happy, of course I was sad.

I had a moment, a real moment of time, where I thought about Mom. Felt what she felt. Not about how *I* would have to take care of her, but how *she* would crumble. What was at stake, not just for me but for her.

Dad stopped kissing Mom's neck for a second to say goodnight to us. I didn't roll my eyes or say, "Ewww." I just smiled. He pecked me on the cheek.

Mom fumbled with the room key and finally opened the door.

That was the last time I saw them.

Empathy was a deep pain that I didn't want.

And now Alinx is groaning. He's hurting, but trying to be brave.

"Stop! Stop it!" I scream.

The kraken does. He's lit up now. Flashing. His eyes are nearly the size of my whole body. "What happened? Why didn't she keep me?" I ask.

I'm being squeezed in from pressure. The memory isn't there. I simply don't have it. I don't know why the Serpent Mistress left me all alone.

The slinus' whispers are slithering. They want my flesh.

I'm dripping with blood.

I feel it now. The gashing, gasping wound. I cry out in pain.

"You don't remember?" he asks.

"No. I don't."

A triangular flash of white. A great, powerful current. That's all I have.

Shocked then. Shocked now. It's all I know.

"Too bad for you!" he shouts. "The Mistress thought you'd be her special one, her pet. The sixteenth try will work, she thought! You didn't like your life. You looked at the sea with longing. She thought that was the answer! Get one who *wants* to come. *Needs* to. She won't want you now, compromised by lava! And uncontrollable too! So I get to eat you!"

Ugh. Nobody's going to eat me.

Alinx shrieks, caught by surprise pain. No time to be brave.

44

Syedahl

I FORCE MYSELF TO LEAVE Joaviz convulsing on the
floor and try not to breathe the dust that she unsettles. There's
nothing I can do to save her from herself, her own memories
and fear. Alinx needs me now. A set of red orbs fuse together
at the top of my staff and I aim the stream of light just to the
side of Alinx's neck where a tentacle wraps around him.

With a sizzle and a pop, the tentacle blackens and releases
him. But it's a small victory. Together Mac and I have only
partially damaged three tentacles.

Alinx sinks to the ground, moaning. The chorus of his and
Joaviz's screams clamps around my skull.

Mac swims up to the kraken again, causing him to flash a
myriad of colors. With his arms pushed out and locked sol-
idly by his sides, Mac zooms past the kraken, slicing him. The
smell is sour. The kraken's glow dims slightly.

A huge tentacle sweeps towards Mac. He evades it, circling
back around to slice the kraken's other side with the sword
bands on his forearms. Mac does this again and again, slicing
and evading. Each time the kraken shudders and dims before
lighting himself again, but otherwise seems unaffected.

The dark slices are nothing more than scratches to him.

A tentacle retracts, ready to strike. The kraken drains his colors. I see nothing but the light from my own staff. I scream Mac's name, my voice louder than Joaviz's and Alinx's helpless groans and the slinus' cheering. Louder than the snapping of the kraken's beak. I must try something, trust myself, and hope.

Blue orbs gather now and I shoot them upwards, focusing on hitting the kraken squarely. A single tentacle glows yellow and blocks the orbs, getting frozen in the process. The black shape that is Mac swiftly knocks against the iced tentacle, breaking it off.

My heart lurches with happiness that Mac is alive. That feeling opens me up and makes me vulnerable to a new round of pressure and pain. The kraken is flashing purple and yellow now. I see Alinx's strong but gentle face, grimacing, knowing that he's about to…

I can't imagine it.

I attack, trying over and over again to hit his body with red jets of steam. But I'm always blocked, withering only a small section of tentacle each time. Soon I'm left with just one set of blue orbs. Fearing total darkness, I don't use them.

My staff glows feebly now, barely even lighting the dusty ground beneath me.

I curse myself for not knowing any healing spells. The smell of blood from Alinx and Joaviz is suffocating, and the slinus all around the skench have taken up a chant. Simple and terrible, "Kill them! Kill them! Kill them!"

They're clutching the edges, hiding themselves. I look behind me, my staff revealing mean, greedy eyes. Still, the slinus don't attack.

I have one set of orbs. Mac has one spear. Nothing he's done has caused the kraken real harm. We've shortened his tentacles, but they still thrash wildly. He launches into a dazzling display, striping his body with color, stunning me. He's laughing, triumphant, snapping his beak.

I steal my eyes away from the lights to see Joaviz hovering, using both hands to cover up the blood that blooms from her wound.

Alinx is covered with deep gashes. I can't bear to look at his body, a mess of life that won't last, so I focus on his eyes and escape for a moment into a fantasy. We have found our own little cave in the wild, are living lawless outside of a city. He hunts and I weave. We have a child.

I inhale his blood as I near him. Joaviz's hand scrapes my underside but I ignore her. Flashes of light from overhead reveal Alinx's mangled form. How much longer?

I kiss him on the lips, trying not to touch any of his skin. Not because I'm disgusted, but because I don't want to hurt him. "Alinx, I'm so sorry. I don't know any healing spells."

My eyes burn.

He lifts a few fingers, his only reply. I lean in and kiss him again, hearing the slinus snicker around me. His blood and the dust swirl in my mouth. His lips are achingly soft.

"I love you," I say. "I have to go…I'm sorry."

He mumbles something and I lean in further, trying not to taste the blood I breathe. "No. Stay. Love you."

"I'm so sorry." I hate that those must be my last words to him, but right now risk is the only way to love.

Bringing up dust that makes him cough, I grab the spear that lies forgotten beside him and swim across the skench to the six slinus who had been prodding and jabbing each other.

Fierce anger and adrenaline course through me. "Move!" I shout, wielding staff in one hand and spear in the other. Their shark bodies wriggle side to side in anticipation, and their big black eyes look up at me helplessly. I'll spare them no mercy. Give them no pity.

Thick and slimy, a tentacle slams onto my shoulder, blinding my eyes with its brightness. I'm spun around, made to endure terrible pain. My muscles are excavated. The hook bores into my bones and there's nothing I can do to free myself. I'm so aware of the beak snapping that I can't hear past it to the words.

I look up, seeing a black shape in the colors. The kraken groans and lets me go. I back away. He's sent his warning. I am not to disturb these guardians.

The kraken's remaining intact tentacles slither towards Joaviz and Alinx, wrapping them up in swirls of green light. The kraken's hooks do not spin, but the coils around them are tight enough to be a death embrace. Alinx's head falls forward, his body already drained of life, but Joaviz is stiff and alert. In her dark silhouette I imagine wide eyes and tiny breaths. Knowing that she's about to die. Aware of it all.

The last set of orbs grows colder in my staff. I feel pressed in from every direction, blinded by green flashing that reminds me of my father's eyes. A decision to spite him? To infuriate him? A decision to save the alee I love or the ala I vowed to protect?

Wouldn't it always have to come to this? Father was wrong to give me a choice between them. Now I'm not so fortunate. Without healing magic I will lose them both.

The voice of the Great Volcán booms louder than my frantic sorrow. *Get the gem.*

I can't save them.

Not either of them.

"No. Please. I can't leave him."

The choice is for me, and for him, and for some future that will soon take over the Eleven Seas. A new war. I'm sure of it now. I can't refuse outright so I ask, "Why?"

Trust in me.

I've always trusted him, but now with Joaviz and Alinx at stake, I can't trust anything.

The kraken taunts me, first bringing Joaviz closer to his beak, then pushing her away and holding Alinx to the center of his tentacles. Joaviz, and then Alinx. I don't know who will die first.

My magic is nothing against him.

"Please save them," I plead.

Get the gem, Syedahl.

The Great Volcán is right there, not in the shape of an alu like some believe, nor an active Deep volcano, but a hot mass. Indefinable except for his beauty. Pure golden light.

I find myself smiling in the midst of pain, nodding my head against my previous indecision.

"Hi," I say stupidly.

In that moment he knows me and I am his. He's with me, outside but just above me, always near. A guide.

The whizzing sound returns, cutting into flesh and bone, evoking screams.

A black shape cuts across the glow again and disappears.

All the tentacles shudder and retract, lighting up Mac's last spear wedged in the kraken's beak. I sense him, unafraid and accepting. He gives a firm kick to get away. Not one of desperation. There's no flailing. It's simply an attempt.

Mac is snatched up.

Joaviz and Alinx are falling, their bodies full of bloody holes.

Mac is squeezed, lifted, rammed inside the beak and snapped in half. A disembodied tail falls limply, black with a green sheen from the glow. It falls to the floor and swirls up dust.

Slinus race by. Knocking me this way and that, fighting for

the remains.

I can't see Joaviz and Alinx. There's no time. The six guardians are unmoving. I ram my spear into a slick, green back and fling the slinu away with all my might. The other five scatter.

The six slivers of light are so beautiful. Sparkling like the strongest moonlight. So pure, so feminine and soft, but powerfully bright all the same. I bring my staff to the silver leaking from the crack in one of the ugly stones. I watch as the light creeps inside the nearly empty glass, filling it, magnifying it, glistening on the fearful slinus' faces. It makes the kraken's size insignificant, his glow dull. My own blue orbs too seem dimmed.

The slinus' frenzy smothers Joaviz and Alinx, memories of a life I used to have and a future I once imagined. I open my lips, expecting a shout of victory to emerge, but instead I laugh.

Laughter shakes me. *I* am triumphant. A slinu skitters by. I'm caught in self-consciousness but know I can't waste this chance.

The kraken swipes at the slinus, trying to clear them from his prey. Seeing me, he comes forward, slapping the ground, rolling and unrolling what is left of him. A tentacle reaches out towards me as my staff vibrates in my hands.

"Xjix," I say softly. A whisper in a language I don't know and have never heard. A command to the mystical power of the Deep.

45

Joaviz

THE COLD, FIRM BODIES of slinus sweep over me. Their claws grip me as they try to get to Mac.

I can't hear Alinx breathing anymore.

Teeth sink into me. I scream. I rub the perforations on my arm.

"She's not dead! They're not dead!" Syedahl shrieks with equal parts desperation and amazement. I'm not dead. He's not dead.

She shouts at the slinus in their language.

Thin long teeth tear at my wounds. A scream catches in my throat.

The bright light of heaven sweeps across my face. All the slinus back away and I'm lifted out of this world.

By an angel with lavender eyes.

The light glows brighter and sprinkles down on me. I jerk around. See Alinx's face.

Then I cough. Gurgle water. I'm shaking, or being shook. The beam of silver light clears and I see the angel's face. "Syedahl."

She holds me, but with one arm.

Alinx is in her other arm, leaning on her shoulder.

"I'm okay," he says. He's moving. Swimming around.

I'm remembering. Afraid. "Where is he? Where did he go?"

The slinus snicker.

Saying a word I don't understand, Syedahl moves her staff to protect us, but they aren't coming at me anymore. I look down and the pain melts away. My body is pale in that light, looking brand new.

"I don't know," Syedahl says. "He just disappeared. I sent him...somewhere. Another realm I think. Somewhere far away, where he will never hurt us."

"Another realm?" Alinx asks.

"I'm not sure."

The slinus are gathered around us. Hovering horizontally or lying on the skench, they start complaining, a sound like fangs scraping stone.

I lift my head. It hurts so badly. What did I do to my head? The breaths I take aren't big enough.

"What are they saying?" I still can't get up. These flukes don't feel like mine.

"They're upset that the kraken's body is gone. They wanted to eat it," Syedahl says.

My temples draw in towards my brain.

"Well why didn't you leave his body here?" Alinx means to sound curious, but Syedahl gets defensive.

"It wasn't my choice!"

That silver light is beautiful like stars. It all comes back to me and I fall from heaven into my body. That light is why we came here and why we have to leave.

"Mac," I say.

Syedahl shouts at the slinus in their icky language. I cock my head, see Mac's bones stripped bare. He was the one who helped me face my fears.

All the memories are with me, not trapped inside. I want to tell him goodbye but don't want to see him. "Thank you, Mac." I say to the surface somewhere. "Thank you so much."

The slinus hold his bones in their webbed hands, licking.

Syedahl continues, "He sacrificed himself for us."

"You were right about the myst gem. So the Serpent Mistress…" Alinx's voice breaks.

"We have to get out of here," I say, coming alive.

Syedahl shouts at the slinus as I push off from the skench.

"She might sense that the kraken died," she says. "They could be connected." Mid-breath, Syedahl switches languages, switches *species* actually, and says something threatening to the slinus.

Right below me is an uncracked gem that I covet. I pick it up and hold it protectively like a baby, my precious little piece of the ocean.

I'm going to take it home. My own amulet. I'll carve a chunk out of it to wear as a necklace. Or give it to my dad.

The slinus start laughing. I can't believe that I know what that horsey, hellish sound is. They're making fun of me.

"They say you'll never be able to open it," Syedahl translates.

Alinx leans over and grabs one. Thank God he is strong again. Obedient or defiant, we never know which. "It's worth a try."

"Please let's go," I say.

The slinus are totally defeated. They do nothing but watch us ascend. Syedahl stays closest to them and points her staff menacingly. Inside, I make out the borders of four silver orbs. The blue ones are faint.

The slinus don't even try to stop us. Only stare, shiny from her bright light.

"Goodbye, Mac. Thank you."

I think of Zeeki and his Hea lover. All this sorrow because of me?

I want to go fast. Go. Go. Go. But Syedahl makes us ascend agonizingly slowly so our bodies can adjust.

"Slinus are scavengers," Alinx says. "They don't attack."

I really don't want to talk about them.

"I know," Syedahl says.

"What's going on?" he asks.

We are in deep blue again and I'm thankful for it.

"We'll go to the Base and get answers." Syedahl's voice is soft and her words are short.

I feel a transition. Syedahl will be his and not mine. "Will it work?" I ask.

I expect her to say, "I hope so." Instead, she says, "I think it will."

46

Syedahl

"WHAT WAS THAT?" ALINX ASKS.

I hear movement, coming from up the current, the direction we must go.

I conceal my staff and take deep gulps of water, not even knowing who I am anymore. A Hea who has killed a kraken and caused an alee's death? Or simply an ala trying to protect the ones she loves? An escapee? A vagabond? A thief? A killer? Somehow I'm less interested than ever in coming up with a label.

"Who is it? What do we do?" Joaviz is already jerking to make her getaway downstream.

The scent of Hea lava is like an announcement. I know they have come for me.

"Help her," I say.

Alinx grabs Joaviz by the tail and she yelps, glaring at him. Then she manages an apologetic grimace until he lets her go.

"What about these?" Alinx asks, holding his unopened gem with one hand. Joaviz clings to hers, though it makes her movements awkward.

I try to think of a good story, but only come up with the

absurd, that we eat them, or that selling rocks has become our profession.

Instead I say nothing and swim forward, against the current.

Henna's luxurious voice reaches me before I see her. "He's here. I sense her as well," she says.

"Did you want her to find you?" I snarl at Alinx, whipping around to glare at him.

"No."

"Did you know she was tracking you?"

He shakes his head. "Your dad told me that once I found you, someone would find me."

I want to slap him, but instead I open my mouth and demand, "And you didn't think to tell me?" in a voice that sounds like Joaviz.

Alinx, Joaviz, and I push ahead towards the sound of Henna's voice, her image still a blur in the blue. I need to meet her as far from the skench as possible, so she doesn't sense that horrible feeling and ask questions.

It must be an effect of so many myst gems. The horror has trailed me but I hope it won't reach Henna.

A smug face appears in the blue. I've never seen this Hea before, but there's something familiar about his thin angles and pale hair.

Henna follows behind him. For a moment I see a flicker of sympathy, but then she hardens her expression to match the alee's.

I remember hoping, before my initiation, that she could give me some advice about my love for Alinx from an ala's perspective. I looked up to her, hoping for a role model.

Now she is an enemy.

Our trio collides with their duo. "Will you come willingly?" the alee asks.

"No."

His astonishment does not hamper his confidence. Two experienced Heas against an inexperienced one isn't even a fight.

"Cutro, let me speak with her," Henna says. "Syedahl, if not the love of this warrior, then what could possibly change your mind?"

The two of them glide forward with the force of the current. Joaviz, Alinx, and I keep straining against it.

I don't answer Henna.

"I've been tracking him since he left. Isn't it enough to be with him? Will you come home? Your father wanted you to come on your own." She doesn't sound like herself. Her words are flat instead of fussed over. "It will look better at your Court trial if you come willingly. You still have a chance."

Court trial.

"I can't," I say and look to Alinx for support. He's compensating for his absolute helplessness against them with clenched fists and a puffed chest.

The blond alee, Cutro, looks at Joaviz with amusement. "Now what could Cualt possibly want with you?"

I angle myself protectively in front of her. "If Cualt didn't tell you, then you don't deserve to know."

"A little pride for your daddy? Yes well, I also try to support Dawein whenever I can." He inclines his head superiorly. "Especially when it comes to serving my city."

So, he is Dawein's son from Untine. Now I see it. The yellowish paleness, the smugness. But Cutro is not nearly as hefty.

Henna can barely look at me.

Tired and unfocused, I realize the current has pushed us closer to the skench.

"What are they holding?" Cutro asks me.

I save Alinx and Joaviz with a question of my own, directed at Henna. "If you're so concerned with taking me home, why did you let me go when you saw me in Kalein?"

Everything about the water changes. Henna deflates like a puffer into a bag of poison. Cutro is cruelly pleased, turning to sneer at his partner.

"I…" She does not continue.

Cutro smiles at me in an oddly friendly way. Getting leverage over Henna seems to have satisfied him. "We will guide you back to Ezkine, Syedahl, where you and Alinx can live a happy life. Just relinquish the ala."

My staff bursts into all of its silvery brilliance, banishing the horror of the cold darkness and my worry that they'll discover my new power.

Here it is. They see it now. This is what I have to defend us. We are directly above the skench. The fact that the kraken is gone doesn't heal the hopelessness rising up from below. I don't know if they perceive it.

"Wh-what is that?" Cutro asks about the silver light.

I stare at it myself. Then he jolts forward, snatches Joaviz, and holds her against his body. As he sputters to keep her under his command, her tail quivers violently and her face turns purple. Henna watches with wild eyes.

Joaviz's stone drops from her hands and falls slowly. Her loss is a catalyst for Alinx. He lifts his stone and moves to smash it against Cutro's head but Cutro gathers red orbs and scalds Alinx's face.

Alinx cries out. His attack had lasted just long enough for Cutro to relax his telekinetic command on Joaviz, who took a breath that turned her face from purple to red.

Henna is swift to heal Alinx with pink orbs, using her principle skill to give him new skin.

I can't be this numb. What I experienced at the skench has

changed me. Mac made sure of that.

Once again, the five of us are locked, stalled, only now Cutro has what my father wants. He lets her breathe.

Joaviz manages to rasp my name.

"I asked you what is in your staff," Cutro says.

"The myst gem."

Cutro stammers a reply, looking from me to the darkness below us, disbelieving and yet so stunned by the brilliance of my staff that something like respect shines in his eyes.

Joaviz's eyes are bulging, her mouth gurgling water that never goes deep enough.

I lock eyes with Alinx and then with Henna, hoping they can hear my silent commands.

"You can't kill her," I say.

Cutro knows I'm right.

The ten blue freezing orbs combine into one silver orb that speaks through my staff, sending a message to my fingertips that then crawls up my arm to my chest, chin, lips. "Xijx," I utter, barely a whisper.

Cradling his gem in one arm, Alinx jolts up and slams his wrist sword down on Cutro's arm, slicing open a gash that blossoms blood.

Henna rips Joaviz away from Cutro just as the silver light connects with his face, revealing in his expression a sick love of fear. The blue behind him is visible. He's gone.

The dessa was right. Once you use a myst gem, the spell is yours forever.

The silver glow is replaced with a golden one. It takes me a long moment to accept what the three floating masses of red-orange are. Then they seek each other out and become one ball of lava.

Henna stirs her staff but I'm faster, slurping the substance up.

Myst gem orbs and now raw Hea power dance and collide in my staff. I expect this new power to evoke the greed I've always hated in my father. Or for my staff to explode. But all is well.

I conceal it and face Henna.

"I didn't want to come here," she says. Her voice quavers, begging for mercy. I liked her much better when she was sultry and confident.

"Now you know," I say.

I know the Serpent Mistress's secrets and Henna knows mine.

Though I care deeply for Alinx and Joaviz, they are far from my awareness in this moment. All I see is Henna, how she keeps glancing below us. By now we've been carried even farther, past the ravine that leads to the skench, to where the water is aquamarine again.

"I won't tell," she says.

"You'll never find them, anyway. I took them all. They are rare. Harvests are…" I trail off, Joaviz's frantic breathing breaking my concentration.

"I believe you. I won't say anything." Henna's eyes are the widest yet, her heavy lids pulled back.

"What do you want? What will you do?"

She stares at my staff. "That lava belongs to Ch'tlan. As does the lava inside of you."

"You won't get either."

She nods, knowing that should she choose to defy me, she too will become a swirling mass in my staff. A twinge of guilt breaks through my cold demeanor, but now is not the time for self-reflection. I grit my teeth.

Henna's outstretched fingertips caress the empty water. "Where did he go?"

I almost answer honestly, but decide not to show my weakness. "His body is simply gone. It is no more."

"That's impossible. Against the laws of nature."

I can't tell if Henna is trying to catch me in a lie, or if she is merely baffled.

"This power goes against everything we know," I say.

Her eyes glide from me to Joaviz, who is cradling water where her gem used to be.

"High Transformation," Henna says wistfully.

"What will you do?" I ask again, trying to deflect to her, but of course the real question is what will *I* do with her?

"My son. He needs me. I'll go home and won't speak a word of it."

I shake my head. "That's absurd. They'll want Cutro. His body at the very least."

"Well, give me his power!" Her voice is shrill.

"No. I won't do that."

"I can tell them I extracted it myself after you killed him. I can blame this on Hasat. Give me his power. It will be better for you this way."

Alinx is staring at me, wondering.

He's the recipient I would choose. Dare I give myself the choice? "The power wouldn't really belong to you," I tell him. "It never does."

He understands the danger.

Alinx is unreadable as he says, "I'm already wanted by Ezkine. Officers aren't allowed to leave."

I can't take my eyes off of Henna for too long, so I take hold of Alinx's hand and turn back to her. "Tell your queen that I had Hasat with me. We overpowered the two of you. You came upon us, not sensing Hasat—inexplicably. He killed Cutro. I wanted to kill you, but Hasat couldn't bear to harm his niece. So, we let you go. You know nothing of the gem. You know nothing of what happened to Cutro's body or when we extracted the power."

Alinx's skin is clammy with disbelief. I myself can't imagine what this means for us—not yet.

"I'll tell them that, exactly as you've said."

"I suppose now you're afraid of me, but what about before?" She lied to the Court that I had achieved my right of passage. She helped Joaviz and me flee Kalein.

"I respect you. That's why I helped you leave, why I warned you about the Kaleinian Hea. Your journey is not for me. I honestly love Tila, and can't wait to return." Her voice has regained its gritty theatricality. "But I never wanted to hinder a Hea from using her power as she needs to. I don't believe in these Tribe laws imposed upon us, meant to make the strongest weak. My second child—an ala…was…" She clutches her chest and hangs her head. "Taken from me. But I'm fortunate to truly desire what's expected of me. To serve my city."

"Thank you." She knows I'm referring to her honesty. Her words are a huge gift. I'm not selfish or irresponsible. I'm simply different.

A traveler.

An adventurer.

Everything I wanted but thought I could never be.

"Did you go to the Lunata Coven in Akati?" Henna asks.

"No."

She smiles. "Their moon magic would mean nothing to you now."

Henna departs, without so much as a goodbye to Joaviz or Alinx.

"Alinx, Joaviz and I need to do this alone." I pull my hand from his. "I'm sorry but you can't come with us."

Joaviz doesn't succeed at hiding her sadness, still stealing glances at her empty hands. "Come on, Syedahl. I know you'll help me. What does it matter if he comes too?"

Alinx fills the void between her hands with his own gem. Joaviz bears the weight with disbelief and thanks him.

He couldn't possibly understand the paranoia that makes her need her own back-up gem, but he sees how important it is to her. I need her to have peace of mind.

I turn to Alinx, my stomach a knot of nerves. "I must learn to journey on my own. I was with you for so long. And then with Joaviz. I'll take her home, and then have time alone to think...to think and decide what to do..."

He nods, but I can see just how much this hurts him. I give him a sweet kiss on the lips, more promise than passion.

I explain to him which currents to take to the base, what mounds and formations he can expect to see along the way. "Tell them you're a friend of Syedahl's and you have news about Mac."

"I have to be the one to tell them? You think that will put me in their favor?"

"The Commander—only share your news with him—will see your respect for Mac when you describe what happened. You can tell him anything. Everything."

His face is so different to me now. That gorgeous bone structure is softened with vulnerability. "You're sure?"

"Yes."

"We'll see." Alinx doesn't trust strangers, not even those I recommend.

Joaviz hugs Alinx and thanks him. He thanks her for taking care of me, which makes us all laugh.

"Promise me. It'll be you and me. Promise." Alinx looks so pale to me now, and his hair so dark. I smile, remembering how exotic his coloring seemed when we first met. There will always be that sweet familiarity with him. But those golden eyes still surprise me. There's now so much we don't know about each other that we both want to learn.

And so the promise escapes my lips.

The fact that he doesn't ask me about initiating him shows me that he loves me and not what I am or what I can provide.

47

Joaviz

WE COME INTO THE CITY farther down from Ertra. All the buildings are made of coral and the alus here have little decorative fins on their tails—more vibrant than the coral and the fish. I'm awestruck. This city is a trippy swirling vortex of color.

"Where else would he have gone when he left Ertra? This is the closest city down current!" Syedahl is saying. She's obsessed with trying to figure out what Mac was doing when he ditched me in Ertra. I don't pay attention to her conversations with the guards. I just look around at all the alus, gorgeous but shy.

I couldn't see Mac when he attacked the kraken's mouth, but I could feel him. I can just picture his eyes, proud and knowing. He knew what he was doing, but why did he do it?

Maybe for Syedahl, so she could protect me and not loose Alinx. But Mac had no guarantees we would make it out alive. I'm really sad for Syedahl's sake that he's gone. She could have used someone like that in her life. Straight-up and wise.

I didn't really get to talk to the Commander much, but she has nothing but good things to say about him. Hopefully he'll be that person for her now.

This city does me in. I admit to myself what I couldn't when I was afraid: I actually like being underwater.

My trauma isn't hiding anymore. Neither are the good things that have happened to me here. The adventure of it. Syedahl.

Then I think about my old life. When Dad is gone, Lily will be the only good part. Even so, I have to see him. I love him too much to just disappear.

When he dies, I'll have to be strong for my mom and sister. I want to live *my own* life, not sacrifice everything for them.

I'm not saying I want to be an ala—I don't think I do. Too vulnerable. It's no fun being prey.

Besides, I miss breathing air. It makes me wonder how all those myths got it wrong. The whole shape-shifting thing. In and out of water all the time. It's so not fair. I wish it could be like that. But it's one or the other, and I'm human.

Syedahl guides me farther into the reef-lined ravine, to where an orator is announcing the news about an oil spill continuing to spread. Everyone in the crowd is shouting angrily, but his voice is loudest. When he finishes, Syedahl describes Mac to him.

"Yes. I saw that alee. Looked like a warrior?" the orator asks. I think of Mac's short hair and enormous biceps, the scars on his chest.

"That's him," Syedahl says. Her voice is low and out of breath. "Did he say anything to you?"

The alee's eyes light up. "I remember. He wanted to know if the Tribe had released a statement about the Annual Hea Convention."

Syedahl's hands dart forward, ready to grab him around the shoulders. He eyes her, and she brings them back down. "Had they? What did you tell him?"

"Not that I had heard. Still nothing, actually." The alee

strokes his double chin. "He thought it was odd that the Tribe hadn't condemned the meeting publicly the way they did last year. He got all quiet and looked…I don't know…like that was a really bad omen."

After he says ten times that he doesn't know anything else, Syedahl finally leaves him alone.

He blasts off on his next story and my ears ring. We leave.

I comfort her as she cries over Mac. It feels strange to be the strong one.

We come to the wide inlet of the Great Canal, guided here by a troupe of performers. They thought we were nuts for wanting to cross it and wouldn't tell us where it was, so we lied and said we just wanted to look at boats. Well, there are tons of boats now. More than I've ever seen in my life. Their bottoms spread out wide and smooth. Cruise ships, fishing boats, and what I guess are cargo ships—gray and flat and huge. We swim as low as we can, looking up at the red, white, gray, and black boat bottoms. I try to ignore the low, monstrous human voices.

Syedahl whips out her staff.

I worry that all the gems will come out at once, but she says just one emerges at a time. She's right. Just a strange word uttered and she has accomplished moving invisibility. No other Hea can do it. I can't see her or myself. "Where are you? Where are you?" The rocks are sharp, the bottom-feeder fish gnarled and ugly.

"Stop thrashing." I hear the soft swishing of her tail. "Follow me."

I'm glad the myst gem in my hands is still visible. I don't want to lose it. Holding on tight doesn't feel like enough. I have to see it to know that it's there.

I listen to her as we swim below a boat, then dart under another and another. We crawl over the rocks, our bodies sinking in the fresh water. We stop in front of concrete gates and wait for them to open. The Panama Canal is more waiting than swimming.

We laugh about how Syedahl is the most powerful and also the least powerful Hea in the Seas. She only laughs for a second though. "Do you think they can hear us?" She's worried. Responsibility isn't funny to her.

"No." I don't want to worry about humans just yet.

Everyone is going to want her now. As if they didn't already.

Trapped in the concrete, we hear the harsh, clipped voices of humans on the boats. I can't understand them. The cars on the bridge above us don't sound the way cars used to. All the honking seems less like impatience and more like a thousand warnings. Syedahl's invisible hand on my arm is shaking.

My two worlds really do collide.

All this time I'd pitied myself. Why me? Poor me.

Now I feel lucky for the first time. I'm one of a very few humans who have been mermaids. And I accept it. I'm stronger now.

I hope I can take this attitude home.

The bad thing is, I've gotten used to this body without realizing it. I love the slick feeling of my scales. The speed...

I was wrong about that memory, about Nicolai. I wasn't just blocking out the transformation, I was blocking out what I didn't want to go home to. Dad wasn't at a poker game when Nicolai broke up with me.

He was getting chemo.

48

Syedahl

WHEN JOAVIZ CONFESSES that she's saving the myst gem for her father, I haven't the heart to remind her that she needs power to successfully wield it. Besides, she'll probably never know the effect of the gem on land. The slinus claim they're the only ones who can open them.

On the other side of the human passage, past the awful thundering noises and fowl smells, the water is instantly cooler and fresher than it is in Kai. The current comes straight from the north.

Something must be terribly wrong with me. I feel no remorse for killing Cutro.

Perhaps it will come later, once I allow myself to fully process what has happened. Once Joaviz is gone.

For now, I'm strong. I have a promise to keep.

I trust myself. My intuition. I know what I must do.

"Can I read your mind?" I ask.

Joaviz does not guffaw nor reveal any inclination to deny me, but still I explain. "To know exactly where to take you. You live near a beach, yes?"

With her eyes closed, she looks good-natured and sweet, the fire in those bright turquoise eyes hidden.

I'm not bothered that it took her so long to trust me. I admire it really, that she was so cautious, so protective of herself. I never thought I'd place myself above others, but when Joaviz and Alinx were about to be killed, I went straight for the gem.

"What is it?" Joaviz asks, opening her eyes, sick of waiting.

"Sorry."

She closes them again.

I search through her memories. It's wonderful to experience everything through her, to see myself with her eyes. There I am, leaning over her, healing her from the kraken attacks, letting her lead the way to the skench, wishing her goodbye on my way to the Convention, telling her that she should stay at the Base and not come to Ertra, soothing her fears in the sea topped with floating seaweed and human trash.

I watch myself strap Fairesa to the table, watch my disapproving stare as I-as-Joaviz kiss Enkirik. I-as-Joaviz am upset with myself for coming to Kalein, angry that I, Syedahl, do everything for Alinx. I'm afraid of Cualt.

I'm afraid of the ocean, of the Deep, but I go to Ezkine—not understanding why.

The Serpent is an echo. Blinding light. Slick skin.

I rush through the human memories because there's nothing to understand in the sheer terror of her transformation. Then comes a memory that begs to be experienced.

I feel weak and limp as I lean against horizontal metal bars, staring out into the invisible night. One word spills from my icy lips. "Daddy."

I bury my face in my hands, feeling the strain in my jaw from keeping my mouth clenched shut all day. "Please don't die."

Memories come in a head-splitting blur.

Finally, I'm on a long beach with coarse multi-colored sand looking out at the gray sea. I walk to a rock that emerges from the water and stand on it, letting the waves hit my skin—my feet. I breathe air and watch the sunset. This is my favorite beach. I've been here a thousand times.

I come out of Joaviz's memories and into myself, panting for water, feeling instantly comforted by it. I hate the way the ocean looks from the air—uniform and unknowable.

"Transportation magic," I say with a forced grin. "Let's try and break yet another Hea shortcoming."

I focus on the place I've seen and say, from somewhere inside me, "Halu."

I won't question the word. Nor judge it. Nor assume this power will make me evil. I'll harness and control it from the place beyond fear.

Silver light erupts and surrounds us in a rounded diamond shape and then solidifies. It bends and takes on the shape of my hand when I push against it.

"It's like putty," Joaviz says, leaning into it and then watching the indentation gradually disappear. The substance looks like a hazy, colorless eye, just a streamlined defect in the deep blue. "Putty in the shape of an eye!"

"What shall we call it?" I ask.

Joaviz surprises me by coming up with the perfect name instantly. "The Current Star." Two wonders we've taught each other about.

"So, you can use it again? On your way back?" Joaviz is still clutching her cracked gem as though it is life itself.

Each gem is a lesson, at least for those who naturally create power. "Yes, with my own orbs once I harvest them."

The Current Star picks up speed and slams us back into its soft shell. I get queasy, but Joaviz laughs and laughs, holding the uncracked gem against her stomach.

We keep far from the shelf, which is good. I have no idea how this would look from the outside. Invisible? A whir of color? We see no cites, just endless blue.

I wonder if there are other alu cities besides Ezkine on top of skenches. I wonder why slinus do not build themselves homes. Maybe they have them elsewhere, down in the Deep. It seems the skenches are just workplaces. I wonder how many skenches there are in the world.

How many slinus? Dessas? Krakens? Anything else? Joaviz has changed my life forever. Now I know why the Great Volcán wanted me to protect her. It was for both our sakes. I thank him silently.

Three days later, the Current Star slows down and moves towards land.

We stop in front of a large boulder that stretches out beyond the surface. The water here churns. Visibility is poor.

Everything is an ugly shade of gray. All I can do is slow the rush of my exhale as the squishy substance of the Current Star disappears, leaving the two of us swaying backwards and forwards, trying not to hit the boulder. I guide Joaviz away from it. My hair obscures my vision.

"I want to see you again," Joaviz says, breaking the silence. "Can you come back and visit me?"

"I don't know when I could. I need to help the Commander—for Mac."

Joaviz nods sadly. "And for you."

"Yes, and for me. I could try to visit…"

Her eyes light up. "How about this? Every full moon, I'll come and sit on this rock at sunset. I'll put my foot in so you can see me. If you're not here, I'll know it didn't work out."

The thought of her waiting for me every full moon is horribly depressing. "I'm not sure," I say.

"This way you don't have to know. Just work it out on some

full moon. Now that you have the Current Star, it shouldn't be too hard. You're the busy one. Don't worry about me. "

I exhale deeply now, letting those last words sink in. I've let her go little by little since Mac told me I must, but now I really have to. "I'll come."

"Don't take too long. At least by the third full moon."

"I'll try."

"Good."

A thought strikes me. "We won't be able to understand each other. You won't be able to tell me about your father, and I won't be able to tell you about Alinx or Zeeki or the Commanders or the Base."

I can't read her face. Something in her hardens. "I know," Joaviz says. "Don't make this worse."

"I'm sorry," I say.

"It's okay. I just want to see you again. Just to know you're all right."

I nod. "Of course."

"Okay," Joaviz says. I know how she's feeling, or rather how she wishes she felt: resolved. I thought all she wanted was to go home, but now I can tell she's conflicted. She could be swayed. I could be the one to sway her.

But that would be wrong. We've both worked so hard for this.

All of this...just so she could say goodbye to her father, so she could go home and live her life on land. I think of what she told me after Mac's death. I need to discover what I want. It seems to me she needs to do the same, but I won't be the one to tell her that.

Going home may not be exactly what she wants, but for a reason I don't fully understand, it's what she needs.

We hug.

"I love you," she says.

"I love you too. Are you ready?"

She pauses, looks at her tail, runs her hand down her gorgeous red-orange scales. Just the sight of it makes me shiver.

"I'm ready," she says.

I take one last look at her, hug her one more time with my eyes closed, and then pull away. I imagine how it would feel to really stand on that rock, to have legs. Curiosity finally wins. I open my eyes and say one word. "Sithair."

Her eyes are locked on mine as the silver light spills over her. I smile, hoping she won't be afraid. As the light covers her eyes, she blinks rapidly as if in pain, but tries to smile back. Her eye scales are gone. The gills in her neck smooth out into skin.

Her yellow top frays to nothingness while the color drains from her tail. It smoothes out and then splits, peels apart into two separate fleshy poles that bend in the middle. Each ends in a fluke of skin. The webbing gradually disintegrates and the flukes become things like long hands with short fingers.

I stare in awe and she stares back, her mouth closed and her eyes bulging. Finally she can take no more. When she pushes off the sand and swims up to the surface, I gasp, thinking of the pain she'll be in with her head out of water. She brings her head back down for a moment. I assume she'll take a sip, but her lips stay firmly closed. She floats at the choppy surface and looks down at me. There is nothing to say. I smile as she turns around, using those ugly, awkward legs to kick the water. She's the strangest thing I've ever seen, but somehow beautiful.

She's my Joaviz.

49

Joanne

I'M NAKED AND FREEZING and I can't move. I just lie on the gritty sand, staring up at the pale blue sky. The sun is up. It's a new day.

For me, it's a new life. The old life anew.

But I just lie here, the powerful ugly myst gem at my side. I have to savor the transition.

I listen to the waves. Something is splashing. I look up in time to see Syedahl jumping out of the water, letting me know it was all real. That she loves me.

She's so beautiful. The sight of her is a bigger message than I could have anticipated. She looks different, though. Unreal. But there she is.

Long black hair clings to her pale body. Light blue scales glisten. She tries to smile but I know she's in pain.

She crashes down into the water, leaving me all alone.

I'm up, afraid for her, but no one else is on the beach. I stand up and fall over. Stand up again. I scream her name.

I know how it must sound to her, but there she is farther out this time, shooting out of the waves for me to see.

She dives back down and I don't see her again. I stare out at the water for a long time. The tears on my cheeks are hot.

They are tears for everything.

I let myself feel it. All of it. I look down at my naked body. Just a skinny teenage girl.

My arms are still tan, my hair long and red. But my legs look pale and brand new. Pink like new skin and just as sensitive. I touch the skin on my eyes, my neck.

What am I now?

I'm not a regular 17-year-old girl anymore. I'm something else. It will take some figuring out.

I can't deny how cold I feel. I'm shivering uncontrollably. My hair is like icicles down my back. The sand is like broken glass.

The myst gem makes me walk lop-sided. I cover myself with one hand as best as I can and walk down the street. I don't feel embarrassed. Not for this body, because it isn't mine yet. I trip and stumble and drag my legs. I don't know what day it is, or even what month. May, maybe? Not warm at all.

A lady runs out of her house.

"You're the girl! The missing girl on the news."

Her words make sense to my brain but not to my ears. I don't want to hear them. I walk past her, shove past the towel she holds out to me.

She follows me, but I keep going like a zombie. Past the houses. Perfect lawns. Parked cars.

I try the words out on my tongue. They don't slur or back up. "I'm going home."

"I'll drive you."

"Fuck off."

She stops in her tracks, turns on her heels and walks back to her house. Now I feel like me again. But I don't want to be a tough girl, not today.

I'm ready to find out if my dad is still alive. I'm prepared for the answer. I'm ready to break down.

Our lawn is dry and long. Neglected by the man of the house. It hurts to walk on it.

The front door bangs open and slams shut again. Instantly I'm covered by a big quilt and my mother's arms. Like squeezing the breath out of me might make me real. The myst gem is wedged between us.

Her head is tilted up towards the sky as she whispers in my ear, "Thank you Jesus. Oh, sweet Jesus. Thank you." Then she pulls back and holds me too hard, shakes me. "Who hurt you? Where are they?" Her mad eyes roam the street.

I just shake my head, saying nothing, looking like what she must have guessed: kidnapped and abused.

Not a naked miracle lost at sea.

She guides me inside.

I recognize the quilt. It's the one that's always on our couch. The couch is pushed farther back to the kitchen to make room for the hospital bed where my dad lies, sleeping and frail.

A bowl of uneaten cereal is on the tray that stretches across his belly.

I hold his hand and wake him up. My mom stands by the foot of the bed.

"Daddy? Daddy, I'm home."

His eyes snap open. It scares me. They aren't his eyes. They aren't strong anymore. But they see me. "I've been waiting, Joey."

I kiss him on the forehead and then back up, taking one step at a time until the couch presses against my calves and I crash into it. The gem is in my lap. "Your green chair is gone."

50

Syedahl

THE SMELL OF ALU BLOOD shocks me into clarity.

The Current Star takes me closer to the mouth of the ravine. Sharks squirm to get into the city. Blood seeps in through the porous Star. I urge it closer and catch a glimpse of a Hea mumbling, ragged and tired. All around him, alus are bleeding with mortal wounds.

They curse the slinus.

I search for the impossibility of their green skin in this sunlight.

I make myself invisible and am jostled through the shark bodies, still protected by my pliable Star. Once inside the city boundary, I look around. About half of the alus within sight are injured. I can hear many more, farther up the ravine, hiding.

None of their stricken eyes are directed at me.

An ala swims up to the Hea and presents a child to him. She begs him to heal her son. The Hea looks away from the boundary, at her, for only a moment, but it's enough to break his concentration. A shark—the same gorgeous species we saw with Mac at the Base—breaks through the boundary and snatches an alee, biting him around his chest and shaking him side to side.

I send red orbs flying at the shark, killing shark and alee alike. The Hea is wild-eyed, utterly perplexed.

Blue freezing orbs transform into healing orbs, a mixture of myst gem and Hea power. I cover the entire city with light. Everything is sparkly and glowing. The scent of blood is gone, leaving only silence. Then stunned cries of joy.

The Hea sobs with exhaustion. He continues to keep the sharks out of his city, but nearly all of them have already turned away, on to find less-protected prey.

The Hea turns to look for the source of the magic, and though I am invisible, I hurry away.

Zeeki's is the first face I recognize. Her brightness has been hollowed out, excavated. I feel the pain of regret but try to make myself strong, remembering what Mac would have wanted.

She bites back bitterness. I know she'll never like me. "There was no telling what my uncle would do—no telling him what to do. I know it wasn't your fault. The Commander said Mac died for a good reason, but he won't tell me what it is. Will you?"

I feel awful that she can't know about the myst gem, but I understand. The less who know, the better. "I'm sorry. We should follow the Commander on this. It really was a good reason. Mac has changed history."

Her eyes light up for a moment with what I think is pride until she says, "I'll figure it out." She starts to turn away but I stop her.

"Are you…a spy now?" I ask.

"In training."

Her presence is replaced by that of the Commander, who grabs me up in his warm dark arms and hugs me tightly. He holds my face in both hands and actually kisses me swiftly on the lips. His pride fills me, too. He grabs my hand and leads me into the tunnels. I ignore the stares of the young warriors who watch us pass by.

We come to the room where we first talked. It feels so long ago. Tasapi, Rew, Greizjo, and Hasat are all here. The Commander and I interrupt their heated conversation. Before I let myself listen or speak, I take a moment to thank the Great Volcán for these powerful and respectful alees who have changed my life and will continue to do so. Can't I have an ala friend too?

They're still speaking, arguing in fact, but when they see that I'm not listening, not even responding to my name, they all slow down and stop talking completely. Hasat hugs me with his giant, scarred arms. I look at his bright white hair and into his wide-spread black eyes.

"Are you here to stay?" I ask.

He shakes his head. "Just sharing what I know."

"And what is it that you know?"

"Greizjo is putting it all together," he says.

Greizjo smiles and bows to me, then begins to hum. It's the low vibrating sound that follows a play, a way to show approval. They all join in heartily now, and I can feel the stress seep out through my pores and through the holes in the coral rock.

"Thank you," I say and then demand that we do the same for Mac.

These are the alees who know about the myst gem, about Joaviz. These are the alees I can trust.

Greizjo swims nearer to me, intriguing me with those green eyes. "The Tribe of All Seas staged slinu attacks on all the cities that sent a Hea to the Convention. Most likely to prove that Heas are too irresponsible to be solely in charge of protecting the citizalus. The Tribe wants the citizalus to vote their Representatives into their city governments."

"You're…" I begin, not knowing what to say.

"Hasat brought news of the attacks, and I know everyone who attended. The cities match up."

"But that city near Ertra was attacked. Recently. I saw it today."

He eyes me strangely, probably wondering how I could have possibly been there today, but ignores it. "A few cities were attacked after their Heas returned. The official Tribe statement is that these are random wild slinu attacks."

My voice is stammering, high-pitched and enraged. "The slinus are scavengers! They eat only dead things. How could it have been slinus?" I gulp, sickened. "Was it alus, disguised? Did they teach real slinus to attack? Why? Create a war to win it…I don't understand."

"You don't need to right now. You need rest." The Commander's eyes are soothing, showing me just how bulging my own tired eyes must be.

I could easily retreat and seek out Alinx, but there's one question that keeps me here. "What could have stopped the Serpent Mistress from fully transforming Joaviz, giving her the power of speech?"

Rew utters, "The mantagon."

"Rew is the only alee I know who has seen him," the Commander says.

"Who is he?" I ask.

"The only creature the Serpent Mistress fears. The mantagon is…" Rew's face breaks into a huge, wrinkled smile. "…just a giant old manta ray." His hands find the ceiling. "Huge!"

I lower my flukes into the opening in the floor.

Hasat coughs. "I knew it was the Serpent Mistress all

along. Sorry I couldn't tell you, pup."

Oh yes, I do remember feeling he was keeping something from me. Now I understand perfectly. He feared that if he told me the truth, I wouldn't believe him—and wouldn't leave Ezkine. He knew I needed the mystery. "Apology accepted. No. *Appreciated*. I appreciate what you did for me."

The Commander's voice stops me from descending any further. "Tell me, Syedahl…did Cutro's power disappear with him? Alinx wouldn't say."

I'm thankful that my staff is concealed. They can't see the shimmering red-hot orb, so much more magnificent than Hea orbs, yet dull in comparison to the myst gem power that swirls around it. It's the only true myst gem orb that I have left.

"What happened?" Tasapi demands.

The energy of the room heightens and stiffens. Unthinkingly, I react by enlarging my staff and pointing at each of them in turn.

The hungriness drains from Tasapi's eyes and he raises his hands innocently. Rew laughs.

Hasat is wide-eyed as usual, watching. Greizjo grimaces, disgusted and disappointed that I should take an initiation upon myself.

The Commander swims right up to my staff, placing its tip at his muscled stomach to show that he's not afraid. "We can't have these kinds of secrets."

"I know." My voice quavers while my hands tighten around my staff.

"What are you going to do with the lava?" Greizjo asks.

"I'm not sure yet."

Hasat smirks. "She's going to see if Alinx wants it."

Tasapi asks, "Why should he get it? He just got here. Shouldn't we have some sort of vote? And what if it's true that it will kill someone who isn't a Hea heir?"

The Commander casts an incredulous smile over his shoulder but keeps his eyes on me. "Syedahl has just gotten here too."

Hasat grunts. "Nevermind all that." He crosses and uncrosses his arms and darts back and forth as much as he can manage in this small, packed room. He mumbles loudly. "Wrapped up…thought so…we'll see…and Henna repaid all her debts and still got away! Cualt doesn't hold much over her anymore." The memory of his shark face is layered upon the moment as he turns to me. "Unless there's something you know?"

"Her…her *debt* to…*Cualt*?"

"She owed us both for the same act. What we did together not so very long ago to get her chosen over my daughter. I wanted to protect my daughter from this life, but she couldn't forgive me for it. But you go. Get out. Get on with it."

Tasapi renews his protests over the lava humming in my staff.

"Let it be!" Hasat thunders.

He's already there on the deck, right in front of me, sparing me the torture of looking for him. I'm in his arms. I pull back and kiss him for all the Rebels to see. "Come with me."

We swim straight up and over the deck, then down, searching for a private place.

A long gray shark resting on a ledge makes me tense. "This kind is harmless," Alinx says.

"Learned much in your time here, have you?"

When he shrugs, I notice that his swirling mass of dark brown hair has grown longer since I left Ezkine. The strands that fall downwards reach his clavicles. His eyes narrow, looking past me. "There." Beneath the ledge, between two crops of orange coral, is the darkened mouth of a cave. Alinx darts inside.

My heart pounds, waiting for him to come back out.

Only an arm emerges, beckoning me inside.

He grabs my face and kisses me, working his hands to the back of my neck, breathing in the water in my mouth, touching his tongue to mine.

I relax, and then… "Ow!" I pull back and examine the spot where I nicked a scale on a sharp rock.

"I like you the way you are," I say, seeing so much of our past in his golden eyes. He has been my solace, my escape to a normal life. "I like that you aren't a Hea. I always liked that you weren't an heir."

He nods but shows no reaction to my words. His face is dark except for his glowing eyes.

"Tell me what you want," I say. "Do you want it?"

"Syedahl, we'll be equals." His voice is far off and pained.

"But the power won't really belong to either of us. It never will. We'll both be property of Ch'tlan, hunted until we're returned, tried, and killed."

"Stop." His hand is warm and rough on my cheek. "That's how it is for us already. I want that life too. Why not, Syedahl? Why are you hesitating?"

"You won't love me anymore."

I have no idea if Heas are truly unable to love, and if I somehow magnificently defied that. Would Alinx work past it too? I don't think I changed much from the power, but more from my journey.

Father was charged with protecting a city, his mother already sick and his grandmother already dead. Of course he was unable to love. He was utterly overworked.

The change is in the lifestyle.

What sort of life would Alinx and I lead together?

"That's just a Tribe tactic, Syedahl," he says. "It's not that Heas can't love, it's that they're not allowed to. You're being naive."

I realize how ridiculous I am, how little I've slept. "You won't think I'm special or unique once you're just like me."

"Yeah sure," Alinx says, closing his eyes.

The absence of his eyes is haunting. "You'll die."

I can hear the Teindahn during one of our lessons. *Only someone descended from the first four hundred can survive the lava and use it.*

Alinx holds my hand. "So, you think it's true."

"No. It must be a lie. Don't *you* think it's a lie?"

He watches a fish leave the cave. "I want it to be."

My staff explodes out of my closed fist, a fury of color and light.

"Wow," Alinx breathes, mesmerized by the glow of the myst gem sparkling against every crag and crevice in this cave. "What will you do with the last gem?"

"It's not for me to decide."

I worry that while I had three initiators, Alinx will have only one. I worry that the lava will not separate into three segments as it is meant to. I worry that the Great Volcán will disapprove.

Stomach. Eyes. Mouth. That's the order in which I was burned.

Am I capable of hurting Alinx? "Great Volcán, help me."

It happens easily, once we've made the decision and I've asked for help. With each separate globe of molten lava that emerges from the tip of my staff and squeezes into Alinx's skin, he shudders softly and grits his teeth. He refuses to groan or cry out.

When it's over, he collapses on the floor of the cave.

"Alinx! Alinx!"

"I'm fine," he mumbles.

"Make your staff or…perform something."

I remember how difficult this part was for me, how I forced

my hands together and then yanked them apart.

I recall Henna's words exactly. *There is something that you will join together.*

Now I see what she meant: Hea and myst gem magic.

Alinx stares at me blankly.

"Are you sure you're okay?" I kneel down and kiss him gently on the lips. My Alinx. One of us. Not that I ever belonged.

Now we can belong to each other.

He pushes his right hand against the floor of the cave and then lifts up, a thick staff growing from the hard, gray stone. Henna is not here to predict something for him, and I have no idea what the action means. Extraction, perhaps? Pulling something magnificent from something dull?

His flukes flap wildly, driving him further into the cave. He slumps against the wall and leans over his staff, just a long cylindrical gleam.

When Alinx brings his fingertips to his lips, ten golden orbs pop out of his mouth to adorn them. He jams the hot, tender things into his staff. The material sucks them up. The ten orbs dance from end to end.

Golden. Transformation.

He tosses his staff from one hand to the other and directs it at a yellow fish, turning it pink.

Only its color has changed. Now I remember Father saying that the longer lava is outside a body, the longer it takes to train its next owner. "I'm sorry Alinx. You would have been able to change its shape too, if I had...I just wanted to be sure. But Greizjo can train both of us."

He leans in and quiets me with a kiss, then stares from his now-empty staff to his hands to the pink fish and back to me.

Acknowledgments

I feel compelled to explain my dedication.
And as all first novels deserve lengthy acknowledgment
pages, I feel vindicated in my compulsion. In 10th grade, my
English teacher Mrs. Markovich wrote on one of my essays,
"You should pursue a career in creative writing."

Not consider pursuing. Pursue.

I managed to turn every essay assignment into a creative one.

I recall comparing and contrasting the heirloom and the
mass-manufactured members of my mom's cow figurine col-
lection. There were spider webs and painted eye lashes and
cheap plastic versus porcelain. I relished in full paragraphs
of description.

For a metaphor assignment, I wrote about how I was a
seed that needed to be watered. (Without getting too auto-
biographical, let's just say that I was having a really rough
time.)

Often, mine was one of the essays that Mrs. Markovich
deemed exemplary. After every assignment, one or a few
pages would be brought in to class in projector form.

My words printed on see-through plastic for all the class to
see. At this point, I don't even remember if the examples were
anonymous or not.

It didn't matter.

I recall the burning heat. The opposite of shame gluing me
to my seat, swelling my heart, and connecting me to heaven
via direct fluorescent light.

It felt good.

Fast forward through emo love poems, novels in my notebook that didn't make it past the second chapter, rants on religion and family life, fictionalization of recent memories, and all the way to my husband telling me not to get a job after college so that I could finish the mermaid novel I had started in a bout of jargon-hating senioritis (while sitting in class).

Thank you, Gabriel, for going beyond believing. For guiding, supporting, cheering, and getting down right frustrated at any and all forms of my own self-doubt. We are of one heart. I see the mountains in your eyes.

Now:

Thanks to Jackie and James Waterfall for deeper love than even we can understand. Your readings of my drafts are filled with light and healing and heart. It's nearly impossible for me to have a sense of who I'd be without you two.

Thanks to my early readers: Chris Stockdale, Lori Van Laanen, and Talitha Mayfield. You offered comments, insight, and encouragement and are the best sort a writer can know: those who never say, "Get a real job." Plus, I love you guys.

Thanks all over the moon to Judy Patton, my friend and tía. The tangible book form of the story would not have happened without you. Your experience, sincerity, kindness, and friendship are stunning. And we have so much fun! Not many people can giggle uncontrollably about commas.

Thank you to Julie Valin for kicking this baby bird out of the nest and making it fly.

Thanks to you, dear reader, for picking up a debut.

Thanks to my mom and dad for naming me after a writer. I know I was supposed to be a journalist, but novelists get to work in their pajamas.

Thank you to B.B. Monster for being the one who woke me up.

ABOUT THE AUTHOR

DAYANA STOCKDALE has stared at the ocean with longing thousands of times, most especially when she lived in Santa Cruz and Honolulu. She now lives with her husband and their baby girl in Gold Country, where she dreams often of the surface as seen from below. Learn more about the series and the author at dayanastockdale.com.